GHOST AGENT

A MATTHEW RIKER NOVEL

J.T. BAIER

PROLOGUE

MATTHEW RIKER HAD TO DIE. The five men around the table were in consensus.

The officers of QS-4 were overly cautious by nature, and strict protocol was followed throughout the facility. But here, in the inner sanctum where the senior most members of QS-4's field operations team gathered, even more stringent measures were taken to ensure privacy. No electronic devices were allowed in the room. The walls were thick, and the only entrance was protected by a retina scanner, a keypad with a passcode, and a former US Marine Corps boxing champion. The room was swept nightly for listening devices. It was as secure as any room in the Pentagon.

Still, Edgar Morrison didn't feel at ease. The topic of their conversation for the past four hours had him out of sorts. He'd recruited Riker to come work for QS-4. He'd also negotiated the terms of Riker's retirement, terms Riker had blatantly broken in New York City when he'd taken down the entire Weaver organization and a handful of Chinese nationals, all to save some politician's daughter.

The price of breaking those terms was clear—Riker had

to die. Killing him wouldn't be easy, and they'd spent most of the day formulating their strategy, a brute force attack that would overwhelm him in his own home. There were only a few more details to hammer out. Then they'd sign the order and put a team in the field. Riker would be dead by morning.

Morrison leaned forward and sighed, going over the handwritten notes on the legal pad in front of him. This on top of everything else that was going on in QS-4 at the moment. He was having a hell of a week, and it showed no signs of improving.

Stone, Morrison's operational second-in-command, watched him with a wary eye. "Having second thoughts?"

"No. Just trying to see the plan from every angle possible. Riker will make us pay for any mistake, so we have to execute perfectly."

"We will. I'm confident we have a solid approach. Riker's smart, but he's rusty. Six years off the job, it's impossible not to lose your edge."

Morrison let out a humorless laugh. "Tell that to the men in the airfield outside New York City. Better yet, tell it to their widows."

He took one last look at his notes. Stone was right. This was a solid plan. Riker was good—he might even take out one or two of their guys—but this attack would be the end of Matthew Riker.

It was time to stop planning and start doing.

Just as Morrison opened his mouth to give the order, a red light above the door came on. The men around the table exchanged surprised glances. Though the light had been there for years, it was rarely used.

Stone got to his feet and opened the door. A tall blond man with a crew cut stood on the other side.

"What is it?" Stone asked.

"There's a phone call for Captain Morrison."

Morrison raised an eyebrow. "A phone call from whom?"

The man looked past Stone, meeting Morrison's gaze. "Matthew Riker."

1

Riker watched through his front window as the Toyota Camry pulled into his driveway. Of course it would be a Camry, the most anonymous car in America, and in silver, the most common color. The driver's door opened, and a man stepped out of the vehicle.

Morrison had more gray in his hair than he had six years ago, but little else about the man had changed. He was still broad and solid, built like a linebacker, and he walked with the same easy, confident stride as he had the day Riker met him. Riker watched until he disappeared from view when he stepped up to the stoop by the front door.

The older man didn't bother knocking, and Riker wasn't surprised. Morrison would undoubtedly know Riker was watching.

Riker opened the door and greeted his old mentor with a nod. The two men regarded each other warily, each subconsciously planning for battle, subtly positioning their bodies for optimum strategic advantage. Morrison wore his sidearm at his hip. That didn't surprise Riker. He would have been more worried if the old man hadn't been wearing his signature piece.

After a moment, Riker held out his hand. Morrison shook it. Then Riker nodded toward the kitchen, and Morrison stepped inside.

"Nice place," Morrison said.

"Thanks."

Riker led him to the kitchen. The table was set for two, with glasses of lemonade, a stack of freshly toasted bread, and a jar of honey. It wasn't often that Riker had company, and he'd never hosted a meeting quite as important as this one. His life depended on the outcome of this conversation. Riker took a seat at the head of the table.

Morrison walked to the fridge and paused, looking at the crayon drawing that hung there. He stared at it for a long while, tilting his head this way and that as if trying to understand what the drawing depicted. Riker gave him no explanation. There were plenty of things he was willing to share with his old mentor, but this wasn't one of them.

Finally, Morrison walked to the table and sat across from Riker. He gestured toward the jar of honey. "Yours?"

Riker nodded.

Morrison put a piece of toast on the empty plate in front of him and opened the honey jar. "I'm not sure if you remember, but I'm a bit of a connoisseur when it comes to honey."

Riker remembered. It was Morrison who'd first introduced him to the strange and wonderful world of fine honey.

"I've eaten Manuka honey in New Zealand. Leatherwood honey in Tasmania, Elvish honey in Turkey, and Sourwood honey right here in Appalachia." He slathered a thick layer of honey onto his bread while he spoke. "All that to say, my standards are high. Don't be offended if yours doesn't stack up to those world-class nectars."

He took a bite of the toast, his face unreadable. Then he took a swig of lemonade.

"Does it stack up?" Riker asked.

A slight smile played on Morrison's lips. "It very much does."

He took another bite, chewing slowly, clearly savoring it, but his eyes never left Riker. After he'd swallowed, he set the toast on the plate.

"You broke the terms."

"Yeah," Riker said.

"And then you called, which is in and of itself another violation."

"Yeah."

"So you brought me down here, halfway across the country. I assume you have a suggestion of how we resolve the situation."

Riker paused, choosing his words carefully. "I don't."

Morrison leaned back in his seat. "Not a great start, Matthew."

"But an honest one. Truth is, I don't need to come up with a resolution. Because you already have one in mind."

"Is that so?" Morrison picked up the toast and took another bite.

"Captain, you trained me to always look at the situation from my opponent's perspective, so that's what I've been doing these past few days. I've been trying to figure out how you see this ending."

"Yeah? And what did you come up with?"

Riker took a deep breath. His life depended on what he said next. If he was wrong in his assumptions or if Morrison thought he sounded insincere in his convictions, he was a dead man. "You put yourself on the line for me once. They let me retire. That never happens. Putting a guy like me who knows the things I know out onto the street had to make a lot of people nervous. You would have had to make a lot of promises. Given a lot of guarantees. The most important of which would have been that you wouldn't hesitate to end my life if I broke the retirement terms."

Morrison's eyes were hard and cold as he stared back at Riker. "Keep going."

Riker knew that it would be a waste of time to recount the events that had surrounded his time in New York City. He'd done what he'd done to help a child. That would be meaningless to QS-4. He might as well have performed a terrorist attack for all they cared. He'd broken the terms. It didn't matter why. So he moved on to the aftermath.

"I knew I only had two options in this situation. I could gear up for a fight I had no hope of winning. Or I could reach out." Riker leaned forward. "You can't let what I did slide. If you looked the other way, we'd both be dead men. But you came when I called. That leads me to believe there's another way out of this."

"You sure about that?" Morrison asked, his voice a low growl. "Maybe I just wanted to do the deed myself."

"Neither of us wants to find out what would happen if you tried."

Morrison stared at him a long moment before speaking again. "You're right about there being two options, but I don't think you'll like either of them."

"Try me."

"One of them is you die. The other is we nullify the deal. It'll be like the agreement never existed. Hence, you never broke it."

Riker struggled to keep any emotion off his face. "Meaning?"

"Meaning you never retired. Meaning QS-4 owns your ass just as thoroughly as they did six years ago."

Riker raised an eyebrow. "Does QS-4 really trust me enough to put me back on a team?"

"Not a team. You'd be Lone Wolf status. A ghost agent."

Riker swallowed hard. Lone Wolf status meant he'd not only operate alone, but he'd have limited support from the company, and none of the usual legal protections they offered their employees if things with law enforcement went sideways.

"I suggest you don't argue. It's the best deal you're going to get. Come back to work, Matthew."

Riker thought a moment before answering. "You must have quite the situation on your hands if the senior leadership team agreed to this."

"You're not wrong." Morrison reached into his pocket and pulled out a small key. He set it on the table and slid it across to Riker. "Leviathan Protocol."

Riker stared at the key, his jaw set. The mere thought of touching that key made his stomach turn. It would mean he was back under QS-4's thumb. It would mean the last six years had been for nothing. His freedom would evaporate as quickly as a drop of water on a hot pan.

Morrison pushed back his chair and stood up. "I should go. Thanks for the honey."

Riker opened a cabinet and took out another jar, this one unopened, and handed it to Morrison. "For the road."

Morrison chuckled. "I'll save it for the apocalypse. This stuff never goes bad, right?"

"This is unfiltered. It has impurities. It will go bad eventually."

Morrison nodded and headed for the door. He paused when he reached it, his hand on the knob. "If you're not on a plane out of Charlotte tonight, I'll have my answer, and we'll do this the other way."

He walked out without saying goodbye.

Riker watched him through the window, waiting until the silver Camry disappeared into the distance. Then he went back to the kitchen, sat down, and stared at the key Morrison had left on the table.

2

Ever since his days in the military, Riker had possessed the ability to quickly and deeply fall asleep on planes. He spent the journey from Charlotte to Los Angeles dead to the world, his body responding to the travel with an almost greedy desire for slumber, as if it knew it would need as much energy as possible in the days to come. The jolt of the landing gear touching the runway woke him, bringing him back to the grim reality that he was about to undertake his first mission for QS-4 in six years. When the seatbelt light turned off, he grabbed his small backpack and touched the front pocket of his jeans. The small key was still safely in place.

Riker made his way to a nearby offsite locker facility and found the locker that matched the number on his key. Inside, he found a cell phone and an envelope containing a California driver's license with Riker's photo and the name Jacob Smith. The ID looked so authentic that Riker wondered if it had been printed by the California DMV. The envelope also contained one thousand dollars in crisp new one hundred dollar bills.

He changed out his ID with the fake and put the money in his wallet. He left his driver's license in the locker and put the key back in his pocket. Trying the phone, Riker wasn't surprised to find that his fingerprint unlocked the device. QS-4 always liked to show off. There were no phone numbers programmed into the Contacts, but there was a ten-digit code in the Notes app.

On his way out the door, he had to sidestep, narrowly avoiding a woman on her way into the facility. She gave him a dirty look that he unsuccessfully tried to defuse with a smile. He hadn't meant to plow through the door, but he felt anger building up inside him. The cloak-and-dagger routine made his current situation feel more real. He had spent the last six years living a normal life. He didn't need to check for a tail anytime he wanted to go to the store. There was no elaborate web of lies needed when he bought groceries or tended to his hives. Now that was all gone.

The logical part of his brain had known that would be the case when he decided to call Morrison, but the rest of him was just making the connection. He wanted to call Morrison and scream into the phone, telling him to just give him a gun and let him know who to kill. No bullshit, no sneaking around. He wanted to punch someone. He also knew none of those were options. He was back in the game and needed to follow the rules.

As he stepped into the cool night air of Los Angeles, he pulled the fake driver's license out of his wallet and typed Jacob Smith's address into his phone's navigation. The Maps app gave him a route to the location five miles away. He considered getting a cab, but he realized that with traffic, he could get there just as quickly on his own two feet. He knew that he may draw some attention running along the shoulder of the road at night, but he wanted to clear his head.

The smog in the air reminded him of his recent trip to New York. Both cities were a harsh contrast to the crisp air he was used to in North Carolina. The pavement dashed by quickly as he jogged down the road, but he didn't push himself hard. He fell into a natural pace and the motion of his body allowed his mind to relax.

When he arrived at the address listed on the ID, he found a keypad on the door. He entered the code from the Notes app on the phone, and the electric bolt hummed as it disengaged. Riker stood to the side of the door and slowly pushed it open.

A voice called out from inside of the house. "Ah, there you are. Please, do come in."

Riker stepped inside and took a look at the man who had spoken to him. The guy was in his late twenties, maybe six foot one, with a slim, athletic build. He was dressed in slacks and a pressed dress shirt. His shoes shined like polished brass. His hair was cropped tight on the sides and back and carefully styled, and he stood a little too straight, as if he was slightly nervous.

"You're the handler, then?" Riker said.

The man stuck out his hand, and the two men shook. "It's a pleasure to meet you, Scarecrow. You can call me Franklin."

Riker pushed down the tinge of annoyance that rose up at the man's use of his old codename. "It's just Riker now."

Franklin stepped past Riker and looked outside, glancing left and then right, as if checking to see if he'd been followed. Then he pulled the door shut and turned the deadbolt. "Yes, well, you're working for QS-4 again. There are certain protocols that prohibit the use of--"

"It's Riker." His tone was a little more insistent this time.

Franklin opened his mouth as if he wanted to argue, but he shut it a moment later.

Riker stepped through the entryway and into the kitchen. He set his backpack on the counter and looked around. "How about you? Handlers don't have assigned codenames. You can call yourself anything you want as long as it's not your real name, right?"

"Yes," Franklin allowed.

"And you went with Franklin?"

Franklin followed Riker into the kitchen and leaned against the counter. "Research has shown that even when you think you're selecting a fake name at random, you are not. Cultural biases, the region where you grew up, and even favorite movies can subconsciously influence the decision. Enemies can use that information to find out valuable intelligence about your background. I wasn't willing to risk that outcome."

"You used a random name generator, didn't you?"

"Yes." A slight flush rose on Franklin's cheeks.

Riker shook his head. He's seen plenty of guys like Franklin in his time with QS-4. The company recruited from only the best schools, which meant Franklin probably had an Ivy League education. They also required military service, a nice little show of patriotism for the board members, so Franklin had served, but one look in his eyes told Riker the man hadn't seen serious combat. If all went well, Franklin would probably move up to a leadership position in QS-4 in a few years. A decade from now, he'd be giving the orders that sent real warriors into battle. He'd send men and women to their deaths with a stroke of his pen. This would be the closest he'd ever come to true fieldwork. Riker had always made it his business to fuck with guys like Franklin as much as humanly possible.

"So how's this work?" he asked, his eyes roaming around the kitchen. "With L.A. real estate prices, even a small house like this has to be worth close to a million. Does QS-4 own this place? Or is this an Airbnb situation?"

"Scarecrow, I hardly see how that's—"

"It's Riker." He spoke a bit more forcefully this time.

"Okay. Point is, there's a mission, and it's time sensitive. We should discuss the details."

"In a minute." Riker left Franklin standing in the kitchen and walked through the house. He wanted to get the lay of the land. In truth, he knew that QS-4 owned this place, just as they owned numerous houses in every major metropolitan area in the country, not to mention most major cities in the world. Not only did the properties serve as convenient safe houses for their agents, allowing them to avoid the paper trail that came with hotel stays, but they also served as nice investments. While the military-industrial complex earned them a healthy and consistent profit, a little diversity of assets was always a good move.

Riker paced through the house, checking the two bathrooms, the three bedrooms. He looked around the laundry room and the living room. He even stepped out back and walked the small, well-maintained yard. He wasn't looking for anything in particular, but he was back in the business now, like it or not. He'd be spending a fair amount of time in this safe house in the coming days, and he needed to be very familiar with the layout.

As he checked the second bathroom, he spotted something in the corner of the light fixture. He immediately recognized it as a tiny camera lens. He shook his head, more at the sloppy placement than at the existence of the camera.

He had to assume that his every move was being recorded and monitored here; there was no such thing as privacy in a QS-4 safe house.

Satisfied that he knew the layout, he walked back to the kitchen. Franklin was waiting exactly where he'd left him, leaning against the counter, arms crossed. Riker walked past him and started searching through the cabinets.

"I'll need a gun. Preferably a SIG Sauer P226, but any small, reliable handgun will do."

"Of course," Franklin said, standing up a bit straighter now. "I have access to a wide range of weapons, including military grade--"

"Just the SIG. And a knife. Something durable, but I have to be able to fit it in my pocket." He found what he was looking for in the cabinet over the sink—a bag of ground coffee and a box of filters. He grabbed one of the filters and stuck it in the coffee maker. Then he held up the bag of grounds, showing it to Franklin. "You want a cup?"

"Uh, sure. If we could discuss the mission--"

"In a minute." Riker found a spoon and started scooping grounds into the coffee filter. Much to his delight, Franklin's lips were pressed tightly together in annoyance now. You had to take joy in the little things in life, especially when it was spinning so wildly out of control.

He filled the coffee maker with water and started it. He waited until the percolator began its rumbly, noisy process, and then he turned back to Franklin. "How long have you been working as a handler?"

Franklin's face reddened at the question. He glanced up at the light fixture over the sink. Apparently Riker wasn't the only one aware that they were being remotely observed. "I understand that you've been out of the business for a while, but surely you know that we are not allowed to discuss personal details."

"You didn't read my file?"

"Of course I did." He seemed almost offended at the implication.

"So you get to know my history, but I don't get to know yours?"

"It's crucial for the mission that I understand your skillset and areas of expertise so that I can advise on the best approach for each situation. It would be irresponsible for me to not have all the information."

"Uh-huh. Did you ever consider that maybe it would be irresponsible for me to follow your precious advice without all the information? If this is your first time in the field, or if you've sent other operatives into harm's way with bad intel, that would be pretty damn nice for me to know going in, don't you think?"

"That's hardly the same thing, Scarecrow. I can assure you that—"

Riker was across the room in an instant. He didn't touch Franklin, but he got as close as humanly possible without doing so. Their noses were less than an inch apart. "I'm not going to tell you again. The name's Riker. The guy whose file you read? That was Scarecrow. You know the things he's done as well as I do. That ain't me. Not anymore."

He gave Franklin a hard look, then stepped back.

The handler let out a breath in relief. He knew what Riker was capable of, at least on paper. No way did he want to piss him off.

But then Franklin surprised Riker. "Listen to me carefully. I don't have time for your conflicted feelings or your guilt. We have a job to do. Scarecrow is the codename you have been assigned by our employers, and I will address you as such. Understand?"

Riker held the man's gaze another moment. Then he opened the cabinet above the coffee maker and pulled out two mugs. "Sure. Cream or sugar?"

"Black is fine."

"Good man." Riker poured two cups and handed one to Franklin. He couldn't help but respect the man a little. Standing up to a guy with as many confirmed kills as Riker wasn't easy. "So are you going to tell me about the job or what?"

Franklin relaxed visibly at that, clearly relieved that things were getting back on track. He reached into a manila folder on the counter and pulled out a photograph. He slid it across the counter to Riker. "This is Simon Buckner."

Riker picked up the photo and studied it for a moment. It was a surveillance photo, but a good one. He could clearly make out the young man's features. The guy was maybe in his mid-twenties. He had a stylish haircut, and Gucci sunglasses hung from the pocket of his designer shirt. "You want me to kill him?"

"No. We want you to protect him."

Riker said nothing. Something wasn't adding up here. Why would QS-4 care about the existence of some rich kid from L.A.? And why would protecting him be a Lone Wolf mission? "Protect him from whom?"

"An organization called Laghaz. Heard of them?"

Riker shook his head. "Not sure if you know this, but I've been out of the game for a bit."

"They're an extremist group. Wants to make the West pay for its meddling in the affairs of their country. The usual. What's not so usual is that they have a splinter cell right here in L.A. Somehow, this Buckner kid pissed them off, and they want him dead."

Riker considered that a moment. "There are plenty of private security firms that would be happy to protect this kid. Why are we involved in this?"

"Because Simon is Albert Buckner's son."

Suddenly, it all clicked for Riker. "Ah. Albert Buckner, the senator."

Franklin nodded. "Senator Buckner sits on the Defense Committee, and QS-4 would very much like him to owe us a favor. Saving his son would be a great way to put him in our debt."

"And I take it we want to keep this on the down low to avoid the public finding out a senator's son got himself mixed up with terrorists."

Franklin nodded. "I can provide logistical support and some equipment, but QS-4 can't get any more involved than that. You'll be acting on your own."

Riker stared at the photo for a long moment. Helping some rich kid who'd gotten in over his head... this certainly wasn't the type of mission he'd been expecting. But what choice did he have?

He met Franklin's gaze. "Consider it done."

3

Eleven years ago.

Matthew Riker had intel that could destroy one of the worst terrorist cells in existence. Now he just needed to get the information back to his bosses.

He'd been part of a two-man team when he located the compound headquarters of Mohamad Izad. But after a surprise encounter two miles south of Izad's compound, his buddy Lando was dead, and he was alone. Which meant it was his sole responsibility to get the information back to Uncle Sam.

A rock outcropping protected Riker from the harsh sun of the mountain desert of eastern Iran. He stayed in the shadow, watching it grow longer and longer. He'd killed the two men who'd ambushed Lando, and so far no one seemed to be looking for them. But he wasn't willing to risk drawing the attention of Izad's men by wandering around in the daylight. He needed to wait for nightfall.

Aside from being discovered by the enemy, Riker's

biggest concern was water. There was a liter left in his pack, but it had taken him two days to hike into the remote area. The riverbeds that he had seen were dry, so rationing the water was a must. Every other hour he allowed himself a small sip.

Once the sun disappeared beneath the horizon and the stars appeared in the sky, Riker started to move. He stayed low, crawling his way along the rocky outcropping. He'd only gone five feet when he bumped into the first scorpion. The arachnid shot its stinger into his camo jacket. He flicked it away and checked his arm, seeing that the stinger hadn't made it through to the flesh.

He looked ahead and saw motion all along the ground. The cool of the night had brought out the creatures of the desert. He resisted the urge to stand up and move quickly—he couldn't risk anyone spotting his silhouette against the night sky. He crawled one hundred yards through the rocks, bugs, and dust. On four separate occasions, he looked back to see scorpions crawling on his legs, making their way up his body. Each time, he used the barrel of his rifle to brush them off.

Sweat was sliding down his forehead by the time he crested the ridge and moved down the other side. His forearms burned from the crawl. At one point, a sharp rock had cut through his pants, and he could feel blood trickling from the wound on his knee. But now that the mountain was between him and Izad's compound, the first phase was over and he could walk under the night sky. He took a long drag of water and immediately cursed himself for drinking too greedily.

Finding his path back to the village where he'd started from was difficult in the darkness. He'd marked his maps on the journey to the hidden compound, but going down the mountains was a harder task than climbing up them had been. He came to a sheer cliff and knew that he was off his path. It took him two hours to find a way around and get back on track.

By the time sunlight peeked over the mountain and touched his face, every muscle in his body ached. Riker knew that he needed to rest during the heat of the day, so he found a rock outcropping to sleep under. It was easier to see markers in the daylight, so he checked his map. He wasn't even halfway back to the village. Disappointed by the slow progress, he grabbed his food rations from his pack. The MRE required him to put water in the pouch. He used half the recommended amount. The result was a thick paste that only vaguely tasted like lasagna. He coughed and choked while trying to force it down his dry throat. He allowed himself one sip of water. He only had a quarter of a liter left.

Resting his head on his pack, he looked at his map one more time. He had twenty miles left to walk before he would reach the village. Once he was there, he could call for extraction. He lay there thinking of his dead brother in arms. The only thing that sustained him was the thought of how it would feel when they finally took down Mohamad Izad. Finally, exhaustion took him and he fell asleep.

Hours later, Riker was startled out of sleep by something crawling across his hand. He swatted at it groggily. He yelled out, thinking for a moment that his hand was on fire. Once his mind finished its transition from the dream world back to reality, he saw where the scorpion had stung him. The area on the back of his hand near the base of the thumb was already swelling. He made a small cut at the sting and tried to push out as much venom as he could. Then he put a piece of gauze and tape over the wound.

The sun was under the horizon, but its glow was still

visible. Riker's sore muscles protested as he stood. He put his pack on and checked his map. His swollen hand burned, but he didn't feel short of breath. As much as he wanted to sit back down, he concentrated on putting one foot in front of the other. After fifteen minutes of hiking, he started to feel normal.

The idea of walking twenty miles before the sun came up sounded doable to Riker. He knew that the terrain for the first eight would be hard, but after that the landscape would level out and he'd be able to move faster. Water was his biggest concern. He knew that he was already dehydrated, but the night was cool and he could push through anything.

Six hours later, he fell for the first time. He tried to catch himself, but his arms and mind had a disconnect. His cheek hit the dirt hard, and he tasted blood in his mouth. He just laid there for a moment, his mind spinning. The moisture of the blood in his mouth felt pleasant. His tongue and throat were so dry that they burned with each breath.

As he pushed himself up, a charley horse hit his calf. The muscle flexed so hard it felt as if there was a steel ball in his leg. He hit the ground again and cursed until the muscle started to relax and the fiery pain dulled.

The adrenaline from the pain cleared his head. He rested against a rock and checked his pack. The last of the water was already gone, but he had one MRE left, a hard square meant to resemble pizza. He ate it in a few huge bites, barely tasting the heavily preserved food. He let himself rest for ten minutes while he looked at the map. He checked his supplies. The pack was down to a first aid kit, spotting scope, and his notebooks. He had a rifle, which he would have gladly traded for food or water.

His muscles told him that he should lie down and sleep, but his mind knew that wasn't an option. He stood up and tried to take a piss. Something closer to snot than urine dripped out of his body. Just another sign that he desperately needed water.

Riker spoke out loud to himself under the night sky. "I don't give a shit what you need, body. Rest and water are not part of the mission. Gaining intel on Mohamad Izad and relaying that information to command is your mission. You will not interfere with or obstruct those orders!"

He realized that yelling at himself in the desert was probably a sign that things were not going well. Still, it gave him the drive he needed to put one foot in front of the other and keep moving.

The night was long, and the pain in his feet and legs was growing worse. Both knees bled from stumbles he had taken, and his thumb was swollen from the scorpion sting. Riker thought back to his time in BUD/S and the pain that he'd gone through in Hell Week. He knew what he was made of and he used the pain he was experiencing to motivate each step.

When the sun came up, he saw a dirt road. A quick check of the map told him that he was only two miles off course. That road would lead him to the village. And a village meant water. The village meant food. His salvation was just over ten thousand feet away.

His pace was incredibly slow, and the day grew hotter with each step. His socks stuck to his feet with a mixture of dried blood and puss. He didn't need to take those socks off to know that the nail on his right big toe was about to fall off. But still, he concentrated on the task at hand—putting one foot in front of the other.

He looked up and saw a building through the waves of heat in the distance. He smiled. The end was in sight. His mind was stronger than his body, and the world would be a safer place because of it.

Then he heard an engine. He kept walking towards the village, but the sound grew louder. He turned and looked back. A truck was coming up the road. He kept walking, hoping that they would go by him. His rifle was slung over his shoulder and hung on his back.

The truck rolled to a halt next to him. Four men hopped out. Each one held an assault rifle, and none of them were shy about pointing them at Riker. All four men yelled at him in Farsi at the same time. The voices overlapped, and each yelled something different. Riker caught most of it which amounted to "put your weapon down" and "who are you?"

Riker raised both hands in the air and turned towards the men. That seemed to calm them a little, and they exchanged confused glances.

Riker's left hand was swollen to twice its regular size. His face was gaunt and covered in dirt. White chunks of dry skin covered his lips. His pants were a shredded mess of dried blood around his knees. He didn't look like any kind of threat. He didn't even look like he should be standing.

"Drop your weapon!" one of the men shouted.

Riker drew in a deep breath. He cleared his mind and made note of the position of each man around him. Four between him and the truck and two more inside. He slowly lowered his left arm and let the rifle slide off his shoulder and hit the ground.

The four men appeared to relax as Riker dropped to his knees. He acted as if he could no longer hold his hands above him, and he rested them on the dirt. In truth he was barely acting. He let his head rest and prepared his body for what it needed to do next.

Two men came over to him. They grabbed Riker under

the arms and stood him up. He let them do most of the work as they lifted him to his feet.

The other two were already lowering the tailgate on the bed of the truck, ready to load Riker in. Riker eyed the pistol in the closest man's waistband. He took a deep breath and made his move.

His hand snaked out, grabbing the pistol, and he fired two quick rounds into the men holding him. The shots entered through the bottom of their chins and exited the top of their skulls.

The men at the back of the truck looked startled and fumbled with the rifles slung around their shoulders, but Riker shot both of them in center mass. The men inside the truck started to open the doors but Riker fired into the cab until all his bullets were spent.

The whole action took less than ten seconds. Six men lay dead in front of him. Riker's legs wobbled, and he almost fell. He dropped the pistol and picked up his rifle, using it for balance as he walked to the cab of the truck. Inside, he saw the most wonderful site he'd ever laid eyes on—a case of bottled water.

Twelve-hours later, he was sitting in an empty mess hall in Shindand Air Base, bone-tired but still too jacked up on adrenaline and emotions to sleep. He had an issue of the *Fantastic Four* open in front of him, but he couldn't concentrate on it enough to read. He was staring blankly at a splash page of The Thing punching Mole Man when Captain Adams marched in, his face a mask of anger. He sat down across from Riker.

"You've been through a hell of a thing, Riker, so I'm going to give it to you straight."

"Sir?" Riker asked, looking up at his commanding officer.

"Apparently the Iranians got wind of your recon mission. The politicians are all in an uproar, of course." He looked down at his feet.

"What is it, sir?" Riker's heart was racing. He was afraid he knew what was coming next.

Adams looked up, and Riker was shocked to see anguish in the tough man's eyes. "They think we'll be able to get Lando's body back, but beyond that... We're not moving on your intelligence. They say it's too risky for us to continue. The Iranians would freak out if they found out we were on their soil. They're calling off the mission and sending us home."

"No." Riker jumped to his feet, suddenly filled with rage. Everything he'd been through over the past few days, everything he'd lost, it would all be for nothing if they didn't finish the job and go after Mohamad Izad. He stalked toward the door, hands balled into fists.

"Where are you going?" Adams asked.

"To find someone with the authority to make this happen, and to change their mind."

He walked out of the mess hall and into the desert air. Sunrise was still an hour away, and the night was cold. The stars shone brightly overhead. The area between the mess hall and the admin building was empty but for a lone figure. The man stood stone still, arms crossed, as if he were waiting for someone.

"You're in a hurry," the man said as Riker strode toward him.

"Very astute observation." Riker angled left to go around the guy, but he held up a hand for Riker to stop.

"Hold up a moment. I think you and I need to talk."

Riker paused, taking a good look at the man for the first time. He was at least ten years Riker's senior, and he was solidly built. He exuded quiet confidence in the way career military men often did, as if he understood he was tougher than just about anyone he was likely to encounter, but he didn't need to prove it. Riker forced himself to measure his words carefully. The guy wore a simple green T-shirt and camo pants, but he could easily be a senior officer. The last thing Riker needed to do was piss off the brass. That wouldn't help his case one bit.

"Sorry, do we know each other?" Riker asked.

The man flashed a toothy grin. "I know you. You're Matthew Riker."

"Okay," Riker said. "And you are?"

The man held up a hand, offering it to Riker. "I'm Edgar Morrison."

4

THE MORNING CAME QUICKLY. Riker's eyes opened before the sun rose, and for a brief moment, he was disoriented by the strange room. Then he remembered that he was in a safe house on the wrong side of the country.

He lay in bed and took five deep breaths. With each one he focused his mind and his body, recalling the layout of the house he was in and the task at hand. On the last exhale, his feet touched the floor and he silently began his mission.

After a quick trip to the bathroom, he entered the kitchen. A manila envelope lay on the counter where Franklin had left it. Riker slid the contents from the package while the coffee brewed.

The life story of Simon Buckner was laid out before him, and very little of it surprised Riker. Simon's life checked all the rich kid boxes. He was a decent student who went to Stanford, where he was in a fraternity. After six years, he graduated with an MBA in Marketing. Now he worked as a consultant for a company called Greyson Electronics.

If Simon had ever been in trouble with the law, it didn't show up in the file. His family was old money—just because there was no criminal record didn't mean there hadn't been any crimes committed. Kids like that could walk away from almost anything without a scratch.

Riker wondered what made this mission special. Franklin seemed to accept that saving a senator's son was all that concerned QS-4. Maybe that was true, but he needed to understand how the kid was involved with a terrorist group. It was possible he knew something he shouldn't, or maybe he'd ripped them off. The answers should come quickly enough once he had Simon.

After a cup of coffee, Riker went to the garage. He laughed when he opened the door. A silver Toyota Camry was waiting for him. He wondered if QS-4 bought them in bulk. Riker hopped in the car and checked the glove box. There was a current registration and an insurance card indicating this was a company car. The address on each was a P.O. Box. In addition, there was a loaded SIG Sauer P226 with an extra clip.

The file on Simon included his home address. Riker put it into his phone's GPS and headed out as the sun crested the horizon.

An hour later, Riker parked down the street from the address. A brand new Mercedes AMG S63 was parked in the driveway. Riker considered that he might be too late. The owner of the Mercedes may have already killed Simon.

Riker got out of the car with his pistol tucked into the waistband of his pants. He strolled towards the house with the gait of a man out for some light exercise. His right hand floated by his side ready to grab the weapon and spring into action. High bushes between the sidewalk and the front of the home obstructed his view. Staring into the bushes as he walked, he could make out the front of the house through the gaps in the plants. There were at least two people in the home. He couldn't get a good look, but he would have a view once he reached the driveway. Riker reached the end of the shrubs with his hand resting on the butt of his pistol. The front window curtains were open, allowing Riker to see inside.

Simon sat at a table in his boxers eating a bowl of cereal. Across from him, a woman sat with her back to Riker. She had on a large dress shirt and seemingly nothing else. Riker moved back to the sidewalk and continued on. If that woman were here to kill Simon, he would die a happy man.

Riker did a loop back to his car. He stayed low and watched the house. An hour later Simon walked the woman to the Mercedes in the driveway. Riker recognized her. He couldn't remember her name, but he knew she'd been in a movie he'd seen the previous summer.

Simon wrapped his arms around the small of her back and drew her in for a long kiss that turned into a minor make-out session. After a few minutes she pushed him back and slipped into her car. Simon watched as she drove down the street.

Once she was out of sight, Riker got out of his car and walked back towards Simon's. When he was half a block away an engine roared and crackled. Riker picked up his pace, but a yellow Lamborghini pulled out of the driveway before he could get there. The engine roared, and the car lurched as it flew down the otherwise quiet street.

For a moment Riker considered running back to his car and chasing him. Instead, he continued walking towards the home. Simon was giving him the opportunity to search the house for any information that would reveal the cause of his current predicament. Simon clearly wasn't worried about his safety yet. When he realized his life was in danger, Riker guessed he would get rid of any evidence that could incriminate him. For now, Riker had a chance to find some puzzle pieces.

The house had large glass windows wrapping around most of the first floor. Riker walked around the side of the house to the backyard. The only movement from inside the home came from a large grey cat. Riker was glad to see that there were no motion sensors inside the home.

When he reached the back door, he used his bump key to unlock the deadbolt. As soon as he opened the door, the cat ran out into the yard. Riker slid into the home, shutting the door behind him.

The interior of the home wasn't exactly what Riker expected. It was modern with nice finishes, no surprise there. What stood out was how well organized it was. The home was clean and nothing seemed out of place. Riker had expected to see an upscale version of a frat house.

The first floor didn't reveal any secrets, and he went to the second level. The first door that he came to was an office. It was as organized as the rest of the home. The only things on the desk were a computer and a tablet. Riker tried the computer, but it was password protected.

The desk didn't have anything of interest in the drawers. The shelves held numerous books, most of them about business and marketing. The rest of the space was filled with photos of Simon with various celebrities. Most of them were in the same age bracket as Simon, but one shot showed him riding a golf cart with Clint Eastwood.

Riker heard a ping and turned to see the iPad on the desk light up. The first line of a text message displayed on the screen.

Viper will be at Avalon tonight.

The message was from Ted V.

Riker searched for Avalon on his phone and quickly discovered it was a high-end L.A. nightclub.

The tablet pinged again, this time with a message from Simon.

I'll be there.

Riker shook his head. All the encryption and passcodes in the world could be undone because people liked all their devices synced.

As he continued down the hall to the bedroom, he heard a car pull into the driveway. The sound of the car was very different from the Lamborghini. Unless Simon had switched cars, this was someone else.

A knock at the front door echoed through the house. Riker waited at the top of the stairs. Then he heard glass break and the door open. Riker could hear the footsteps of two men entering the house. He slid into one of the bedrooms, pressing his body against the wall just past the light switch. The only sound was the motion of the intruders. Whoever was in the house hadn't spoken a single word.

Riker heard footsteps on the stairs. He pulled the gun from his waistband and slid his finger inside of the guard. The footsteps of the intruders moved closer. Riker kept his breath shallow and steady. He stayed silent as the men moved to the hallway outside of the bedroom.

Riker heard the door to the office across the hall creak open. One of the intruders checked the office from the doorway. Riker slipped from his room and into the hallway behind the man. In one fluid move Riker put the barrel of his pistol against the back of the intruder's head.

"Don't move," Riker said in a whisper.

The man stood perfectly still for a moment. Then he spoke in a thick Middle Eastern accent. "Don't shoot." He lifted his hands slowly. His right held a 9mm pistol with a silencer attached to the barrel. "We were just sent here to talk with you."

"Do you always talk while holding a weapon? I suggest you drop it if you want to live."

"Of course."

The man loosened his grip on the weapon, and it fell from his hand. Before it hit the floor, he turned and brought his left forearm around in an attempt to knock Riker's gun out of his hand.

Riker knew the move. It was one he had used several times himself. He could have pulled the trigger, but he didn't want to kill this guy until he knew who he was. Instead, Riker stepped back, avoiding the blow.

The intruder pressed the attack. He charged towards Riker, attempting a tackle. The man wore a ski mask over his face. Riker smashed his pistol into the bridge of his nose. The cartilage crunched and shifted sideways. The momentum of the attack stopped, and the man wavered on his feet.

Riker didn't waste the moment. He moved to the man's back and put an arm around his neck. He held his pistol to the side of the man's head while keeping pressure on his neck. Riker could feel blood soaking through the cotton mask and painting his forearm red.

"I have a gun pressed to your friend's temple," Riker yelled. "If you want him to live, I suggest that you leave the house. There is no need for either of you to die."

A man yelled his response in Farsi.

Riker understood the language. The man had said, "Where are you?" Riker kept quiet. He didn't want them to know he could understand.

The man with Riker's arm around his neck answered in

the same language. "He has me in the hallway at the top of the stairs. He is not the man we were sent for."

"English only," Riker yelled. "You can leave now with your life. If your friend cooperates, I will release him too."

Riker watched the stairs and held his captive close to cover him.

Then the voice called out again in Farsi. "Stomp your foot."

The man did as he was asked. The moment after his foot pounded the floor, splinters of wood shot up next to them. Riker released the masked man and jumped back down the hallway. From below them the puffs of the silencer burst out in quick succession and bullets shot up from the hallway below them.

One bullet tore into the calf of the man Riker had punched. The man dove forward, tumbling down the stairs. Bullets continued to shoot up through the floor.

Riker ran down the hall away from the stairs and bullets formed a dotted line in the floor coming after him. He reached the end of the hall and shot two rounds into the floor towards the direction of the shots.

The man with the broken nose yelled out in a nasal tone. "I'm hit. We have to get out of here."

Riker heard the front door slam open. He moved cautiously to the stairs. Then he heard the car start and he picked up his pace. Riker reached the front door and saw a black Chrysler sedan pulling out of the driveway. A trail of blood led to the spot it had been parked a moment before.

His arms pumped as he sprinted to his car. He wasn't about to let these guys get away.

5
―――

Miro Chatti stood in front of the floor-to-ceiling window of his downtown penthouse apartment, staring at the city below. He wore only his silk robe, which he hadn't bothered tying. He liked the way the material clung to his shoulders and brushed against the bare skin of his legs. He took a sip of his morning tea, savoring the fragrant liquid as it rolled down his throat.

Chatti made it a point to pay attention to his body, and to all the sensations and pleasures it reported to his brain. After all, what else was there? Life was pleasure and pain. Too many people dulled their senses, ignoring both. Not Chatti. He maximized every experience, savoring agony as well as ecstasy.

Still, he found his mind drifting to the place it always went near the completion of an important operation—loose ends.

This operation had gone almost too smoothly. He'd assumed that his quest to find someone inside Greyson Electronics would take weeks, and then that it would take months if not years to cultivate that relationship and get them to sell out their company secrets. Such work was not easy, and it required a deft touch and a patient mind.

But then he'd discovered Simon Buckner, a man who was practically begging to be manipulated into an act of corporate and national betrayal. In less than three months, Chatti had gone from first contact to having the devices in their hand. Operations this smooth didn't happen every day.

Now that they had what they needed, there was the question of what to do about Simon. Which wasn't really a question at all. Yes, he had a powerful father. An important family name. But what did that matter to Chatti? Simon's family name would do very little to stop the bullet Chatti's operatives were currently placing between his eyes.

Chatti felt neither guilt nor pleasure at the thought of what his men were doing to Simon Buckner. Like any other part of the job, it was simply something that had to be done. The man had seen too much to be left alive.

"Miro?" a voice called from the bedroom. "Come back to bed."

A wave of revulsion ran through Chatti at the sound of Tracy's voice. It was before noon, and she was already high.

Not that he was against his women using drugs. In fact, he encouraged it. Most of his conquests were party girls who'd arrived in the city with dreams of stardom and little-to-no cash. He brought them into his opulent lifestyle and supplied them with designer drugs far more powerful than anything they could get on the street. Before long, they were hooked on both the drugs and the lifestyle. That made them eager to please, willing to comply with any request of which his fertile mind could conceive. And it could conceive of some very creative requests.

Still, when they started shooting up before lunch, it was time to move on. He'd soon send Tracy back to the cheap studio apartment she'd been sharing with two roommates when he met her. If she could kick the drugs, maybe she'd even grow as a person from this experience. If not...well, she was still young and pretty. There were ways for her to earn her heroin, at least for a few years until the drugs aged her. Then maybe she'd find a pimp to introduce her to a less discerning class of clients. Either way, it wasn't Chatti's problem.

"In a minute, darling," he called.

He turned back to the window and stared at the city stretching before him. His mind returned to Simon Buckner. The men he'd sent would have done their jobs by now. He just needed their confirmation that it was done. Then it was on to phase two. The pieces were in place. All he needed to do was to keep things moving and ensure everything went according to plan.

It was almost time for the world to learn the name Laghaz. Soon, they would all see what his new weapons could do.

Riker threw the Camry into drive, his eyes fixed on the black Chrysler speeding into the distance. These assassins could be the key to finding the group that wanted Simon dead. If he got his hands on one of them and spent some quality time with the man, he could have all the answers he needed. With any luck, he'd be back home tending to his bees by the end of the day tomorrow.

But that meant he had to catch these men.

He raced after them, speeding down the residential street, grateful that he'd taken the time to get the lay of the land before going inside Simon's house. He had a clear map of the area in his mind, and he knew where the assassins were heading. They were taking the quickest route possible out of the neighborhood. Their vehicle was much more powerful than his, but that was okay. As soon as they left this neighborhood, they'd hit the famed Los Angeles traffic. When that happened, they'd be forced to slow down and Riker could find a way to disable their vehicle.

As he reached the intersection of the first major road, Riker smiled. Just as he'd expected, traffic was heavy. They'd be lucky to go more than thirty miles per hour on this road. That would give Riker all the opportunity he needed.

The black Chrysler was going as fast as possible on the crowded street, riding tight on the bumper of some SUV, honking at the soccer mom behind the wheel to go faster. As if that were possible.

Riker took the turn hard, positioning his Camry two cars back from the Chrysler. This was a game of patience now. All he needed to do was hang on their tail and wait for his opportunity to strike.

Suddenly, the Chrysler surprised him. It slowed for a moment, creating a little space between itself and the SUV, and then the driver punched the gas. The car hopped the curb and sped down the sidewalk.

Riker cursed. It appeared these guys were more desperate to get away than he'd assumed. He had no choice but to follow. He stomped the gas and turned the wheel hard. The Camry lurched its way onto the sidewalk. He kept his eyes on the target, clutching the wheel as he drove down the narrow sidewalk. It was thankfully empty of pedestrians, but the Chrysler crashed through a few carts of products lining the streets. This slowed their car a little, letting Riker's less powerful vehicle keep up.

As they reached a corner, Riker saw the car begin to

turn. Once again, he consulted his mental map of the area. If he were trying to escape, he'd want to get as far away from this crowded street as possible. If they followed the backroads, they had a path to the Hollywood Hills and the less populous areas beyond them. Riker had to assume that was where they were going.

He hesitated for only a moment, then he turned down the street before the one the Chrysler had taken. If his guess was right, he should be able to cut through and catch them at Burbank Boulevard, the last major intersection before they reached the hills.

He gripped the wheel with sweaty hands and focused on pushing the car hard. Up ahead, a Lexus was cruising along at just above the speed limit. Riker weaved around it, earning himself a honk and an angry middle finger.

He reached Burbank and took a left. Just as he was turning, he saw the Chrysler blaze through the intersection, and he let out another curse. If he'd just been a little bit faster, he might have been able to blindside them. As it was, he'd have to do something more drastic.

The Camry lurched into the right lane, cutting off a Subaru and earning another blare of the horn. Riker reached into his waistband and pulled out the SIG. Then he pressed a button on the door, and the driver's side window slid down. He took the turn hard, and his wheels skidded on the pavement. He was behind the Chrysler now.

Steadying the wheel with his right hand, he leaned out the window, raised the SIG, and took aim at the Chrysler's rear left tire. They were driving sporadically, but Riker was patient. He waited until they stopped weaving for a moment, and he prepared to fire.

His finger was on the trigger, starting to press, when he

heard sirens and spotted flashing red and blue lights behind him in the side-view mirror.

"You've got to be shitting me." He leaned back into his car and lowered his weapon, hoping the cops hadn't seen it. Almost automatically, his priorities shifted. This mission had changed from one of pursuit to one of evasion. As frustrating as it was, getting away from the police was more important than catching the men who'd tried to assassinate Simon Buckner.

He glanced down at the SIG clutched in his left hand. He had to assume the weapon was black market. If he were arrested, QS-4 wouldn't want the cops to have a paper trail that led back to them or their more official employees.

If the cops hadn't seen him pointing the weapon, there was a chance they'd follow the Chrysler instead of him. If they had, he was definitely their primary target. There was only one way to find out.

As the Chrysler barreled onward, weaving in and out of traffic, Riker eyed the next intersection up ahead. A moment before he reached it, he wrenched the steering wheel to the left. The tires screeched, and Riker thought he was going to lose control of the small car. But it held the line he'd set it on, and a moment later he was speeding down another side street.

The police car followed behind him, its cherries flashing.

"Asked and answered," Riker muttered.

His eyes scanned the road up ahead. He was now well outside the area he'd studied prior to going to Simon's. The police would undoubtedly know this area far better than he did. He needed to make a move fast.

While he was still considering that, he heard another sound over the siren, one that sent even more adrenaline rushing through his veins—a helicopter. He scanned the sky through the windshield and confirmed what his ears had already told him. A police chopper was flying overhead, tracking him. Any chance of losing the police with fancy driving had just gone up in smoke.

His mind flipped through options like a dealer flips through playing cards, but he didn't see any he liked. He knew that he didn't have long. With the helicopter tracking him, additional police cars would soon be in his path. They'd probably even form a roadblock.

Though he didn't want to, he couldn't help but wonder what would happen to him if he were arrested. Would Morrison's patience finally run out? Riker had to assume it would. Since he had no intention of dying in a Los Angeles jail cell, he needed to find another way out of this.

He spotted something up ahead, and an idea began to form. Not perfect, but it was all he had. He stepped on the gas and headed back toward Burbank Boulevard. He was less than a block away before he confirmed that the concrete building was what he'd suspected—a parking structure.

Keeping his foot on the gas until the last minute, Riker eyed the rearview mirror. The cop car was far enough back that it wouldn't collide with him when he slammed on the brakes. As he reached the entrance to the parking structure, he did just that, spinning the wheel so the car slid ninety degrees. Then he stepped on the gas again and bolted into the parking garage.

He sped past the ticketing machine, ignoring the blaring lights and slamming through the bar that attempted to halt his unauthorized progress. He drove the Camry into the dim confines of the parking garage, going up the spiraling path, following the signs that guided him but ignoring the suggested speed limit.

He was at the second level by the time he heard the police sirens echoing through the concrete structure. The police car was back on his trail.

Riker pressed on until he reached the fifth level. He estimated the police car was two floors below him. That would have to be good enough. He pulled into a parking spot and quickly backed out again, changing direction. With the nose of his vehicle pointing down the ramp, Riker put the car in neutral and pressed his foot on the brake. He forced himself to wait, counting to ten, and then he opened the door and hopped out of the car.

The Camry began to roll down the ramp, picking up speed and momentum as it went. Riker didn't bother watching. He ran to the interior edge of the ramp and threw his leg over the rail. He waited until the cop car sped by, and then he dropped down to the next level.

The sound of metal crunching metal echoed through the parking garage as the police car slammed into the driverless Camry. Riker didn't even pause to look. He dropped down to the third floor. Then the second. Then the first.

He waited in the entryway until a group of businessmen walked past, and he joined them, falling into step, willing himself not to look up at the helicopter overhead. He walked with them for two blocks, and then he disappeared into another building, headed for the parking garage, and hotwired himself a new ride.

6

MATTHEW RIKER HAD FOUGHT in jungles, deserts, mountains and war-torn cities. None of that had prepared him for The Avalon. He stood at the corner of Hollywood and Vine cringing at the buildings in front of him.

Night clubs and Riker were mutually exclusive. He'd gone from high school to the military. When he went out, it was with brothers in arms, they went to bars with cheap beer and local girls. He had never seen a live DJ or been in a club with multiple levels. That would all change tonight.

Riker arrived at 9:00, but the club hadn't even opened the doors. Two spotlights beamed towards the heavens and neon lights screamed out the name of a DJ. He looked over a line of young beautiful people snaking out in front of the building. Simon was not among them.

After waiting forty minutes in line, Riker entered the club. He planned to find Simon and see who he was meeting. Once Riker was inside, he found a table in the corner and waited. He hoped that this Viper was the key to the connection between Simon and the terrorist organization Laghaz. With any luck, there would be answers this evening.

The more the room filled up, the more Riker started to stand out. He noticed that he was the oldest person in the room. He was also dressed differently and the only person sitting alone. Worse than the uncomfortable nature of the club was the logistics. There was a large open floor in front of a stage. An upper VIP area overlooked the floor and bars lined the walls. Simon would be an easy target almost anywhere in the club.

Watching the entrance became harder as people packed into the building. The main floor filled with bodies, and at eleven the DJ started to play. Lights, strobes, and lasers traced the walls and ceiling. The bass pounded in Riker's chest—he began to wonder if he'd even be able to hear a gunshot over the music.

Riker's head was starting to hurt from the incessantly loud music. He was starting to wonder if Simon would show up when the young man stumbled right past him. Riker did a double take. There was no chance that he'd come through the main entrance. Riker had made note of every person that came through those doors. He stood up and traced Simon's path back to a set of stairs with two bouncers in front of them. A sign read VIP access only. Apparently, there was another entrance for the privileged.

Simon had his arm around a girl who barely looked old enough to drink. She was swaying and pulling him in different directions. He kept redirecting her and moving towards the exit.

Riker felt sick to his stomach. The thought of saving this piece of shit sickened him. This wasn't the girl from that morning's make-out session. She was clearly past the point of coherency, and this asshole was dragging her out of the club.

Riker followed them through the crowded club to the

front entrance. When they tried to walk down the three steps to the sidewalk, the girl stumbled and both crashed to the ground.

Riker stood above them fuming. "Are you two okay?"

Simon looked up at Riker, taking in his large frame. "Actually, I could really use a hand." He got to his feet but the girl that he was with stayed down. "I think my friend was drugged. Her sister is on her way to pick her up, but it's a little hard to walk with her. Could you help me get her to the parking lot?"

Riker paused for a moment. "Yeah, I can give you a hand."

"Thanks a lot, man. I didn't realize how tough it would be to carry a one-hundred-and-twenty-pound girl."

Simon tried to pick the girl up off the sidewalk. She slipped back onto her back, and Simon was barely able to stop her head from hitting the concrete.

"Let me." Riker bent down, grabbing the girl's right arm and leg. In a quick motion, he twisted and pulled her onto his back, positioning her in a soldier's carry. "Where do we need to take her?"

"Wow, I wouldn't have thought of picking her up like that. Do you want me to support her back or something?"

Riker realized that picking up an unconscious person wasn't something that most civilians were taught to do. "I've got it. You said that her sister is here?"

Simon pulled a phone out of his pocket and checked the screen. "Looks like she'll be here any minute. She'll meet us in the lot."

Riker carried the girl down the sidewalk to the parking lot. Simon walked by his side. "I'm Simon." He stuck out his hand before realizing that both of Riker's hands were occupied.

"I'm Riker." He nodded in Simon's direction.

They reached the parking lot and an SUV rolled to a stop in front of them. The woman got out and rushed over to Simon.

"Oh my God. Is she okay?"

Simon opened the rear door, and Riker put her into the seat.

"I think she got drugged. She was fine one second and barely able to stand up the next. I can come with you if you need help."

She gestured toward a man in the passenger seat. "It's okay. I've got Chuck with me. We'll take her to the ER. Thank God you were here, Simon."

She gave him a quick hug and jumped back in the car.

Simon watched the car pull away. "Wow, that was trippy." He stuck his hand out again, and this time Riker shook it.

"Thanks a lot, man. It's good to see that people still help each other out. You don't see that much anymore."

"Yep, it seems to happen less and less."

"Come have a drink with me. I've got bottle service upstairs." Simon started to walk towards the entrance past the line of people. "You deserve a good karma drink after that. Besides, I'm hanging out with some good people. You'll have a blast."

Riker thought of the Viper and followed Simon back into the club. The bouncer just nodded and allowed the two of them past the line.

Simon led Riker past two more sets of bouncers and up the stairs to the VIP area. Riker noticed two NBA players and a movie star on the way to the table. Four people sat on plush couches with three bottles of high-end liquor on the table between them.

"Is Steph okay?" asked an olive-skinned woman in a low cut dress.

"I think so. Her sister picked her up." Simon tapped Riker on the chest. "I was stumbling around with her and this dude just threw her over his shoulder, caveman style. Carried her to her sister's car. His name's Riker."

"Don't be shy, Riker. Have a seat." The woman patted the couch next to her and winked.

Simon threw an arm around Riker like they were old friends. "You've got to watch out for that one. They don't call her Viper for nothing."

Riker snapped his head toward the woman, looking at her more closely now.

"My name is Miranda. No one calls me Viper except these two fools." She pointed to Simon and another man across from her.

The man shot Riker a wide grin. "We call her that because she is deadly to any man that comes within striking distance. I'm Ted."

Riker had seen evil men and women around the globe. He'd spent his life hunting dangerous individuals, and all it took was a glance to see that this group didn't fall into that category. They were just young and privileged.

Simon was pouring shots for everyone in the group. Riker grabbed his arm and spoke into his ear. "We need to talk. I don't think you want your friends around when we do."

He stopped pouring drinks and scrunched up his face. "What?"

"You need to come with me, Simon."

"Listen, I don't know who you think you are, but I don't *need* to do anything."

"You are in danger. I'm here to figure out why."

The color drained from Simon's face. "What are you talking about?"

"I'll tell you all about it, but not here." He started to pull Simon towards the stairs.

Ted stood up. "Hey, is everything okay?"

Simon regained his composure. "It's fine. I just figured out that me and my man here have a mutual business connection. Top priority stuff. Don't finish those bottles before we get back."

The two reached the top of the stairs. From that vantage point, Riker had a good view of the entire club. Most of the patrons were jumping up and down to the rhythm of the music. A different kind of motion caught Riker's eyes. Three Middle Eastern men were at the bottom of the stairs that led to the VIP area. Two of them were up in the bouncer's face, and the third was slipping past him, taking advantage of the distraction and heading up the stairs.

Riker glanced around the club and spotted four other Middle Eastern men positioned next to each emergency exit and the front entrance.

He pulled Simon back from the stairs and locked eyes with him. "You are in immediate danger. There are several men here that want you dead. I need you to do exactly what I say. Understand?"

Simon's eyes widened. "What the hell are you talking about? No one wants me dead."

The man reached the top of the stairs, his eyes locked on Simon. His only focus was his target. Riker was about to teach him a lesson about observing the entire area.

Riker stepped to the side and casually moved towards the attacker. The man reached under his jacket and pulled out a pistol. Simon stood frozen, watching the weapon that was about to end his life. Riker shot out a lightning-quick jab, and his fist slammed into the attacker's throat.

The man dropped the gun and grabbed his throat with both hands. Riker smashed a hard right hook into the back of his head. The force knocked him facedown onto the floor, where he lay motionless.

Simon stood frozen, unable to process what he had just witnessed. Riker picked up the gun and stuck it into his waistband. A few people looked at the person on the floor, but no one reacted to what had just happened.

Riker grabbed Simon's shoulder hard. "We need to get out of here. There are at least six more of these guys between us and the exit."

Simon looked around frantically. "Why don't we just go out the VIP exit." He pointed to a door in the back of the VIP area.

The two men went out the door, Riker leading the way. Apparently, the men hunting Simon didn't know any more about club access than Riker. After going down a set of stairs and through the kitchen, they entered an alley behind the building.

"My car is parked a few blocks over," Riker said. "We need to move quickly and stay low."

"We should just take my car. It's right here." Simon gestured toward several cars parked along the wall of the building. The third one down was a yellow Lamborghini Huracan.

"That isn't exactly subtle," Riker muttered.

"You said you wanted to get the hell out of here, right?"

A noise at the entrance to the alley caused Riker to look up. There was a man dressed like the other attackers, and his hand was reaching into his jacket.

Riker turned to Simon. "Give me the keys. I'm driving."

7

They'd only driven four blocks before Riker realized they were being followed. A motorcycle pulled up behind them, and it was soon joined by two others.

"I don't believe this," Simon muttered.

"Well, you'd better start believing."

It was the wee hours of the morning, and for the first time since Riker had come to LA, the traffic was blissfully light. There would be no repeat of that morning's police chase down crowded streets.

Simon stared nervously into the side-view mirror, his gaze locked on the motorcycles hot on their tail. Then he glanced out the windshield, seeming to notice their surroundings for the first time. "My place is the other way. We need to head south."

"We're not going to your place."

Riker took a left, guiding the car onto the 101 Freeway. Despite all his many and varied experiences, this was the first time Riker had ever been behind the wheel of a Lamborghini. Driving the supercar so soon after the Camry was a bit of a shock to the system, but a pleasant one. The vehicle was so responsive that it almost seemed to anticipate his moves before he made them. If it hadn't been for the men pursuing them with intent to kill, he would have been in heaven.

"If we're not going to my place, where are we going?" Simon asked.

"North."

Even with all the Lamborghini's power, the motorcycles were having no trouble keeping up with them on the Freeway. The bikes weaved around the other cars, their motors whirring loudly as they clung to Riker's tail. If he was going to lose their pursuers, he needed to get somewhere where the roads were narrow and winding. He'd spent a good portion of the afternoon studying a map of the city, and he had just such a destination in mind.

He glanced over and saw Simon raising his cellphone to his ear. Riker's hand shot out, slapping the cellphone down.

"Hey!" Simon shouted.

"What exactly are you doing?"

"I'm calling my dad."

Riker grimaced. Of course he was. What rich kid wouldn't call his parents at the first sign of trouble? "That's not a good idea."

"My dad is kinda important. He can help."

"I know who your father is. He's not going to be able to help you in this situation."

"But—"

"Listen to me, because I'm only going to say this once." The frustration was clear in Riker's voice, and he didn't try to hide it. "If you care about your father even a little, you will leave him out of this. This is a life-and-death situation, and dragging him into it will ruin his career at best. At worst, he'll end up dead alongside you. Understand?"

There was a long pause. Then Simon slid the phone back into his pocket. "Yeah. I read you."

"Good." A wave of relief swept through Riker. Simon might be a spoiled rich kid, but at least he could follow orders. That was something. "Your best chance of getting through this isn't your father. It's the guy sitting next to you. You're going to have to learn to trust me."

Simon let out a bitter laugh. "Oh really? You do this sort of thing a lot? High-speed chases through the streets of Los Angeles?"

"Second time today."

Simon looked at him wide-eyed, as if he was trying to figure out whether he was serious.

Up ahead, Riker saw the exit he was looking for, and he slid the Lamborghini into the right-hand lane.

Simon raised an eyebrow. "Cahuenga Blvd. You taking us to the Reservoir?"

"Yeah. Hang on." While studying the L.A. map, he'd made a mental note of the Hollywood Reservoir's location and layout. It was an oasis of hiking trails and hills in this urban jungle. And with the hills came a maze of winding, narrow roads. The kind where he might be able to put the Lamborghini to the true test and maybe lose their pursuers.

"Listen, man," Simon said. "You should know that I never meant for things to go this way. What happened at Greyson... the circuit boards and all that... there's an explanation. I wasn't trying to hurt anyone."

Any fondness or sympathy Riker had been feeling toward Simon suddenly drifted away. The man had clearly gotten himself in over his head. Riker would dig into the details, but he needed to focus. "Honestly, I don't give a shit. Lucky for you, someone wants to keep you alive enough that they got me involved. How about you keep your explanations to yourself and let me concentrate on doing my job?"

Simon slid down in his seat a little, arms crossed, but at least he stopped talking.

Riker focused all his concentration on the road ahead of him. He turned off Cahuenga and onto San Marco, a much narrower road that took them close to the reservoir. The Lamborghini rocketed through the curves.

A burst of gunfire rang out from behind them. Riker recognized the sound of an automatic weapon. The men on the motorcycles weren't messing around.

"What the hell!" Simon shouted. "They're shooting at us?"

Riker didn't bother responding. The more isolated roads were allowing the assassins to be bolder. That was all right. It would allow Riker the same opportunity. As they turned onto another winding road, he drove onto the gravel shoulder. He eased off the gas a moment, allowing the motorcycles to get a bit closer. Then, when the bikes were behind him, he slammed his foot down on the accelerator.

Rocks flew back, propelled by the Lamborghini's powerful wheels, showering the men behind them. As Riker angled back onto the road, he saw two of the motorcycles go down. They'd been pushing fifty miles per hour; those men wouldn't be continuing the pursuit any time soon.

"Holy shit," Simon whispered, his eyes locked on the fallen men.

Riker was more focused on the one still upright. He needed to end this fast. The gunfire and the racing vehicles were sure to attract police attention eventually, and the last thing Riker wanted was another encounter with Los Angeles' finest.

Up ahead, he saw just the spot he needed. A short

stretch of straightaway on a narrow road. He lowered his window and turned to Simon. "Hold on to something."

Simon's face was pale. "Like I wasn't before?"

Just before he reached the spot, Riker hit the brakes and turned the wheel. The Lamborghini slid, turning ninety degrees until it was perpendicular to the road. Riker raised his SIG, aimed at the motorcyclist rocketing toward them, and fired three rounds. Every one of them landed center-mass.

The motorcycle went down, sliding across the pavement and just missing their car.

"You shot that guy!" Simon shouted.

Riker said nothing. He opened the door and trotted over to the fallen man.

The right side of the guy's face and body were a mess of road rash, and there were three bullets in his chest. He was dead. Riker gave his body a quick search, but found no identification, just a wad of cash, a pistol, and the assault rifle strapped to his back.

Riker walked back to the Lamborghini and climbed inside.

"What do we do now?" Simon asked.

Riker put the car in reverse and turned around. "We go check on the other guys, and we hope one of them is still alive."

When they reached the spot where the two motorcycles had fallen, Riker let out a soft curse. One of the men lay face down on the pavement, ten feet from where he'd gone down. He wasn't moving. The other man was gone, though his bike remained. He must have managed to stumble off into the woods.

Though he wasn't hopeful, Riker got out and checked the fallen man. As he'd expected, the guy was dead.

Riker stood on the empty road for a moment, considering his options. He could go after the injured man. Chances were, the guy wasn't moving fast. Still, a search like that would take time, and it would mean either leaving Simon alone or dragging him through the woods. Riker didn't relish the thought of either option.

"Oh my God. I can't believe this shit."

Riker glanced back and saw Simon standing next to the Lamborghini, inspecting the bullet holes in the rear portion of the vehicle. Riker felt a wave of anger rise up in him. He'd just saved this guy's life against incredible odds, and the man was worried about his car? He should be thanking God he was alive, not stressing over the damage to his precious status symbol. Protecting this guy was the last thing he wanted to do, but he didn't have any choice in the matter, did he? He was once again an instrument of QS-4. He did what they told him. Or he died.

Sirens blared in the distance, making Riker's decision of what to do next an easy one. He stalked over and grabbed Simon's arm.

"Come on. We're leaving."

Simon took one last look at the exterior of his Lamborghini Huracan, shook his head, and climbed inside.

As Riker was pulling the vehicle back onto the road, Simon turned to him.

"Hey, listen. I don't know why you're doing this, but thank you. Sincerely. You saved my life, man. That's... No one's ever done anything like that for me before. And I won't forget it. Not ever. Thank you."

The words caught Riker by surprise. "Yeah. You're welcome."

"So what now? The police?"

"Not a good idea," Riker said. "Our best bet is to lay low

tonight. You and I need to have a conversation about everything you know about this group if we're going to make that happen."

Simon thought for a moment, then nodded. "Yeah, okay. Let's go back to my place. You can crash there. I'm so exhausted that all I want to do is lie in my bed and sleep for about twelve hours."

"Sorry to tell you this Simon," Riker said as they pulled onto the freeway, "but we can't go to your place. You're not going to be seeing your own bed until this thing is over."

8

MIRO CHATTI WALKED the length of the facility, considering how to kill Simon Buckner. He had to admit that things were not going according to plan. Normally, that didn't bother him. In fact, he considered his adaptability one of his greatest assets. Still, he couldn't help but be a little annoyed. Of all the things he'd thought might go wrong with this mission, all the possible roadblocks he thought he might encounter, he had never considered that killing the spoiled rich kid would be one of them. And yet, here he was.

It was nearly four in the morning, and the majority of the facility was empty. The gun range was quiet. The state-of-the-art workout room was dark. The computer area was a ghost town of glowing monitors. Chatti couldn't help but be a bit annoyed by this too. It wasn't that he expected his people to work all hours, it was just that he couldn't quite understand their desire not to. Some of them seemed to be succumbing to the odd, Western view of work that saw a vocation as something to be tolerated. Chatti looked at things differently. His job was his reason for living. He believed it kept him young and strong, and he poured everything into it.

Laghaz was well-funded and his people were well-trained. Still, as their leader he had to watch out for the unexpected pitfall. He couldn't let the laziness of the culture they were embedded in seep into his team. It was his duty to protect them from themselves.

He'd reached the end of the facility and was about to turn around and start walking the other direction when his phone buzzed in his pocket. He pulled it out and glanced at the screen before answering.

"Nigel, do you have good news for me?"

"I found him," the man answered in a raspy voice.

"Alive?"

"Yes, but he's badly hurt. He needs a hospital."

Chatti grimaced at the suggestion. "That's not in our best interest. As you well know."

"Right. Apologies. It's just that... he's in rough shape. He crashed his motorcycle and then stumbled into the woods. It's a wonder that he had the strength to call us at all."

Chatti waited for Nigel to continue.

"He's... he won't last much longer, Miro."

"Then I suggest you drive fast." With that, he ended the call. Feeling more discombobulated than ever, Chatti headed to the front entrance of the facility.

He wasn't a religious man—that wasn't what Laghaz was all about, unlike most groups the United States government classified as terrorists. When they eventually used the devices Simon Buckner had helped them acquire, the message they'd be putting out would be one of nationalism and a statement on the global overreach of the West, not one about any particular god.

Still, if there was anything Chatti believed in with a religious fervor, it was self-improvement. He had been born into poverty, and he'd work very hard to get to where he was today. Times like this, when his emotions threatened to spin out of control, reminded him that he was not yet perfect. He had flaws that raged wildly inside of him, flaws that needed to be tamed. And the only way he knew how to tame them was through the discipline of pain.

He reached the entrance of the facility and found a man name Yasuf positioned near the door, standing guard.

"Hello, Yasuf."

The man looked startled that Chatti had spoken to him. He was the lowest of the low on the hierarchy of power within Laghaz, and Chatti wasn't sure the two had ever exchanged a word between them. But the man was big, and his muscles pressed against the arms of his T-shirt. He was perfect for what Chatti intended.

"Hello, Miro," Yasuf replied.

"Nigel will be arriving in a few minutes with Dion. I'm told he's badly injured. We may need your help to get him inside."

"Of course."

Chatti smiled. He felt his mood already improving at just the thought of what was about to happen. "In the meantime, I'd like to play a little game."

Yasuf blinked hard, confused.

"I call this game Three to One. I invented it myself. Are you willing to play it with me while we wait for Nigel and Dion?"

"Yes, sir. Of course."

"Good." Chatti took a step closer and shook his arms out, widening his stance in preparation. "The rules are quite simple. First, you punch me three times. I will make no attempt to defend myself. Three solid hits. The face, the stomach, whatever. It's your choice."

The color drained from Yasuf's face. "You want me to hit you?"

"Yes. Three times." Chatti was beginning to wonder if there was a reason Yasuf was working the door. He didn't appear to be the brightest member of their little family. "Then, after you've hit me three times, I will hit you once. That's why it's called Three to One. Understand?"

"Yes, but—"

"Good!" Chatti took a deep breath and relaxed his body. "Go ahead whenever you're ready."

Yasuf stared at him for a long moment, trying to figure out if he was serious.

Chatti said nothing, but he gave the man a look that left no question that his patience was running thin.

Yasuf drew back his right fist and threw a half-hearted punch. It hit Chatti in the chest.

Chatti frowned. "Is that a joke? You are supposed to be a warrior. If that's your best shot, I'm not sure we can use you. We may have to send you back home."

Yasuf's face reddened. He drew back his fist again and let it fly. This time, his fist landed on the side of Chatti's head, causing him to stagger. He felt a moment of blissful pain. But only a moment. The second hit was an improvement, but not by much.

"Let me explain something to you, Yasuf. You have three punches, and you've already wasted two of them. You only have one punch left. I suggest you give it your all. Because when I hit you, I will not be holding back. The more damage you do to me, the less I'll be able to do to you. Do you understand?"

The big man nodded. A few beads of sweat stood on his

brow, and he unconsciously licked his lips as he raised his fists again. The mental struggle he was going through was clear on his face.

"I'm serious," Chatti said. "Prove to me that you belong here."

Yasuf drew back his fist one more time. Then he let it fly, twisting at the hip, putting his body into it. His big fist landed on Chatti's stomach, knocking the air out of his lungs.

The pain came in a sweet rush, and he doubled over, savoring the sensation as his body fought to breathe. He fell to his knees and finally managed to pull in a gasping breath. He stayed there for nearly a minute, letting the discomfort fill him, making a mental note of every twinge and ache.

Then he got to his feet. The pain had done its job. He felt whole.

Yasuf stared at him, his face pale.

"That was good," Chatti said in a weak voice. "Very good. You've shown me something here today. Now it's my turn." He paused for a moment, setting his feet. "You will feel the urge to raise your hands to protect yourself. Resist it. That would incur a penalty."

"A penalty?"

"Trust me, you don't want to find out."

To his credit, Yasuf kept his arms down.

Chatti put everything he had into the punch. His fist smashed into Yasuf's face, and he felt the bones shift. The big man let out a cry of pain as he went down.

Chatti put a hand on the big man's head and gently caressed his hair. A wave of gratitude rushed through him. Yasuf had given him the gift of pain, and he'd returned the favor.

The door buzzed. Chatti glanced at the monitor next to it and saw Nigel standing outside.

He glanced down at Yasuf. "Don't bother getting up. I got this."

He opened the door and Nigel nodded in greeting.

Nigel's eyes went to Yasuf, still wriggling in pain on the floor. "What happened to him?"

"Three to One," Chatti said.

"Ah." Nigel gestured to the car. "I'm going to need some help with Dion."

Chatti followed him out to the car. The nice thing about using a converted warehouse in Santa Monica as their headquarters was that no one ever complained or questioned the odd hours and strange noises that came from their facility. This was the heart of the movie industry. Long hours and gunshots were a normal part of the movie-making process. Just another thing Chatti loved about Los Angeles.

Nigel opened the vehicle's back door, and Dion let out a groan. Chatti grimaced. Nigel hadn't been exaggerating about his condition. The entire left side of his face was torn to shreds. His lower lip hung loosely in three ribbons, and a good portion of his ear was gone. The entire left side of his body was a bloody mess.

Working together, they carried Dion inside. The man groaned and even cried out in pain a few times, and he seemed to be slipping in and out of consciousness. They carried him to the workout room—the soft mats that covered the floor in one section were the closest thing the facility had to a bed.

"Dion," Chatti said when they'd set him down.

A groan was the only response.

"I don't know, Miro," Nigel said. "He's pretty out of it."

Chatti knew what he had to do. Dion needed the clarifying power of pain just as surely as Chatti himself had. He raised his right boot and placed it against Dion's torn up arm. Then he began to press.

Dion's eyes shot open and he cried out.

"It's okay, friend. You're safe." Chatti eased off the pressure, but kept the boot where it was.

"It hurts."

"I know. We'll give you something for the pain. But we need to talk first. What happened with Simon?"

Dion squeezed his eyes shut as if trying to force his brain to remember. "There was someone with him. Dark hair. Over six feet tall. He had training."

Chatti raised an eyebrow. This had to be the same man his people had seen at Simon's house that morning. "A bodyguard."

Dion nodded weakly.

It didn't make sense to Chatti. Simon had no reason to suspect them. He'd thought he was doing business with a Silicon Valley startup firm looking to get a peek at some industry secrets. He had no idea they were Laghaz. He had no idea what the devices were capable of. So why would he hire a bodyguard?

"What else can you tell me?"

"He was a skilled driver. Smart. Led us away from downtown and picked us off."

"Could you identify him if you saw him again?"

Dion thought a moment, then shook his head. "It was dark."

Chatti sighed. Dion had nothing more to give him. It was time to provide him with his relief. He walked to the office and returned a moment later with a black bag. He pulled out a syringe and filled it with morphine, more than enough to end Dion's suffering. Then he stuck the needle in the man's arm.

He turned to Nigel. "We need to find Simon. That's our top priority now."

"Even above the Senhold project?"

"For now, yes." He gave Nigel a hard look. "I don't expect this to take long. The man drives a yellow Lamborghini. How hard can he be to find?"

"Yes, sir. We'll make it happen."

On the floor in front of them, Dion's body was fully relaxed now. They watched as his breathing slowed and then stopped altogether. It was always sad losing a soldier, but in this case, it was for the best. They couldn't take him to a hospital, and Chatti didn't want to use his precious resources nursing a man with half his face torn off back to health.

He needed to use those resources to find Simon Buckner. There was no choice. Simon had seen Miro Chatti's face. He had to die.

9

ONCE THE SIRENS had faded into the distance, Riker stopped the car. He checked all the usual locations for trackers and found none. While he searched, he replayed the events of the day in his mind.

The first assassins hadn't seemed to know that Simon had left his home that morning. That meant they didn't have a tracker on him at that point. They did find him at the club, however.

"Simon, did anyone know that you would be at the club tonight?" Riker asked when he got back in the car.

"Seriously?" Simon looked at Riker like he was a thousand years old.

"Why is that an odd question?"

"You don't go to Avalon VIP on the down low. You gotta flex if you want to get the right eyes on you. I've been talking about it on Instagram, Twitter, Facebook and TikTok. Everyone knew that I was going to be there."

Riker shook his head. The dangers of the world were so hidden from the elite that they didn't even know they existed. "Let me see your phone."

Simon cautiously handed it to him. Riker powered it down and removed the sim card. Simon's eyes widened. "Um, how long do I have to keep that powered down? That is literally my connection to everyone."

"It stays off until you are safe. You can't communicate with anyone until this is over. If the men that are chasing you think one of your friends knows where you are, they might use them to get to you. If they track your phone or credit cards, they will find you and kill you. Do you understand?"

Riker handed the phone back to Simon but put the sim card in his own pocket. Simon nodded, and they drove back to Riker's place in silence. By the time they arrived, Simon was snoring in the passenger seat. Riker could barely wake him up to get him to go inside the house. The combination of alcohol and adrenaline was more than the kid could handle. Riker guided him to a bedroom, and Simon kicked off his shoes and fell onto the bed.

Riker sent a message to Franklin, letting him know that he had Simon. It was 1:30 in the morning, and Riker allowed himself to sleep until 6:00.

Once a pot of coffee was ready to go, Riker shook Simon awake. The young man wasn't thrilled, but he stumbled his way to the kitchen table and Riker put a cup of coffee in front of him.

"I need to know everything about what you did and who you interacted with," Riker said.

Simon yawned and took a sip from his mug. "Like, ever? And do you really need it right now? It's a bit early."

Riker shook his head. "For someone who has a team of skilled hitmen gunning for him, you're really taking this lightly."

Simon shook his head. "Okay, that was totally messed

up, but this is just some kind of misunderstanding. I just need to make some calls to figure out what is going on."

Riker kept his gaze on Simon. He watched for any ticks in his face or hands. He'd expected the kid to lie about what he had done, but it seemed that he was telling the truth.

"We need to talk about how you got mixed up with these people."

"What people? This isn't about Tom, is it?" Simon paused. "Should I have my lawyer here for this?"

"Not unless your lawyer can keep a terrorist organization from killing you. I really don't care if you go to jail or party at night clubs for the rest of your life. My mission is to keep you alive, not to arrest you. The only way I will be able to do that is to find and stop the men who are after you. The best thing you can do is to be honest with me."

Simon sat back in his chair with a blank stare. "I don't understand any of this. Why would a terrorist organization want me dead?"

"If you really don't know who is trying to kill you I think we need to start from the beginning. You mentioned Tom. Who is he and what were you involved with?"

Simon thought for a moment. "Okay, listen. I work for a company called Greyson Electronics. I sort of borrowed something from them. I probably shouldn't have done it, but I figured I'd have it back before anyone noticed."

"What did you take?" Riker asked.

"A couple pieces of new tech from their R&D department. Some kind of communication devices."

"Some kind of communication devices? You don't know what you took?"

"Hey, it's not my area of expertise. It was a case with four parts in it. Two separate pairs of devices. I looked inside, but I have no idea what they do."

"Why did you take it if you didn't even know what it was?"

"First off, I borrowed it. I'm going to put it back. I took it because Tom Segman asked me to get it for him."

The name sounded familiar to Riker. "Who is Tom Segman?"

"Damn, you really don't get out much. He is the owner of SimCom. They make wireless tech. The new Interlink home system is his design. He's worth a couple billion. Ringing any bells?"

"Okay, so why would a billionaire tech designer need your help?"

"He knew that I worked for Greyson. I run their social media marketing division. Tom came to me and asked me to help him out. He told me that Greyson figured out a new kind of wireless communication. They don't operate in the same space as SimCom so it wouldn't even hurt their business if he copied it. He gave me a part number and I got it out of storage. It was just four little devices. Two communicators and two receivers. He wanted to look at them and that's it. Just a big misunderstanding."

"Why did you do it? Don't you have enough money?"

Simon shook his head. "It wasn't about money. It was about a job. Tom said he'd hired me if I helped him out."

Riker shook his head. "A better job. That's what caused all of this?"

"My dad got me the gig with Greyson." Simon looked at his feet. "Just like all my other jobs before that. I decided it was time to earn something on my own."

"And you figured committing industrial espionage, a felony, by stealing an unknown device was a good way to stand on your own two feet?"

Simon turned red. "You don't have to be a dick. It sounds

bad when you say it like that. I was just helping out a friend. No harm, no foul."

"Except there is some harm directed at you. The people chasing you are part of a terrorist network. You are on their radar, and unless you've committed some other major crimes lately, it must be related to the device you took. Did anyone other than Tom know about what you did?"

"No. He asked me to get it, and I gave it to him in person."

"Then Tom wants you dead."

"No way. Tom Segman is a progressive. He'd never hurt anyone. We aren't best friends, but I know that much about him."

"Either he sent the guys to kill you, or there are also guys on the way to kill him. No matter what, he is part of this in a big way."

"Then he's in danger. I know he wouldn't kill anyone."

"You'd be surprised what people are capable of." Riker took a sip of coffee. "We need to figure out what you took. I'm guessing that it is more than just a communication device."

"What else would it be?"

Riker looked at Simon. His sheltered life was astonishing. He had taken something without bothering to know what he was doing. It never even occurred to him that there could be major consequences.

"You're right. They were probably just prototype iPhones. Now that they have them you don't serve a purpose and you need to die."

"Ha ha." Simon didn't look amused.

"Tell me about the exchange."

"I already told you. I gave the case to Tom directly."

"I need details. Did anyone else from Greyson know what you took?"

Simon thought for a moment. "No. I paid a few of the guards to look the other way when I entered the secure area, but they didn't know what I was there for. Tom told me not to tell anyone about what I was doing."

"Where did you meet with him?"

"We met at one of Tom's factories. I just drove up and gave him the case with everything in it. I thought that we were going to meet in his office, but he just met me outside."

"So it was just the two of you?"

"No, not exactly. Tom had some guys with him in his car. There was a driver and some bodyguards in the backseat. I remember that Tom was really nervous the whole time, but I just figured he was worried about getting caught with another company's proprietary tech."

"What makes you think that the guys in the backseat were bodyguards?"

"They were big guys that didn't say anything. I also saw that one of them had a gun."

Riker looked at Simon as if he just stepped off the short bus. "Didn't it seem strange to you that the bodyguards stayed in the car?"

Simon sat up straight. "Well, no. I mean, it does now. At the time I figured that there was no need for protection once Tom saw that it was just me."

Riker shook his head. "Did you get a good look at the guy in the backseat?"

"Yeah, I was standing right next to the car. He was a Middle Eastern guy, about your age."

"Would you recognize him if you saw him again?"

"Yeah, man. I got a good look at him. I'm sure we can ask

Tom who he was." He paused. "Jessica got a good look at him too."

Riker set his cup down. "Jessica?"

"Yeah, she was there with me. I mean, she wasn't involved. I just brought her along."

"You brought a girl with you to a drop?"

"No. I mean, yes. I didn't think of it as a 'drop.' I've known Jessica forever. She's old money, and I know that she likes Tom's company. Hell, everyone thinks he's a genius. I asked if she wanted to meet him and she said yes, so I brought her along."

"Where is she right now?" Riker spoke with urgency.

"I don't know. I'm not her keeper. Besides, you took my phone. It doesn't matter anyway. Like I already said, she isn't part of this."

"Are you an idiot? She was at the drop. Whoever ordered you killed is probably tying up all the loose ends. She is a loose end. My guess is she's already dead."

The color left Simon's face. "We have to save her. I didn't mean for any of this to happen. What about Tom? We have to save him too."

"I hate to be the one to tell you, but Tom probably ordered your death. He may seem like a nice guy, but he is clearly involved in some very bad shit. We will get to him as fast as we can, but I intend to keep the civilian casualties to zero. What's Jessica's last name?"

"King."

Riker picked up his phone and called Franklin. "I need you to find out if a woman named Jessica King is still alive. If she is, get me her location."

10

"This is humiliating," Simon muttered as he squeezed into the vinyl bench seat.

"Yes," Riker answered dryly. "I can hardly think of a worse fate."

The city bus lurched forward and they started down the road.

It was only after much discussion and many protests from Simon that they'd decided to take the bus across town to Jessica's. Riker had considered other methods. The fastest would have been taking Simon's Lamborghini, but that brought a number of issues along with it. Not only would they be likely to be spotted in the distinctive yellow vehicle, but there was a chance they would lead the killers directly to Jessica. Franklin had assured them she was still alive—or at least she had been two hours ago, based on her latest Instagram post—and Riker intended to keep it that way. Calling an Uber was another possibility, but Riker didn't want an electronic paper trail tying even his fake identity to the safe house.

Besides, he didn't exactly hate watching Simon's discomfort at having to take public transportation.

After Franklin had confirmed via social media that Jessica was still alive, they'd given him the part number for the items Simon had taken from Greyson Electronics. Riker hoped he'd be able to get them more information. In the meantime, Riker was focused on keeping both Simon and the woman he'd foolishly involved safe from Laghaz.

"How does this even work?" Simon asked. "Is this bus going to Jessica's neighborhood?"

"Nope." Riker pulled the bus route map out of his pocket and traced their path with his finger. "We have to transfer over to the orange line at the bus station downtown."

Simon groaned as if the news were causing him physical discomfort.

"What should I know about Jessica?" Riker asked.

"Like I said, she's old money. The real kind of rich, where no one even remembers how your family got its wealth. I've known her since we were kids." Simon smiled a little. "She's one of the few people who won't put up with any bullshit from me."

"I like her already."

The smile disappeared. "You don't think those guys are really going to hurt her, do you? Because of what I did?"

"We're going to do everything we can to keep that from happening."

The bus rolled to a stop and a group of three older women got on. Riker glanced around and saw there were no empty seats. He tapped Simon on the arm.

"Come on. We're standing up."

Simon looked confused. "What? Why?"

"We're giving these women our seats. It's something you do on busses. Trust me on this."

Riker soon discovered that watching Simon tightly clutch the handrail as the bus bumped and lurched along was even more amusing than watching him squeeze into the vinyl seat.

One bus transfer and thirty minutes later, they made it downtown. Riker and Simon got off the bus and walked a block to the nicest apartment building in the area. As they approached, Riker spotted the doorman, a big, burly guy who wore a polite smile but probably had no problem making sure uninvited guests never crossed the threshold.

Simon nudged Riker. "Why don't you let me handle this? You might be the master of stinky city busses, but we're in my world now." He walked up to the doorman and held out his hand. Riker caught a flash of green against his palm, but he didn't catch the denomination of the bill. Simon quickly glanced at the man's name badge as they shook hands. "Ralph, my man, how's it going?"

"Very well, sir." Ralph made the cash disappear into his pocket, then smiled politely, waiting.

"We're here to see Jessica King. Tell her it's Simon."

"Of course. Is she expecting you?"

"Not exactly."

"I understand. One moment." He retreated to a small podium near the door and lifted a phone to his ear. Though they were only six feet away, Ralph somehow managed to talk in a voice they couldn't make out. After a moment, he set down the phone and stepped around the podium. He walked to the door and pulled it open. "You can go up."

The expression of relief on Simon's face was not lost on Riker. As they walked through the beautiful lobby with its marble floors and columns, he turned to Simon. "You weren't sure she'd let us in. What aren't you telling me?"

Simon hesitated a moment before answering. "It's

possible we didn't leave things on the best terms last time we spoke."

Riker said nothing, but he couldn't help but frown. When they got into the elevator, he said, "What floor?"

Simon looked at him like he was an idiot. "The penthouse, of course."

Riker pushed the button for the top floor and waited as they glided into the sky. When they exited the elevator, Simon led them to the left, to one of only two apartments on this level. The door was already open, and the most beautiful woman Riker had ever seen stood in the doorway. Her long dark hair hung loosely around her shoulders in a style that somehow looked both effortless and immaculate at the same time. She was tall, maybe only three inches shorter than Riker, and her casual outfit couldn't hide the curves of her fit body. She looked pissed.

"I can explain," Simon said immediately.

"Honestly, I don't need to hear it. I'm more interested in what you're doing here." She glanced at Riker. "Who's your friend?"

Riker held out his hand. "Matthew Riker."

She shook it, looking a little perplexed. "Jessica King." She turned to Simon, and the annoyance reappeared on her face. "I guess you two better come inside."

They followed her through the door, and Riker stepped into an apartment that looked like it had sprung to life from a high-end magazine spread. He'd visited his share of wealthy homes lately—chiefly Dobbs' mansion and Weaver's brownstone back in New York—but this place was a whole different level. Twenty-five-foot floor to ceiling windows on every side of them gave Riker the feeling that they were floating above the city. Every piece of furniture was perfectly selected to add to the clean design. Jessica led them through the main living area, past the dining room with its long table and glass-walled walk-in wine room. Then she took them upstairs and through a set of glass doors to an outdoor terrace that looked large enough to host a small wedding.

Jessica gestured to some chairs next to the infinity pool, then sank into one herself.

Simon took another, leaning back in the chair and getting comfortable. "Look, about the other night."

"No apology necessary. Tell me what all this is about."

Riker couldn't help but be a little curious as to what Simon was apologizing for, but he decided to let it go for now. He turned to Simon. "You want to tell her, or should I?"

Simon hesitated, then leaned forward. "So listen, you know last week when we met up with Tom Segman?"

"Yeah, you helped him out with that communication tech."

He shifted in his seat uncomfortably. "I wasn't entirely honest with you. I wasn't delivering the stuff as a favor to my boss. In fact, my bosses don't know I did it."

Her brow furrowed in concern. "Are you telling me you stole company secrets?"

"Uh, it's a little worse than that, actually." He paused and turned to Riker.

Though Riker wasn't eager to bail Simon out of this awkward conversation, time was a factor. "It seems there's a terrorist organization involved with whatever Simon handed over to Segman."

"My God." She pulled her feet up under her as if she were suddenly cold.

"I didn't mean to!" Simon said. "I was trying to help Segman out. I'm sorry I can't be going around saving the world all the time like you, but I'm doing my best here."

"Saving the world?" Riker asked.

"Yeah, she runs a charity that gives bottles of water to poor kids or something."

"We build wells to get clean drinking water to remote villages in third-world countries," Jessica clarified.

"Whatever, same thing. Point is, I screwed up."

"More importantly, you're in danger," Riker added, looking at Jessica. "The terrorists want Simon dead, and since you were at the exchange, there's a good chance they'll come after you as well."

Jessica said nothing for a long moment. "You're government."

Riker scratched his chin, amused. "What makes you say that?"

"In the unlikely event that Simon took this seriously enough to hire security, he'd go for dumb muscle. A bouncer at one of the clubs or maybe a former MMA guy. Someone flashy. That's not you."

Riker said nothing.

"That means someone caught wind of the exchange and decided they didn't want a senator's son getting killed, even if he maybe deserves it." She paused, thinking another moment. "But they'd want deniability. It wouldn't look good if it came out that they protected a guy who helped terrorists."

A thin smile crossed Riker's face. He was impressed, not only at how quickly she was putting things together, but with how she'd immediately jumped to problem solving when she'd been told that she was in danger.

Jessica leaned forward, her bright green eyes appraising Riker. "No, you're not government. Not officially, anyway. You're an outside contractor. Someone close enough that they can trust, but distant enough that they can disavow if things go wrong."

Simon stared at Riker, wide-eyed. These were clearly questions he'd never even thought to ask. "Is that true?"

Riker shrugged. "Ghost agent is the official term. Who I work for hardly matters. Point is, I'm here to help."

"He did too," Simon confirmed. "Some guys came after me last night. We did this whole chase through L.A. thing. It was wild as fuck. They shot up the Lambo, but Riker took them down like he was John Wick or something."

Jessica's face darkened. Her eyes were still on Riker. "And what about me? Am I part of your mission?"

Riker shook his head. "I didn't know you existed until an hour ago."

"I understand. Then I need to disappear for a while. I have my annual fundraiser on Friday, but I can get out of L.A. until then. I've got a place in the Alps where I can lay low."

"I don't think that's a good idea. These guys have resources. Once they figure out who you are, they'll check every property you own. They'll track your credit cards. They won't give up until you're dead."

"Then what do I do?"

Riker considered that. The reason he was here was to do the job QS-4 had given him and hopefully get out from under their thumb. This woman was nothing more than a distraction from that goal.

And yet, he couldn't stop the words that came out next.

"I said you weren't part of my mission, but that doesn't mean I'm not going to help. The best plan is for us to stick together."

"And then what?" Simon asked. "We wait for the terrorist group to grow old and die?"

"No," Jessica said. "We have a responsibility here. We need to find out what you gave them." She turned to Riker. "Am I wrong?"

He smiled. "You are not."

"Good. Then what's the plan?"

Riker's phone buzzed in his pocket. He glanced at the screen before answering. "Franklin, what do you have for me."

"Not good news." Franklin's voice was even more serious than usual. "I was able to trace the items Simon stole through the part numbers you gave me. They're not communications tech. They're weapons."

11

Eleven years ago.

Riker and Morrison sat in silence for nearly five minutes. Morrison sipped on bad coffee and looked Riker up and down. Riker's foot silently tapped under the table. His mind worked on the puzzle of this man, turning the possibilities of him like a piece that didn't seem to fit.

Riker broke the silence. "You're ex-military. I'd guess Delta Force."

Morrison's lips turned up in the slightest smile.

"If you have an offer for me, the answer is no. I've got something that I need to do." Riker started to get up.

"I was in Delta, though I'm out now. What made you guess that?"

"You have the movement and rigidness of a military man, but the formal habits are gone. You don't salute like it's your job, because it isn't any more. I guessed Delta because you're contracting in an anti-terrorist location. I think I would have heard if a recent DEVGRU retiree was on base so I doubt you're a SEAL. Plus you've got the Beckwith brow. All you Delta guys have it. I think they beat it onto your faces."

"That's exactly how we get it. You can sit back down. I'll save you the effort of the walk across base. The admiral is not going to let you finish your mission. It's not even worth ruffling his feathers." Morrison spoke as if it was a foregone conclusion.

"I can be very persuasive." Riker didn't sit down, but he didn't leave either. "The admiral may be a hard-ass, but he respects the lives that we've lost to Izad. He doesn't want that to be for nothing."

"That man holds his position because he can care about those lost soldiers and still fall in line, keeping the political balance top of mind."

Riker stared at Morrison. "Are you suggesting that following command is a bad thing?"

"Not at all. Men like the admiral are necessary for the world to keep spinning. Countries need to deal out proportionate responses. They need men who pull back when economic or political pressure tells them to do so. Men like that make the world feel more stable."

"What kind of man are you?"

"I'm the kind of man that does what needs to be done. The kind of man who knows Mohamad Izad is sitting in a compound ninety miles from here. I'm also the kind of man with the resources to do something about it."

Riker took a sip of cool coffee, taking in this stranger. "Then what are you waiting for?"

"I understand that you're skeptical. I was too when I sat where you are. Don't worry. I'll give you evidence about my legitimacy, but first I want to be sure you're the man I think you are."

"Who do you think I am?"

"I think you are the exceptional among the exceptional." Morrison paused for effect. "I'm not just concerned about the things you can do. I read your file. I know you excel with weapons and have completed most of the training the SEALs have to offer. I need to know if you have the mind to achieve the next level."

Riker said nothing. On the surface everything this man was saying sounded like bullshit, but the way he said it made it very believable. "I know the Delta guys think they are hot shit, but I'd argue that there isn't a level higher than DEVGRU."

"I have full respect for everyone in DEVGRU, but you need to open your mind. The SEALs, Delta, Rangers all of them, they are pawns on a board. The players decide where they should go and push them around. You are all skilled warriors, but your actions are limited by the rules of the game and the people who play it."

"So what are you then? A player who moves the pieces around?"

"No, I work with a group that can see the board. We are a new element that plays by a different set of rules. The warriors that I bring in are more than pawns. They have more freedom in the field than any government operative will ever have."

"So your operatives have a license to kill? A bunch of double-oh-sevens running around causing chaos in the world?"

"No license to kill. Just their own discretion. If the team's mission is successful, then we know they did what needed to be done. Nothing less, nothing more."

"You don't think a lack of accountability is an issue?"

"Not with the right men. That's really the point. We need

men that are focused on task, not self-glory and not destruction."

"But they also need to be capable of said death and destruction."

Morrison nodded.

"What about the missions? Do you just let these operatives do whatever they want? Something like a group of vigilante soldiers running around fighting for justice? If so, you should really be wearing an eye patch."

"I don't get the reference. Look, the world is complicated. We do what we do for money, but we don't take just any job. We also strive to make the world a better place."

"Sounds like the admiral and your organization are in the same position. Just trying to keep the balance of powers happy."

"Our positions are very different. The admiral is bound by the rules of the board. His pawns move forward one space at a time. Our operatives can move in any direction, any amount of spaces. They are free from the constraints that have been beaten into their minds."

Riker frowned. "I don't know if you're for real, and if you are I don't know if I'm the guy you're looking for. Either way, this is a waste of time. I already signed up for my next six years. The contract is done and on file. Come back and see me then."

"You're still thinking like a pawn. Take a seat, and I'll give you the evidence that I mentioned."

Riker considered walking away, but he couldn't help but be curious. He reluctantly sank into his chair.

Morrison opened up a small laptop and entered a long passcode. He turned the screen so that Riker could see it.

"I assume that you know who Dimitri Yahontov is?"

"Yeah, the Red Ghost."

"That's right. He works under Putin. One could argue that the invasion of Ukraine was his work. He is a master at manipulating world events."

"He's also a fucking psychopath," Riker observed. "He'll kill an entire village of people just to drum up some civil unrest. Everyone knows who he is."

"Then why don't we do something about him? I mean if he is such a monster and causes so much damage, why don't the fine men of DEVGRU knock on his door and put a bullet into his eye?"

Riker stared at the photo, wishing it were so. "They don't call him the Red Ghost for nothing. He almost never leaves Russia, and when he does, it is only briefly. He disappears before we have time to move." Riker thought for a moment. "I know what you're going to say. Why not get him in Russia? You also know the answer. We can't risk the political fallout from an attack on Russian soil."

"Now you're starting to follow along."

Morrison brought up a video clip. The footage was the green and black image of a night-vision camera. It was mounted to the head of a man moving cautiously through the interior of a large home. The shaky first-person POV turned from side to side. The operative was alone in the hall. His hand pushed open a door and revealed a man sleeping in a bed.

Riker recognized the sharp jaw and bushy eyebrows of Yahontov. His breath was steady as he slept. A hand holding a silenced SIG-Sauer P228 came into the frame. The flash made the night vision screen go white for a moment and the whisper of a shot came through the speakers. The image adjusted back to the green and black to show a hole where one of Yahontov's eyes should have been.

The operative opened the window and slid out onto the

ledge. He closed the window behind him. There was a wire mounted to the side of the building. He hooked onto it and slid across to the adjacent building.

Morrison shut the computer. "That was on Russian soil. Now he really is a ghost."

Riker's mouth hung open. "When did that happen? It's going to start a war. Russia will blame us whether or not the US officially sanctioned it. The fallout will be massive."

"That happened three days ago. No one will ever hear about it from any official Russian source. Just after the target was eliminated, the building was attacked by a small Russian mafia group. They took credit for the kill. Putin's official stance is that he doesn't even know who Yahontov is. You are one of the few people on earth that will know this ever happened.

"The thing that I can't show you is a village in Ukraine. I suppose the correct statement is that I *can* show you the village. It was supposed to be destroyed by an attack that was to be blamed on rebel fighters, and Russian forces were going to come in to calm the civil unrest. The attack didn't happen without Yahontov. The men, women and children that would have died didn't, and the conflict that would have happened in the aftermath never occurred."

Riker sipped his coffee even though it was now room temperature. The gesture gave him a chance to calm his reeling mind. "I'm guessing that you knew my papers had been signed for my next contract. Are those rules open to change?"

"I wouldn't be here if they weren't."

"What's the catch?"

"No catch, but there is always a cost. If you decide you want to be part of the next level, there is no going back. We are our own family, so a wife and kids are off the table. You cut ties with everyone from your old life. That shouldn't be hard for you. There's no contract. You're in until you need to retire or until you die. The second is more likely than the first."

Just like that, Morrison laid it out. No bullshit, just giving it straight. Riker liked the way he operated.

"How long can I think about it?"

"Not long. I need an answer by tomorrow morning. You do get a kind of bonus if you sign on."

Riker smiled. "After that sweet pitch, I can't wait to hear what the bonus is."

"In four days we are going to take out Mohamad Izad and his entire terrorist cell. I will lead a strike force into Iran; we will decimate his infrastructure and prevent all of his future plans. If you say yes, you'll be part of the mission."

Riker's eyes lit up. Though it was difficult, he managed to keep his composure, touching the cold coffee to his lips to hide his smile.

12

"Two explosive devices," Franklin said. "It's next-generation tech. Powerful, but difficult to detect. Invisible to everything from X-ray to bomb-sniffing dogs. It can only be detonated by using the paired device. That was what was in the case you took, Simon. Two bombs. Two detonators."

Riker's expression was grave. "How powerful are they?"

"Each bomb contains one kiloton of explosive power."

"That can't be," Riker said. "From what Simon told me, the devices are light weight and the size of a laptop computer."

"That's what makes them so special. Have you ever heard of a Z-pinch?"

"Yeah, but only in experimental nuclear propulsion. I've never heard of it used in weapons technology."

"Greyson Electronics apparently cracked that nut. I don't understand all of the physics of it, but the idea is they use magnetic forces to compress plasma. The pressure causes extreme heat. The heat is enough to cause a fusion reaction in the core material. This device uses an AI to time and control the direction of a thousand micro forces from different axis, which allowed them to miniaturize the process. It's the first of its kind."

Riker's mind was reeling at the thought of a terrorist organization in control of such technology. "Do you know if there is a way to disable or block the detonators?"

"That's the icing on the cake. The signal receiver and transmitter use neutrinos. It prevents the signal from being blocked by virtually anything. It is a brilliant system."

Riker shook his head. "How come all the brilliance in the world seems to end up creating things that can destroy it?"

Riker talked to Franklin a little while longer, working the problem, before hanging up the phone and conveying the information to Simon and Jessica.

Simon's face was pale. He said nothing as he stared down at the floor.

"We have to do something," Jessica said. "Can't you call your bosses? Have them send in the Marines or something."

"Franklin, the guy who just called me, is working on it."

In truth, Franklin had already contacted Morrison, who had told him in no uncertain terms that they were to concentrate on protecting Simon Buckner, and not to worry about the weapons. Riker had been wrestling with that message since Franklin had given it to him. It sounded decidedly unlike Morrison.

Was it possible that Morrison actually wanted him to go after the weapons? It would explain why he'd sent him across the country on a mission to protect a rich kid. But then why tell Franklin to back off?

More importantly, did Riker care about Morrison's orders? Not with all the lives on the line. If there was a chance of him being able to recover the weapons, he had to try.

He glanced at Jessica. "Pack whatever you need to get through the next few days, but do it quickly. I want to be out of here in ten minutes."

Jessica nodded and disappeared into the apartment.

Simon frowned. "You sure we can't stay here? This place is safe, and it beats the hell out of your house."

Riker shook his head. "If they come for Jessica, this is the first place they'll look."

Simon sighed and headed for the kitchen. He returned a few minutes later with a plate full of fruit.

Jessica came out of a hallway with a small travel bag. It looked like it was made of some expensive material with a designer name stitched all over it. Riker guessed it cost more than the old Ford he had parked back in his driveway.

Simon saw the way Riker was looking at him and responded with a mouth full of strawberries. "What? These will be bad by the time you get back here. I just don't want good food to go to waste."

Jessica turned to Riker. "Listen, I may have some resources that can help us. I have connections and my family can provide almost anything. Sorry if that comes off as boastful, but it needs to be said. If those weapons are out there, we need to use everything at our disposal to get them back, right? It may be your mission, but I think we should have more than one guy."

"You're right. This task would be more suited for a team. The problem is our enemies. They are not going to play by the same rules that we do. Each person that you contact will be in danger. If you speak to your assistant, they might torture him to get information. If you reach out to your parents, they may be kidnapped to get back at you."

Jessica's eyes focused on Riker's face. She didn't know what to think of him. "What about the FBI?"

"I debated contacting them. Here is why I chose not to. The people that took the weapons are after Simon. They will want to tie up that loose end as fast as they can. That means they will focus on him and expose themselves until he is dead. If a government strike force is called in, the people we are after will disappear. Most likely it will accelerate their plans. We have a better chance of finding and stopping them on our own."

Simon stopped eating. "Are you saying that you want the guys to come after us? That plan sounds horrible."

"I'm saying that I want to stop an attack that may kill thousands of people."

Jessica threw her bag over her shoulder. "Then we need to make sure they don't get a chance to carry out an attack."

As the three of them waited for the elevator, Riker remembered that they'd taken the bus from the safe house. "Jessica, do you have a car here?"

Jessica glanced at Simon and the two gave Riker Cheshire cat smiles. "Yeah, I've got a car."

She swiped a key card in the elevator and hit the button labeled PP1. The door opened and the three stepped out into an underground parking garage. It was the nicest garage that Riker had ever seen. The floor was sealed and had a glossy shine. Soft white light filled the room, causing the car's colors to pop brilliantly. Instead of cars crammed into slots that gave just enough room to open the doors, the cars sat five feet apart.

Riker looked around at the selection of vehicles. He could identify about half of them. The others were high-end sports cars that he couldn't name. He hoped that her car was more practical than Simon's.

"Which one's yours?" Riker asked.

"This is my garage," she said with a smile.

"Yes, and which one is your car?"

Simon patted a hand on Riker's back. "No man, this is *her* garage. These are her cars."

Riker turned and looked around. He counted twenty-four cars. One was an old Porsche, but the rest looked brand new. There were SUVs, sedans, coupes, and exotic looking sports cars.

"Which do you want to take?" she asked.

Riker continued to take in the collection of vehicles. "We need one that can hold three people, has good acceleration, handling, and doesn't stand out." He pointed to one of the cars, it was a black sedan. "That will work."

"Ah, the AMG E 63 S. Good choice. Not too flashy, but it's got a little over six hundred horses under the hood. It will get you to sixty in three seconds flat." Jessica smiled proudly as if she was talking about a child. She put her thumb on a scanner next to a metal cabinet on the wall. When a light on the cabinet turned green, she opened it and took out a key fob. She tossed the key to Riker and gave him a wink.

Riker loved his old truck, but he had a hard time keeping the smile off his face when he slid into the driver's seat. The exhaust roared and crackled when he started the engine. He could feel the power and the torque as the car accelerated out of the garage.

Once they were a mile from Jessica's place, Riker reached into his pocket and pulled out Simon's sim card. He held it up so Simon could see it from the backseat.

"Do you think you will be able to contact Tom?" Riker asked.

"No problem. We need to warn him about what's happening."

"Like I said, he knows what's happening. The question is, how involved is he? Tom is probably the one who wants you dead. If he isn't going to use the bombs, he knows who is. Either way, he isn't the guy you think he is. I need you to set up a meeting with him. Tell him that someone tried to attack you, and you think it might be over your deal."

"If he's as bad as you think he is, won't he just kill me when we meet up?"

"I'm sure that someone will be there to kill you. That's who I want to find. Just set up the meeting and don't mention Jessica or me."

"Of course not. I'll get the meeting. That is something that I've always been good at." Simon put the card in his phone. As soon as it powered up, a constant stream of beeps and buzzes erupted from the phone. Simon watched the screen as dozens of notifications streamed by. He scrolled through the text messages and then paused. "I've got a bunch of messages from Tom." He read the texts aloud. "Are you okay? Call me as soon as you get this. Where are you? Call me back ASAP."

Jessica glanced at Riker, then turned to Simon. "Well, call the man."

He put the phone on speaker and hit the call button. Tom picked up on the first ring.

Simon spoke in a calm voice. "What's up, man? I got your text."

The three listened as Tom spoke. "Thank God you're okay. Has anyone come for you?"

"Let's just say it's been a pretty weird day. What the hell did you get me involved with?"

"I'm sorry Simon. We can't talk about this on the phone. Do you remember my beach house?"

"The one in Malibu?"

"Yes. How fast can you get here?"

"Maybe an hour. Depends on traffic."

"Just get here as fast as you can. I'll explain everything."

As soon as Tom finished speaking, the line went dead.

Jessica looked at Riker. "He didn't sound like he was trying to set Simon up. He actually sounded scared to me."

"You're right. I don't think he's the mastermind."

"So who is?" Simon asked.

"I don't know yet, but I do know that Tom is a link in the chain. The odds are he is setting up a trap for you."

"We're not going to walk into said trap, are we?" Jessica asked.

"Not exactly. We'll scope out the place and see what we're up against. If it looks like I can get Tom without too much trouble, I will. If there are too many guys there, we'll come up with another plan."

Riker held his palm up to Simon. "The card."

"Give me two seconds. I need to write a couple posts."

"Really, Simon?"

"Yes, Jessica. Everyone is asking about me. I don't want anyone trying to track me down. I'm sending a message about getting away with a new fling for the week."

Simon finished his cover story and posted it to all his social media. Then he took the sim card out and handed it to Riker. Simon directed Riker to the beach house.

While they drove, Riker's phone rang. He glanced at the screen and answered with a simple "Yes?"

When Franklin spoke his voice was just loud enough for Jessica and Simon to hear. "How did it go with Jessica King? Did she have any information that we need?"

"No, but she was at the exchange. Laghaz could be coming for her. She's with me now."

"If she isn't useful, you shouldn't have her with you. She is not part of the mission and will most likely be a liability."

"So I should have left her to fend for herself? Possibly die?"

"What I'm saying is that she should not concern you. You have orders, and protecting her is not one of them. You need to focus on protecting Simon."

"I don't leave innocent women to die. And she seems perfectly capable, definitely an asset not a liability. Also, I really don't give a shit what you think."

"You need to remember who you are working for and what the mission is."

"I'll keep that in mind if I ever have to save your ass. I'll check and see if it's part of the mission."

Riker ended the call and silenced the phone.

Jessica's mouth turned up in a slight smile. "You've got good judgment. I am a valuable asset."

Riker returned the smile and kept driving. He weaved in and out of traffic, getting them to their destination quickly.

When they were a quarter-mile from the home, he pulled the car over. Houses were built shoulder to shoulder along the beach. Steep hills capped with mansions stood on the other side of the road.

"You two wait here," Riker said. "I'm going to get a vantage point and scope out the house. If it's clear, I'll get Tom."

"We're coming with," Jessica said.

"What?" Simon asked.

"If it is just Tom there, you will need Simon. He isn't going to talk to you alone. He has no idea who you are. Besides, I want to see this for myself. You pulled me out of my life. I'm not going to just sit here like a child."

Simon opened his door and got out of the car.

"Get your ass back in here," Riker said.

"Trust me, man, she already made up her mind. We can either fight her for ten minutes and then agree, or we can cut to the chase."

They both started to walk up the hillside. Riker got out of the car and followed, shaking his head.

They climbed until they had a good vantage point of Tom's house and its wrap-around, floor-to-ceiling windows. Perfect for taking in the sunset over the ocean. Riker pulled out his scope and looked through the windows of the second floor.

"Do you see anything?"

"Yeah. I need you to verify if that's Tom." Riker handed the scope to Simon.

It took Simon a moment to locate the correct house. When he did he gasped.

"Which one is he?" Riker asked.

"He's the one with the gun to his head."

13

Riker stared down at the house, considering his next move. He'd seen three gunmen through the window, but there might have been more. He'd need to proceed carefully. "This changes things. I'm going to get Segman. I need you two to wait here. No excuses. No arguments."

Simon shook his head sadly. "You'll get no argument from me, man. My policy is to stay as far away from gunfire as possible. But good luck convincing Jessica. I've known her since kindergarten, and I've yet to see her change her mind on anything."

Riker turned to Jessica and waited. The woman met his gaze, her eyes searching his for a long moment.

"All right," she said. "We'll wait."

Simon's mouth dropped open. "What the hell? How'd you do that, Riker?"

Riker ignored the question. He tossed the car keys to Jessica, and she neatly snatched them out of the air. "Stay here. Stay low and don't do anything to attract attention. If you see anyone but me leave the house, run back to the car and get the hell out of here. Understand?"

Jessica nodded. Simon just shrugged noncommittally.

"I'll take that as a yes. I'll be back in five minutes with Segman."

With that, he started toward the house.

The house was even bigger and more impressive up close than it had seemed from their observation point. The floor-to-ceiling windows were already concerning Riker. It made approaching undetected challenging, but it also let him keep his eyes on his targets. Luckily for Riker, all three of the gunmen had their attention on the billionaire in the chair. Riker didn't like their posture. They looked like men sent not just to intimidate, but to question and clean up.

Riker crept up the steps to the front door. He was about to pull out his bump key, but then he decided to try the door first. The knob twisted freely in his hand. The gunmen hadn't locked the door behind them. He pulled the SIG out of his waistband, checked his pocket to make sure he had the spare clip, and stepped inside.

The layout of the house immediately made Riker grimace. Like so many modern homes, it had an open floor plan. Great for entertaining and for giving the living space an airy, expansive feel. Not so great for covert approaches. Riker was going to have to walk through the entryway, dining area, and massive main living room to reach the stairs, all the while completely exposed to anyone who happened to glance over the railing and down to the lower level. He took a deep breath and started forward.

His eyes shifted between the upstairs and the downstairs as he moved through the house, gun held in a two-hand grip, moving as quickly as he could while still minimizing the noise his feet made on the tile. There was a good chance they'd left someone on the first floor to stand guard, and he didn't want to be caught unaware because his attention was focused on the upstairs. He did a quick sweep of the lower level, checking the kitchen, the bathroom, the pantry. He found no one, so he headed up the staircase.

A man's panicked voice drifted down to him. "I did what he wanted. You have everything you need."

"Not everything," another voice answered, this one deep and strong.

"I called Buckner and told him to meet me. It's only a matter of time. You'll have your man." The guy sounded drunk as well as terrified.

"And what about the girl who was with him? This Jessica King."

"I told you, I never met her before that night. But she won't be hard to find. She's got this foundation, and she does all these charity events."

As Riker reached the second level, he froze. There was a man in the doorway to the bedroom, one Riker hadn't been able to see from the first floor or from outside. That put the number of bad guys at four. Riker didn't love those odds, but what choice did he have? They needed Segman alive. The good news was that the man in the doorway was facing into the room. Not only did that mean he wouldn't notice Riker, but his body gave Riker a bit of cover from anyone in the room who might glance out.

He paused at the top of the stairs, picturing the layout of the bedroom as best he could from what he'd seen through the window. Once this started, it would happen fast.

"So you don't know the King woman, and you already set the meeting with Buckner. I'm trying to figure out why we need you alive at this point."

"Please. I can't... I don't want to die. I'm not..." His voice broke, and he began to cry.

"My God, can you believe how soft these people are?" one of the men muttered.

Riker crept forward. He doubted he was going to get a distraction better than a grown man weeping. He reached the doorway, paused to gather himself, and threw an arm around the man's neck. He pulled hard, locking the chokehold tight in an instant. Only a tiny grunt escaped the man's lips, and that was thankfully covered by Segman's loud sobs. Riker pulled him backward. The man's hands came up, grabbing the arm around his neck, but only for a moment. Then he went limp.

Riker dragged him away from the doorway and laid his unconscious body on the floor. The other three men still had their attention on Segman. Riker had been lucky so far. He couldn't count on that luck continuing. From here on out he needed to perform flawlessly. He stayed in a low crouch and positioned himself next to the doorway.

"What do you think?" the man with the gun to Segman's head asked. "Don't we need him for the meeting with Buckner? Or what if Buckner calls? We need him to answer the phone, right?"

"You kidding?" another man answered. "The guy can't even stop blubbering. You trust him to talk to Buckner on the phone again?"

"You're right. Let's end it."

That was Riker's cue. He couldn't wait any longer. He peered through the doorway, raised his SIG, and fired two rounds. The man with the gun to Segman's head fell, the contents of his skull splattered on the floor-to-ceiling windows behind him.

The remaining two men had their weapons out in an instant. Riker ducked back behind the door frame. In less than thirty seconds, he'd brought the odds from four-to-one to two-to-one, but things would be more difficult now. He'd lost the element of surprise. These men had training. He could tell that from the way they held their weapons and how quickly they'd reacted to his surprise attack.

"You're the guy, aren't you?" the man with the deep voice said. "The one who's been protecting the Buckner kid."

Riker didn't bother responding.

Segman was still weeping, but softly now.

The man with the deep voice chuckled. "Look, I don't know why you have this obsession with protecting rich kids. Maybe you're looking for reward money or something, but I'm telling you, it's not worth it. We are not people you want to mess with. It won't end well."

There was a long pause.

"I don't think he's feeling very talkative," the other man said.

"No, it doesn't seem that way. Let's see what we can do about that. Okay tough guy, here's the deal. I'm putting my gun to Segman's head, and I'm going to kill him if you don't-_"

Riker was already in motion. A gun to Segman's head was one that wasn't pointed at him. He ducked around the doorframe, took a split second to draw a bead on the deep-voiced man, and fired three rounds into his chest.

The last man stood to Segman's left. His gun was still pointed at the ceiling, but he was bringing it down, a look of determination in his eyes. While the deep-voiced man had seemed to be the leader of this little group, this last man struck Riker as the true warrior among them. He'd stayed mostly quiet, and even now after three of his friends had fallen, he wasn't panicking. In an instant, Riker decided he didn't want to get into a standoff with this man. He needed to end this now.

But the final man was already in motion, shuffling to his left, putting Segman between himself and Riker.

Riker followed suit, moving to get an angle on the gunman. In these close quarters, whoever fired first would likely come out of this confrontation alive, but he couldn't risk hitting Segman.

The man raised his weapon, but instead of aiming at Riker, he put the pistol against Segman's head.

"No!" Riker shouted.

But it was already too late. The man pulled the trigger, cutting off Segman's breath mid-sob. The billionaire's head fell limply to his chest.

Riker pushed down his fury, forcing his mind to focus. The man they'd come to talk to was dead, and there was nothing he could do about that now. He needed a contingency plan. If Segman wasn't able to give them the information they needed, he'd have to get it from someone else.

Riker let his SIG fall to the floor and he charged, covering the ten feet between the door and the gunman in a second. The gunman tried to raise his weapon, but Riker had already reached him. He wrapped his arms around the man, pushing his arms down and pinning them to his side. He drove his feet hard and fast, pushing the man backward, slamming him against the window behind him.

When they hit the glass, Riker let go of his bear hug and grabbed the man's wrist, twisting until he heard a crack and the hand went limp, dropping the gun. The man brought his other hand around, throwing a punch at Riker's face, but Riker ducked inside it. They were in tight now—grappling territory. And few men could grapple like Riker.

In an instant, Riker had his arms around the man's legs, using gravity and his own weight to make the takedown as impactful as possible. The air rushed out of the man's lungs as he hit the floor.

Riker twisted, forcing the man onto his stomach. Then he brought his arm across the man's face, getting his arm around the man's neck, and applied pressure. Like his friend who'd been standing in the doorway, he was out in seconds.

Riker got to his feet, trying not to think about the blood and tissue splattered on the walls and floor. Segman was dead. He'd failed in his goal, but there was still a chance at achieving his desired ends in another way. He picked up his SIG and walked downstairs.

He found Simon and Jessica waiting on the hill where he'd left them.

Simon looked pale. "Holy shit. That was the most fucked up thing I've ever seen. I can't believe Tom's dead. And the way you killed those guys."

Jessica's face was dark, but she said nothing.

Riker hadn't considered that they'd be watching everything that happened through the window. He wished they hadn't. Especially Jessica. He wasn't proud of the part of himself that seemed so well designed for violence.

Still, there was nothing to be done about it now.

He turned to Jessica. "Get the car. Bring it up to the house and open the trunk."

Jessica nodded.

"Why?" Simon asked. "What are we putting in the trunk?"

"Two terrorists."

14

Palm trees and blue skies rushed past the car on the drive back to the house. Tan, beautiful men and women jogged along the streets. People walked their pets, enjoying the day. Jessica sat in the passenger seat staring at her lap. She looked a little pale. An occasional thud came from the back of the car, startling her every time.

Simon broke the silence. "I can't believe Tom is dead. This can't be real."

"We watched that guy kill him. He just put a gun to his head and pulled the trigger. Everything that Tom had to offer the world is gone." Jessica turned to Riker. "And you, you killed two guys."

Riker kept his eyes on the road while he spoke. "Yes, I did. I'm sorry to say that they will probably not be the last two men that die before this is over. I did everything I could to save Tom and I will do everything I can to save both of you."

"It's that easy? You just kill who you think needs killing? I don't mean to sound ungrateful that you are helping us, but I've never seen anyone kill a person before. I'm trying to wrap my head around it." Jessica sounded as if she was trying to solve a puzzle. "Would you kill me if that was your mission?"

Riker's mind flashed back to missions in his past. He thought of all the targets he and his team had taken out. "No, I wouldn't. I have a feeling that you already understand that the world is a complicated place. I have met some of the vilest men ever to cast a shadow and looked them in the eyes. The things they did were pure evil. I never lost a moment's sleep over any of their deaths. But life isn't always that simple, and I used to believe I didn't have a choice." Riker turned his head and looked into Jessica's emerald green eyes. "It took me a long time to understand that we have more choices than we let ourselves believe. I was told not to protect you, but I'm doing it anyway. If I have to end some lives so you can live, I will."

Jessica kept her eyes locked on his. "That's your world. One made of violence and hard choices. You couldn't leave that world if you wanted to, could you?"

Riker shifted his eyes back to the road and said nothing. The rest of the drive was silent.

When they got back to the safe house, Riker dragged the men inside one at a time, their hands bound and pillowcases over their heads. He put them in back-to-back chairs in the bedroom farthest from the street. He zip tied each arm and leg to the chair that they sat in. Riker had turned off the AC, and the room was already hot. Simon stood watching over the two men while Riker gathered supplies in the kitchen.

He laid out various items on a cooking tray. There was a flathead screwdriver, plyers, steak knife, and wooden skewers. Jessica watched while Riker looked through the drawers in the kitchen for more items.

"You're really going to torture these guys? I mean, doesn't that make you the bad guy?"

"Maybe, but all the people we save aren't going to care. Besides, I may not do any actual torture. Sometimes the threat is enough." Riker had seen these two in action and knew that last statement wouldn't apply to them. "You may want to put some headphones on and chill out in one of the other rooms."

"No. If you can't do whatever you're going to do in front of me, then you shouldn't do it."

"Your presence isn't going to change my actions. I just don't want to scar you for life." Riker put a nutcracker onto the tray.

"You're not the only one who wants to stop this attack. I'm not just in for the soft parts. If this is what it takes, then I'm going to be there for it."

Riker looked at Jessica's small frame. She continued to surprise him. Her perfectly groomed soft and feminine appearance covered a much harder core.

"Suit yourself, but if it gets to be too much, you can always walk out."

"I don't live my life in a tower." She paused thinking of where she met Riker. "Well maybe I do at times, but I've been all around the world. I've seen the aftermath of attacks on villages. I've been on the aid teams and helped tend to the wounded. I don't think anything you do will be too much."

Riker couldn't look away from those intense green eyes. "Okay. Let's go get some answers."

When they walked into the room, Simon looked at them warily. "What the hell are you going to do to these guys, Riker?"

"That depends on them. I'm going to ask questions until I get answers. I'm prepared to ask hard."

Riker put the tray down on the bed next to the chairs. He let it fall the last inch so that the metal of the objects rattled on its surface. Part of this game was letting fear build. The human mind always went to darker places than reality would allow.

Riker tapped the side of one of the hoods. The man flinched his head away from the touch. His arms and feet reacted, but the restraints were secure enough that the chair didn't even move an inch.

The man that Riker had choked out before the fight had even begun yelled out from under his hood. "I'm going to kill you! Take this fucking hood off my head and look me in the eyes you son of a bitch!"

The man who'd killed Segman spoke up. He didn't yell. Instead, he used the voice of a commanding officer. "Shut up, Raven. I don't want to hear one more word come out of your mouth."

"If he's Raven what does that make you?" Riker asked.

"Sparrow. I know bird names aren't exactly creative. Is that you, tough guy? Are you the one who broke my wrist?"

"I am. I've got some questions for you and your feathered friend. Please answer them. I don't want to do any more damage to you."

"That's the asshole that killed Tom," Simon said in his best tough-guy voice. "I say, do some damage and then ask the questions."

Sparrow spoke up. "Do you have surgical equipment, or is it stuff you found lying on that tray? My guess is it's stuff you found."

Riker stayed silent. He wanted to see where this was going.

"I've been where you're at, tough guy. I was taught with the same playbook. You are doing great. Keeping us in the dark, uncomfortable, letting the fear build in our minds. I have no doubt that you can work nerve endings like a surgeon."

"Since you know how this ends, why don't we cut to the chase? Tell me everything that you know."

"Not a problem. I'll tell you everything. My mission was to kill Tom Segman and Simon Buckner. Since you were there, I'll keep the debrief short. We succeeded in killing Segman and failed in killing Buckner. Upon interrogation of Segman before his death we acquired a third target, Jessica King. Now you know everything."

"Thanks for recapping the events that I witnessed. What I need is the location of the weapons. Where are they?"

"I have no idea what weapons you are referring to. I have no information outside of my mission. If you feel the need to torture me, I understand. But we're just mercs following orders. I was told exactly what I needed to know to take out my targets. Nothing more."

"There are two things that you haven't told me yet. Who do you work for and what is your contact channel?"

"You know I'm not going to tell you that."

"What happened to telling me everything," Riker said in a sarcastic tone. "You will answer both of those questions. If I'm right about what you are, we don't need to use any of the tools on that tray. The weapons that I mentioned are bombs. The kind that hit infrastructure targets for massive damage. The intended targets are on US soil. Did you know that you are a link in a terrorist chain?"

"Bullshit," Raven said.

Riker motioned to Simon and Jessica to leave the room.

Once they were gone Riker took the hood off Sparrow's head.

"Since we're being honest with each other I figured that we should do it eye to eye."

Sparrow glanced down at the tray on the bed. "Ha, I knew it would just be shit you found lying around."

Riker bent down so their faces were on the same level. He spoke in a soft voice while locking eyes with Sparrow. "I get it. You served and when it was over you had skills that didn't fit into normal society. Your targets probably deserve it. Nobody sends guys like you after innocent people, or at least that's what you get to tell yourself. I understand that. I also understand that under all the layers of shit you're covered with lies a true patriot. You may have a taste for killing, but you're not going to bomb a hospital or a school. You sure as hell aren't going to blow one up on US soil. You may not know it, but that's what you are part of right now."

The man didn't look away. He watched Riker's face. He stared into his eyes.

Riker continued. "I can tell you aren't one for bullshit. That's why I'm just giving it to you straight. Your bosses might kill you for giving me the information that I need. If they do, you'll have an honorable death. If you don't tell me, whatever part of you is holding onto honor will die instead."

Five minutes later, Riker walked into the kitchen holding the tray with all its unused items. Simon and Jessica were sitting at the table.

"Did you get what you needed from them?" Jessica asked.

"Yes."

"These guys aren't who you thought they would be, are they?" Jessica said, already knowing the answer.

Riker was amazed at how perceptive she was. "That's

right. The people that want you dead sent mercenaries in to clean up. They put an extra layer in between us and them. I was expecting to deal with the terrorist directly. The fact that they have enough resources and connections to hire out killings and the foresight to distance themselves from their actions makes me nervous."

"Why does that change anything?" Simon asked.

"They aren't martyrs blinding following a goal," Jessica said. "They are an organized and well-funded group. Finding the weapons and the leaders will be much harder."

"That's right. I did convince the guys in the other room to tell me who they work for. It's a long shot, but we may be able to follow the chain back to the source."

"Great, whose legs do you need to break to find out?" Simon asked.

"Unfortunately it is a little more complicated than breaking legs. Finding out will take pressure from the right people and information that you can only get through back channels. I've got someone that may be able to help us."

Jessica glared at him. "Please tell me that you aren't talking about that asshole that wanted to leave me to die."

Riker put a hand on her shoulder. "Assholes like that are the kind of people we need right now."

To Riker's surprise, Jessica put a hand over his. "Can I at least bust his balls when I meet him?"

Riker smiled. "I wouldn't have it any other way." He pulled out his phone and tapped Franklin's number. "There have been some developments. You should get over here. I'll fill you in when you arrive."

Franklin responded. "What is Simon's status? Did you get rid of the girl?"

"See you in a bit." Riker hung up.

15

Miro Chatti sat behind the driver's seat watching through the windshield. Down the street, he could see the circus of police vehicles and camera crews. He was parked not far from where Riker had sat a few hours prior, though he did not know this.

He glanced at the clock on the dashboard and saw it was 11:28. Not quite time.

He turned to the man sitting next to him. "Did you know that back in the late 1800s, a man declared himself emperor of the United States?"

Nigel raised an eyebrow. He was used to Chatti telling his strange historical stories while they waited, but he hadn't heard this one before. "No. I did not."

"It's true. He was an English businessman named Joshua Norton who'd lost a fortune in an ill-advised rice trading scheme. He came to the US and settled in San Francisco. He got the idea that he wanted to be emperor, and he declared it so. He even printed his own money and called for dissolution of Congress."

As he spoke, Chatti watched the house down the road.

The body of Tom Segman had already been carted away, so had the bodies of two others, but a half-dozen police vehicles were still parked near the house. Officers milled around, some collecting evidence, some taking photographs, some not doing much at all as far as Chatti could tell. Nigel seemed nervous with so many officers of the law so close by, but it didn't bother Chatti. These guys had no idea what had really happened at this house, or why. Likely they never would.

"In any sensible nation," Chatti continued, "a man declaring himself emperor, printing his own money, and calling for the dissolution of Congress would be considered a treasonous enemy of the state. He'd be arrested and questioned. Probably executed like the usurper he was. But what do you suppose happened to Emperor Norton in the United States?"

"I'm guessing not that," Nigel said.

"Correct you are, my friend. Rather than arresting Norton, the people treated him like some odd folk hero. They sold coins and stamps with his face emblazoned on them. Mark Twain wrote a fictionalized version of him. When he died, they lined up in the streets to pay him honor."

Nigel said nothing. He kept his eyes on the house.

Chatti glanced at the clock. 11:31. Any minute now.

"I tell you all this to say, our circumstances are nothing new. The US has never taken threats against their nation seriously, not going back hundreds of years. When I told my plan to some in our organization, they thought I was insane. To attempt such a thing on US soil was madness, I was told. It was suicide. I believed differently. I still do."

Nigel shifted in his seat uncomfortably. "I understand, Miro, but these police..."

"They'll be gone soon."

Two police officers trotted from the house a moment later, got in their car, and sped away. Their sirens blared as they raced past Chatti and Nigel's parked vehicle. Another car quickly followed. And then another. The press and paparazzi followed after the police cars. Soon, there was only one car left in front of the house.

Chatti smiled. It had gone according to plan. All it had taken was orchestrating an active shooter situation ten blocks away. Granted, he would probably lose a good man, but that was the price he had to pay. He needed to recover what was inside that house.

He waited another minute, hoping the last police car would leave as well, but not entirely surprised when it didn't. He opened the car door and turned to Nigel. "I'll be back in five minutes."

"Are you sure you don't want me to come along?"

"That won't be necessary." He got out of the car, taking only a small baton and the pistol concealed at his waist. He marched down the street, not bothering to appear casual or to hide the fact that he was making a beeline for that particular house. Time was of the essence, so he would proceed as directly as possible.

When he reached the driveway, he paused for only a moment, looking up at the bedroom window. The warmth of anger filled him. He had paid good money for high-level mercenaries to complete this job. Yet a team of men had gotten the drop on them. Chatti guessed that the attacking team had at least four members. It would be the minimum number of operatives he would use to attack a group with a solid defensive position.

The biggest question in Chatti's mind about this new enemy was not *who* but *why*. The who hardly mattered in the greater scheme of things. But these people were protecting a man he wanted dead. They had attacked and killed mercenaries in his employ and captured two others. Chatti's men were already in the process of tracking the missing mercenaries. Perhaps they would find answers.

If Chatti could only figure out why, he might be able to get some insight into when they'd strike again. It was clear that they intended to do more than protect Simon Buckner. Today had proven that. The next few days were too important to worry about some unknown enemy attacking at any time. He was hoping that the item he was here to retrieve would shed some light on the situation.

He walked through the house, moving quickly and quietly, his baton at the ready. The room he needed to access was on the upper level of the home. No one was left on the first level.

He paused at the base of the stairs, hearing a soft, repeated click. It took him a moment to identify the sound as a camera shutter. Chatti moved swiftly up the stairs towards the sound of the camera. Stepping into the room, he saw a tall, African American police officer with a digital camera, snapping photos to document the scene.

Chatti didn't hesitate. He swung his baton hard, catching the man in the back of the head. The man went down, letting out a cry of surprise and pain as he fell. Chatti struck again, hitting him near the temple this time. The man went limp.

Chatti took a step to his left, putting himself just inside the doorway.

"Parker, you okay?" a deep voice shouted.

Chatti raised his baton. When the second officer stepped through the door, Chatti swung hard, hitting him in the side of the knee.

The officer howled in pain, tumbling to the floor. To his credit, he reached for the gun at his belt rather than his injured knee as most men would have. Chatti stomped down on the hand, crushing it before it touched the weapon. Then he brought the baton down three times, hitting the officer in the head until he stopped moving.

Chatti watched the two fallen officers for a moment. Both were still breathing. That was fine with Chatti. He had no desire to kill the men. Dead police officers would raise the profile of this crime even higher than it already was. Chatti didn't want the headache of the extra attention. At the same time, he wasn't going to lose any sleep if these men died.

One at a time, he rolled the men onto their stomachs, zip-tying them at the wrists and ankles. He was fairly certain the first man would survive. The sporadic breathing of the second man didn't bode well for his future. He left the two men in the room and headed down the hallway.

The last door led to an office. Chatti was relieved to see the intelligence he had on the location was accurate. This room held the closed-circuit security system for the home. Apparently, the recently deceased billionaire didn't want any possibility of a remote hack for his camera system. The only way to see the footage was from this room.

Two monitors displayed video of the interior and exterior of the home. A paper cup of coffee and a notepad sat next to the screens. Apparently one of the officers had already been going through the security footage. The notepad held only one note.

8:06 am - the assailants arrive.

Chatti frowned at the note. He had ordered the men to arrive prior to 8:00. If he was able to find them, he would be sure to make them aware of his distaste for tardiness.

He glanced at his watch. It had only been three minutes since he entered the home. The images of his adversary were on the drive next to him and he desperately wanted to see them. Now was not the time. Taking evidence from an active crime scene was risky enough. He was patient and there was no need to press his luck.

He unplugged the hard drive, slipped it into his jacket pocket, and left the house. He wondered what wild conspiracy theories the police would come up with for this crime. The death of a prominent billionaire, the attack on the crime scene. He was sure that whatever reasons they imagined would have little ties to the truth.

The drive back to their Santa Monica warehouse was quiet, though Nigel's relief was palpable. When they reached the building, Chatti ignored the numerous hellos and updates that were shouted at him. Everyone wanted his attention, but he wasn't going to give it to them. Not yet.

He marched back to his office and plugged the hard drive into his computer. He scrolled through the footage, not saying a word, though he could hardly have been more surprised by what he found.

The attack had been carried out by one man. A man with the strategic prowess to subdue four well-trained mercenaries. Chatti watched carefully, often scrubbing backward and pausing the footage at key moments. Studying the tactics, the fighting style. As he watched, a pit of concern formed in his stomach.

Chatti had thought the *who* didn't matter. That theory was disproved now. The *who* mattered a great deal. Because he recognized the man in the security footage. Though he hadn't seen him in many years, Chatti would never forget that face.

Somehow, impossibly, it was Matthew Riker.

16

Twenty minutes later, Riker watched through the picture window in the dining room as the QS-4 handler pulled his nondescript sedan into the drive, parking next to Jessica's car. He trotted to the door and entered without knocking. There was sweat on his brow. Considering L.A. traffic, Franklin had made it to the safe house impressively quickly. Riker had to admit the man was taking his handler duties seriously.

"Is everything all right?" he asked Riker as he stepped through the door.

"You're the guy huh?" Simon asked. "I thought you'd be taller. Or maybe British."

"We're fine," Riker said. "We've got a couple houseguests tied up in the back bedroom."

Franklin stared at Riker in surprise for a moment, then nodded.

He introduced himself to Jessica and Simon, but his voice seemed a few degrees cooler when he did. He held the handshakes no longer than absolutely necessary. Then he turned back to Riker.

"Tell me."

Riker explained what had happened since they'd last spoken, detailing the fight at Segman's house, Segman's death, and the capture of the two mercenaries.

"You don't think they're Laghaz?" Franklin asked.

"No. They're mercs. They didn't even know who they were working for."

"Or so they say," Franklin said.

Riker ignored the comment. "I can't keep them here. We have work to do. Let's get them in your car."

"Hold on. Before we do that, I need to talk to you for a moment. Alone."

Riker kept his face blank, but he was annoyed. This was the downside of a handler who took his job seriously; they tended toward micromanagement rather than letting their operative do what he did best. "Sure."

Riker led him to a small bedroom on the other side of the house. He took the only chair. Franklin sat down on the bed, looking anything but comfortable. Riker just waited, feeling no particular urge to end the handler's discomfort.

"I need to understand more about why you brought Jessica into this," Franklin said after a moment. "And how we get her out of it."

"I'm fairly certain we already discussed this."

"Right. It's because she's an innocent who's in danger. I'm sure her stunning good looks have nothing to do with it."

Riker didn't respond, but his annoyance was mounting.

"Look, what's done is done," Franklin continued. "Let's focus on the future. What do we do with her now?"

"She stays with us until the weapons are safe, same as Simon."

"She's not the job. Neither are the weapons."

"No, but it's the right thing to do." Riker leaned forward, glaring at the other man. "Do you have any idea how difficult this assignment is? You want me to protect Simon, which means I have to keep him with me at all times. I'm also going to recover the weapons, which means putting myself into dangerous situations. Accomplishing both these tasks at the same time is proving a bit taxing."

"We're not supposed to worry about the weapons," Franklin said, his face reddening.

"Your green is showing with that answer. That's not the real world. Are you telling me that this rich guy's life is more important than the thousands at stake if this weapon goes off? We do this my way, Franklin."

"And your way involves dragging along a rich girl who looks like a supermodel?" There was a bitterness in Franklin's voice.

Riker sensed a wound there, and he was in the mood to press on it. "Let me ask you something. Where'd you go to college?"

Franklin tilted his head in surprise at the non sequitur. "You know I can't give out personal information."

"Please. You think I couldn't find out if I wanted to know? Humor me."

Franklin hesitated. "Brown."

"Uh-huh. A lot of rich kids at Brown. Ivy League school."

"I hardly see what that has to do with anything."

"Only that you weren't one of them." Riker paused, gauging the reaction, seeing that he was right in his guess. "You work your ass off to get to Brown, then you show up and find a bunch of spoiled brats who got in because of daddy's money. I bet it irked you."

Franklin grimaced. "Let's stay on topic."

"We are on topic. You've got a thing against people born

with too much money, and you're letting that affect the way you see the mission."

"That's not true."

"Oh, it's not?" Riker raised his eyebrows in mock surprise. "So it's possible that you don't like rich kids, but also that you can put this aside to accomplish the goals of the mission?"

"Yes," Franklin admitted.

"Just like how I can acknowledge my attraction to Jessica, but also want to keep her safe because it's the right thing to do, not because I'm looking to get laid."

Franklin said nothing, but it was clear from his expression that he got the point.

"We done here?" Riker asked. "Can we get back to work?"

Franklin nodded.

"Good." Riker stood up and walked back to the dining room. Franklin followed close at his heels.

"You girls get your interpersonal issues worked out?" Simon asked.

Franklin ignored the question. "Here's what's going to happen. We are going to put the two men in the trunk of my car. I'll take them to a facility where they will be detained and interrogated further."

"Oh, you mean exactly like Riker said the moment you walked in the door?" Jessica asked mockingly, an innocent smile on her face.

Franklin cleared his throat and continued on. "In the meantime, you two will stay with Scarecrow. You will continue assisting him in finding the weapons, and in return, he will continue to keep you alive. Any questions?"

"Yeah, just one," Simon said. "Who the hell is Scarecrow?"

"Him." Franklin nodded to Riker. "It's his codename."

Simon stared at Riker for a long moment, then burst out laughing. "Scarecrow is your codename? How the hell did you get that? Were the Tin Man and the Cowardly Lion already taken?"

Riker sighed. "Can we please focus?"

"I too would like to know how you got that name," Jessica said.

"It hardly matters at the moment," Franklin interjected. "Our priority is—"

Riker held up a hand, cutting him off. Out the window, he saw something—a white, unmarked utility van parked a few houses down, just within his line of sight. It hadn't been there a few minutes ago. He got up and looked down the street in the other direction. He spotted another white van.

Then he saw a shadow alongside the house.

"Everybody down!" he shouted, diving to the ground.

Franklin hit the deck immediately, his hand going to his waistband and pulling out the pistol concealed there. Jessica quickly followed. Only Simon remained in his chair, a confused expression on his face.

As if on cue, the front door flew open with a crash, revealing a handful of men dressed in black body armor. The man in front held the battering ram he's used to break the door open. A similar crash came from the kitchen, where the backdoor was located.

The men at the front door didn't come rushing in. Instead, they tossed something inside. Though Riker only caught a glimpse of the object, he recognized it immediately. He only had time to shout one word.

"Flashbang!"

As he said the word, he grabbed Jessica, covering her eyes with one hand and her left ear with the other. He squeezed his eyes shut and buried his face in her hair, trying to protect himself as much as possible.

The stun grenade went off, and the world disappeared, enveloped by pure white light and the loudest noise imaginable.

Riker opened his eyes. For a moment, he couldn't see or hear anything. Then he regained the ability to make out shapes. He knew they only had moments.

He pulled out his SIG and fired at the picture window next to them. Then he grabbed the nearest dining room chair and hurled it through the glass. He gestured to the others, waving his arms wildly toward the opening.

Franklin and Jessica both nodded in response and headed for the window.

Simon was another story. He lay huddled on the ground, eyes squeezed shut, hands over his ears as he wriggled in pain. Unlike the rest of them, he'd taken the full force of the flashbang grenade. He wouldn't be able to hear or see anything for the next few minutes.

In the living room, men rushed through the door and began sweeping the house. Their eyes hadn't yet settled on the dining area.

Riker grabbed Simon by the collar with one hand and the belt with the other and tossed him through the open window. Riker's hearing wasn't back yet, but he saw the young man's mouth open in a surprised scream.

As Simon hit the grass outside the window, Riker leaped after him. He grabbed him again, this time pulling him to his feet. He dragged him along to the driveway where Franklin and Jessica were already standing.

Riker's eye shifted quickly between the two cars. Jessica's or Franklin's? His mind raced for the right answer, knowing he only had a moment to make the decision. He didn't know how these men had found them. Perhaps they'd tracked Jessica's car. Maybe she had some kind of driver assistance service they'd been able to hack. Or maybe they'd followed Franklin here. It was also possible neither of those was correct. Riker briefly considered the likelihood of each scenario, then he gestured toward Franklin's car.

The four of them hopped inside, Franklin behind the wheel, Jessica in the passenger seat, and Riker hauling the still-disoriented Simon into the backseat with him. He pounded on the back of Franklin's seat, urging him to drive. The handler started the car and threw it into reverse. The sedan sped out of the driveway and onto the street just as the attackers poured out the front door, running after them.

Riker watched through the rear window as the house—and their best clues for recovering the weapons—disappeared into the distance.

17

THE CHRYSLER'S tires screeched as they took the corner at forty-five miles an hour. The heavy sedan wanted to spin out of control, but Franklin kept it on the road. He accelerated, weaving between two cars and missing both by inches. Then he slammed the brakes and turned hard onto another street. Riker was impressed by his ability to control the car. He wondered what Franklin would be capable of in Simon's Lamborghini.

"What the hell is going on?" Simon screamed the words much louder than necessary.

Riker's ears were still ringing, but his hearing was coming back quickly. "It was a flashbang grenade. You'll be fine in a little while."

"What?" Simon yelled back.

"How was the house compromised?" Franklin asked while taking another quick turn.

"If I had to guess, we were followed from Segman's. It is also possible that they found a way to track Jessica's car. I'm not sure, but we need to be more cautious going forward. I think we should start by getting a new ride. They saw this one already. We can take one from long-term parking at the airport."

"You want to steal a car?" Jessica asked.

"We need to get rid of this one and replace it with something that can't be traced back to us. I don't consider myself a car thief, but this situation calls for drastic measures. Especially when those measures might keep us alive."

"I don't like it. There is always another way."

"Sorry to drag you into the grey area, but we need to make sure to lose these guys. Part of that will be getting a new vehicle. We should park this thing in an underground garage and hop on a bus to the airport."

"We could just lose them at the gym," Simon shouted.

Riker spoke a little louder. "Simon, don't say anything else until you can hear the conversation."

"I heard you. I'm telling you we can ditch them at the gym."

"What are you talking about? Why would we try to lose them at a gym?"

"He's right," Jessica said. "That's a great idea, Simon."

Riker and Franklin exchanged confused glances.

"Trust me," she said. "I know how to get rid of any tail we might have and get a new ride."

Jessica directed them to downtown Los Angeles. They drove under the shadows of skyscrapers until Jessica instructed them to pull into one of the parking garages. It was under one of the taller buildings, and Franklin followed the parking ramp down to the bottom floor.

"This is a bad idea," Riker said. "We are trapping ourselves."

"Trust me, we aren't going to stay down here long," Jessica said with a smile.

On the bottom level, there was a guard booth with a

rolling metal door behind it. Jessica instructed Franklin to pull up next to the guard.

Franklin rolled to a stop and lowered his window. The guard's hand rested on a pistol that was holstered on his hip. "Can I help you?"

Jessica leaned over from the passenger seat, coming into view of the guard. "Hey, Charlie."

"I'm sorry, Ms. King. I didn't see you in the car."

"How many times do I have to tell you, call me Jessica?"

"At least one more, Ms. King. How many guests will you be bringing with you today?"

"Three."

The door behind the guard booth slid upward, and Franklin drove through. There was a small parking garage behind the door with only a few cars inside. After they parked, Jessica let them to an elevator. She placed her hand on a biometric reader and the doors opened.

Riker glanced at Franklin, and then looked at Jessica. "Are you part of an agency?"

She tilted her head, confused. "No, this is just my gym."

Once inside the elevator, Riker noticed that there were no buttons. Jessica put her hand on a scanner that was identical to the one outside. After a moment there was a pleasant ding, and the elevator accelerated upwards.

The doors opened to a lobby. A receptionist sat behind a desk directly in front of them. Behind her was a large open training area. Through the glass windows behind the exercise equipment, Riker could see the city stretched before them, and he realized that they were on the top floor of the building.

The receptionist was a fit woman in her early thirties with short brown hair. "Great to see you, Jessica. Will your friends be joining you for your workout?"

"Hey, Gloria. I know this is a little odd, but I'm not going to be working out today. I just need a discreet exit."

"Of course." Gloria picked up a phone on her desk. "Hi, Ms. King and three guests will need a ride." She paused and listened for a moment. "I'll let her know." She hung up the phone. "They will be ready for you in fifteen minutes. Would you like anything while you wait?"

Simon spoke up, only a little louder than necessary. "If I could get an organic fruit smoothie with some vegan protein powder that would be awesome." He turned to Riker and Franklin. "You guys want anything?"

Both men shook their heads. Gloria told Simon that his drink would be right out.

Riker walked over to the main entrance of the training facility. The equipment was amazing. They had all the standard weights and machines of any modern gym, but that was just the tip of the iceberg. There were a gymnastics training area, rock climbing walls, yoga area, wire work stations, and what looked like a weapons training area. Riker spotted five people working out. Each person had at least three trainers with them. He recognized four of the five people. Three were actors, and the fourth was one of the richest tech billionaires in the world.

Then Riker's eyes settled on a sixth person, and his jaw dropped. It was another actor, the star of his favorite Marvel movie. He'd never been starstruck in his life, but there was Captain America working a heavy bag. It felt as if he just stepped into an Avengers movie.

Jessica looked at Riker and laughed. "Do you have a crush? I don't think he's into guys, but I can ask."

Riker turned red. He didn't realize that he was staring. "No, I just happen to be a big Marvel fan. I wasn't expecting to see him here."

The smile grew a little bigger on Jessica's face. She waved to the actor, catching his eye. He stopped hitting the bag and said something to his trainer. Then he walked over towards Jessica. Riker felt his stomach tighten.

"Jessica, how have you been? Still out saving the world?" He went to give her a hug, but she pushed him back.

"I'm good, but I'm not in the mood for a sweaty hug, goofball."

He looked down at his tank top and realized he was covered in sweat. He laughed it off. "Sorry, forgot that I was already deep into my workout."

"Jessica's such a prude." Simon came in and gave the actor a big bear hug. "How's it going, big guy?"

"Good, man. You still getting into trouble?"

"You have no idea. I actually have this lunkhead watching my back lately." He motioned towards Riker.

"Really?" The actor turned to Riker. "Are you security? Like a bodyguard?"

"More like what you were to Bucky in *Winter Soldier*," Riker said with a smile.

"Right. Like the Captain America thing." He reached out and shook Riker's hand. "Always good to meet a fan."

"Sorry, I didn't mean to come off like a fanboy. I really do like the way you played that role."

"Riker's actually a pretty cool guy," Jessica said. "He's saved Simon's life twice." She gave Riker a wink.

"That sounds interesting." He shot Jessica the smile that had lit up movie screens worldwide. "Why don't we grab a cup of coffee, and you can tell me all about it?"

"I'll take a rain check on that. We are in a bit of a rush right now."

"Okay, I'm going to hold you to that. I've got work to do.

Take it easy, guys." He walked back to his trainer and started to work the bag again.

A few minutes later Gloria came to let them know that their ride was ready. Jessica led the way up a flight of stairs, and they came out onto the roof. A chopper was waiting on the helipad.

Franklin looked at Jessica and Simon. "Is this part of your gym membership? They just have a chopper on standby ready to take you wherever?"

Jessica shrugged. "It comes in handy for last-minute meetings, avoiding the paparazzi, and apparently losing a group of killers."

Franklin shook his head and climbed into the small bird. Once everyone had their headsets on he asked, "What options do we have for drop locations?"

"I already have that arranged," Jessica said.

"Don't you think you should have consulted me first?"

"I did. You and Riker said you needed a ride that couldn't be traced back to us. We're going to get one, and we don't even have to steal it."

The chopper took them to a small landing pad next to a car dealership. The group got out and was greeted by a man wearing a suit.

"Jessica, great to see you. I've got something that I know you will love. I haven't even sent out the message, but we just got a LaFerrari delivered. It's number 200 in gunmetal grey. A truly beautiful piece."

She gasped. "You know I've been trying to get one."

Riker cleared his throat. "Something with at least four seats would be preferable. And more low key. We don't have a lot of time to shop."

The man gave Riker an annoyed look. Riker didn't know

what the profit margin on a limited exotic sports car was, but he guessed more than most people's annual salary.

"Sorry Sam," Jessica said. "He's right. I'm actually in a big hurry and could use a favor."

"Sure. What do you need?"

"I need a car for a couple of days. Something quick with four seats. Not too flashy and... lots of trunk space."

"Let me see what I've got."

The four waited in a showroom loaded with rare cars.

"Will your name be on the paperwork for the vehicle?" Franklin asked.

"No, this is just a favor," Jessica said.

"What do you mean?"

"I mean he's just getting me a car to use. There isn't any paperwork."

Just outside the window, a BMW M5 pulled up. The group met Sam as he got out. "Will this do the trick?"

"It's perfect, Sam. I'm not sure exactly how long I'll need it. Maybe a week. Is that okay?"

"Just bring it back when you're ready."

"You're the best. And Sam, don't sell the LaFerrari to anyone else."

"It'll be here waiting for you."

Once everyone was in the car Jessica turned to Riker "See, a fresh car with no records. It's that easy."

"You live in a very unusual world, Jessica. I don't think you realize how different your life is."

She tilted her head and thought about it for a moment. "I watched you fight four armed men, killing two of them. I think your world is very unusual as well."

"And I thought you were a badass," Simon chimed in. "But then I saw you make a fool of yourself in front of

Captain America. The world is just full of surprises. Now that we are kind of safe again, where are we going?"

"We're headed to Franklin's place," Riker said.

Franklin shook his head. "Bringing anyone to my safe house is against protocol. Especially civilians."

"Just drive. We need a safe place; you have one. Like it or not, we're in this together."

18

THE CAR PULLED into the driveway of a house in the hills just outside of LA. The home was surrounded with high concrete walls. At first glance the decorations on top of the walls added to the aesthetics of the home, but Riker spotted the sharp spikes and surveillance equipment hidden there. The two-story home was at least twice the size of the safe house where Franklin had stationed Riker.

"This is your safe house?" Riker asked.

Franklin nodded. "It is secure, and we'd be able to run a command center from here if needed."

Riker's eyes narrowed. "You dick. It looks like you were willing to take advantage of the company's perks."

Franklin's cheeks turned a slight red color. "I assigned you the more central location. It made sense. I'm not supposed to be the boots on the ground. You may have needed to reach unknown destinations quickly."

Simon laughed from the back seat. "You can't bullshit a bullshitter. I'm sure that you just happened to think the better house made more practical sense. It clearly had nothing to do with you staying in a sweet pad in the hills."

Simon clapped a hand on Franklin's shoulder. "How many girls did you bring back here?"

Franklin kept a steady tone. "I assure you that I did not abuse my position or risk the mission trying to impress girls."

"So you couldn't get any of them to come back with you? You really need to work on your game. Anyone with a house in the hills should be able to score at will."

Jessica shot him a look. "Believe it or not, some guys focus on things other than trying to get laid."

"Relax, I'm just busting his balls. I know Mr. Leave People To Die If It's Not Part Of The Mission would never use this place for fun."

"That's right," Franklin said. "I mean, he's right that I take this job very seriously."

The inside of the home matched the exterior in quality. The furnishings were high end, but the home had minimal decor. It was clear that no one actually lived here. Simon and Jessica went to find bedrooms to claim. Riker walked the home and the exterior looking for blind spots and tactical advantages. He quickly realized that this place had been designed for defense. The windows were bulletproof and there were two panic rooms. Hardwired cameras covered every inch of the house and exterior. There were a few small decorative structures in the backyard. Riker guessed that the fountain and the berm held weapons in or underneath them.

Riker found Franklin in an office on the first floor. There were three computer monitors on the desk in front of him, each with encrypted screens.

"I see why you didn't give me this house. I assume that you will catch hell for bringing us here."

"Yes, I'm not looking forward to telling QS-4 that a

command house has been compromised by two civilians. This home is a substantial investment and it will take time to equip another like it in the area."

Riker sat on top of the desk next to the monitors. "They'll act pissed, but this mission is important, and you helped save Simon today."

"You make it sound so simple. Like telling your boss that traffic made you late."

"In a way that's all it will be. They don't tell the new guys, but once you have done this for long enough, you realize that the missions are mostly chaos. There is no rule book for tracking down targets or evading criminal organizations. Most of the time just getting the mission done is a minor miracle. The quicker you learn that all the parameters and desired secondary effects are basically wishful thinking, the better you will do at this."

Franklin stopped typing and turned to Riker. "It sounds like you are talking about disobeying orders. I doubt that makes for a long career."

"I'm just saying that you need a very open mind to stay alive and complete the missions. I had one target that I was supposed to eliminate. The mission was to shoot down his private jet just after takeoff. The surface-to-air missile that I was supposed to use was compromised. My orders were to kill him before he left the country. I ended up destroying the private airfield's radar equipment. While they were trying to fix the equipment, I set fire to his mistress's apartment. I had done my research, and I knew that she was a bit crazy. He went to her place to calm her down, and I got him just as he arrived.

"I was never given permission to disrupt air traffic or to damage a residential building. I caught a little hell for doing both. I also received my next mission the following week."

"I see what you're saying," Franklin responded, "but I am supposed to be the guy who keeps the agents grounded. I am supposed to make sure you are staying on task."

"Realizing that there is no clear path to success is the most important thing you can do to help. Don't be afraid to think about different solutions. Once you open up your mind, this will get easier. So don't worry about compromising this location. It is already done. Think of ways to use the things and the people that you have. Jessica has already proven valuable."

"She has proven that she has a cheat card for life. That wasn't a skill that she provided."

"What she has is assets and the ability to think on her feet. She didn't curl up into a ball and cry when we were attacked. She kept her wits and used what she had at her disposal. Like it or not, she is part of our team now. We would be fools if we didn't recognize her abilities."

There was a tap on the door behind them, and Jessica peeked in, a smile on her face. "Sounds like I might get to learn the secret handshake."

"You should not be in this room," Franklin blurted out.

Riker shook his head. "I think we should let Franklin work. You hungry?"

"Starving." She nodded her head in the direction of the kitchen. "Let's have a little dinner."

As they were leaving the room, Riker turned back to Franklin. "Do all of your communications with QS-4 go through Morrison?"

"Of course. He's my point of contact."

"You haven't reached out to anyone in any other division for help or information?" Riker asked.

"No, the parameters were clear. All communication goes

through Morrison. It's standard protocol on a mission like this."

Riker smiled. "Of course, and you always follow protocol." He closed the door as he left.

Making dinner wasn't as easy as Riker had thought it would be. The fridge was empty except for a few condiments and milk. After some searching, they found a few frozen dinners and some dry goods in the pantry. Riker and Jessica eventually sat down to a gourmet dinner of cereal.

"Thanks for sticking up for me," she said. "I know Franklin doesn't want me here."

"I meant what I said. You're a natural at this. Most people lose their minds when they're threatened. They look for help and stop thinking about possible solutions. I hate to say it, but when I first saw you I thought you would be a burden."

"Oh, really. Because I'm a woman?"

"No, because you literally live in a tower looking down on everyone. Most people who grow up around that kind of privilege forget how to fend for themselves. You looked the part as well. Wearing designer clothes. It was easy to think you were just another rich kid, but then I heard you speak."

She gave a soft smile. "I have to admit that I misjudged you at first too. I thought that you would be cold and heartless. Shut down from the rest of the world. But you're not."

Riker laughed. "I wouldn't be so sure about that. My normal life is spent on a plot of land in the middle of nowhere, avoiding human contact."

"This isn't your normal life? Don't you do this all the time?"

Riker considered what he should or shouldn't say. He looked into Jessica's piercing green eyes and decided that he was tired of pushing everyone away. "Actually, this is my second day on the job. How am I doing so far?"

"I *know* that's not true. I've watched the way you handle yourself. Those abilities don't come quick or easy."

"Fair enough. I used to be in the military, then I worked for a private company. I got out. I've been keeping to myself for the last six years."

"Why did you come back?"

"Leaving this life isn't easy, no matter how hard you try to get out."

Her eyes turned down for a moment. "I feel a little silly saying this, but I get it. I know my life isn't the same as yours, but I hold a position that I couldn't leave if I wanted to."

"Really? Seems like you can literally do whatever you want."

"So can you, but there are heavy consequences for both of us. Yours might be more final than mine, but walking away isn't easy for me. After I graduated college, I wanted to do some charity work. One of my friends had been in the Peace Corps, and they asked me to help them in South America.

"We were helping women in Colombia who had lost their families in the drug wars. It was the first time that I'd experienced that kind of poverty and destruction. I wanted to do anything I could to help. I asked my father to donate to the relief efforts. He told me that I would forget about their problems a week after I got home and there was no need to waste the effort. That more than pissed me off. I decided to stay and continue the work we were doing. I gave my phone away and didn't contact my parents for the next two weeks.

"At the end of the second week, a man found me while I was working in the village. My father had sent him to get me. Of course I refused to leave, but he knew that would be my response. He said that if I came back home, the charity that I was working with would get a sizable donation. If I didn't leave, their non-profit status would be revoked and their work would stop. I said goodbye to my friend and left."

"You still do charitable work," Riker pointed out.

"Sure, but the way the trip ended taught me a lesson. Even though my dad won the battle, the charity got the money they needed. I still go around the world and help, but I can do just as much or more using my resources here. I stay in this world of wealth to make connections and bring awareness to people with power. I feel like a hypocrite sometimes, but in the end, I do the most good that I can."

"I see your point, but it's still a lot easier than taking a bullet to the head."

She smiled. "Okay, so maybe it is a little harder for you to get out." She put a hand on top of his.

Riker's heart skipped a beat. Until that moment he hadn't considered that Jessica might be interested in him. That wasn't something that came up in a normal mission. It wasn't something that Riker had considered in a long time. He smiled back at her and wondered if he was reading too much into the simple gesture.

Franklin walked into the room. "I've got it. I've got the location."

Riker pulled his hand back and took his bowl to the sink. "Which location?"

"I found the address of the client that hired the mercenaries. I used some back alley connections, and I have a location."

"How did you get that without leaving the house?"

"I have some sources on the dark web, along with a friend at QS-4 who was willing to help off the books."

"Are we sure the information is good?" Jessica asked.

"No, but we happen to have a recon agent who can find out."

Riker looked at Franklin. "Nice work. I'm going to need some more gear. There will be a lot of unknowns, and I want to be as prepared as possible."

"Not a problem. Follow me."

Franklin led Riker outside and to the backyard. He opened a shed that was attached to the home. Inside he moved a rug and opened a trapdoor in the floor, revealing a short staircase. Underneath the shed was a ten-by-twelve foot room. Various weapons hung on the wall and hard plastic cases sat on shelves.

"You should find anything you might need. Go ahead and gear up before you head out."

19

Eleven years ago.

Four days after his cup of cold coffee with Morrison, Riker found himself sitting in the belly of a plane surrounded by twelve other men. Morrison was one of the twelve and led the team. Each man had a full set of gear, night vision goggles, an oxygen tank and a parachute. They flew thirty-thousand feet above Iran in the dead of the night.

Riker had been introduced to the team three days ago. To his surprise, he knew one of the members, Connor Jackson, an Army Ranger. Riker had heard that Jackson went MIA on a mission and was presumed dead. Apparently, death was one way out of a military contract.

Every team that Riker had ever been a part of had one thing in common—the new guy was tested. When he'd joined the varsity wrestling team he was hazed by the seniors. SEAL teams beat you down when you were green. There was always an alpha that challenged you and made you prove yourself. This team was totally different.

Morrison had brought the team together to meet Riker in a small tent outside of an airfield on a sweaty afternoon. When Riker arrived, Morrison said, "This is Riker he's one of us now."

Riker shook hands with everyone on the team. Each stated their names, nothing else, and each name was accompanied by a subtle head nod. There was no hazing, no testing him. They all knew he wouldn't be there if he didn't belong on the team. They had faith in Morrison. If he said Riker was in, then he was.

The team spent two days going over the strike plan that Morrison had devised. The objective was to eliminate Mohamad Izad and every operative at the base. This would cripple the organization and leave no witnesses. Once the targets were eliminated, the infrastructure would be destroyed so that the compound was no longer usable.

The plan was straightforward, but Riker guessed that there were at least seventy members of the terrorist group working out of a heavily fortified cave system. He counted thirteen men including himself for the offensive. The numbers didn't look good to him.

Then Morrison went over the details of the plan. His strategy was impressive.

Now they sat on benches in the hollow belly of a plane, waiting to put the plan into action. Every man was silent except for one. He whistled, "The Ants Go Marching." The whistling annoyed Riker, and the man doing it was going to be his wingman on the op. Riker couldn't remember his actual name, but everyone called him Timber.

Morrison stood up and yelled loud enough for the team to hear above the roar of the plane. "We are T-minus 10 minutes until drop. I want radio silence until everyone is in position. When I give the signal, we move. Any questions?"

A few moments of silence followed. "Check your gear and get ready."

Riker did as instructed, and he saw that every man did the same. High Altitude Low Opening, HALO, drops were intense. Riker had done several but there were not a lot of special operatives trained in them. Jumping out of a plane at thirty thousand feet, knowing the shoot wouldn't open until you were at four thousand feet was a harrowing experience. But as far as Riker could tell, every member of the team looked as relaxed as a jogger in the park.

Each team member filed out the back of the plane through the cargo door without a word. When it was Riker's turn, he did the same. Wind screamed around him as he raced towards the earth at terminal velocity. There was no chance of any interference from anti-aircraft weapons.

When his altimeter told him it was time, he pulled the shoot. Once he was on the ground, Timber found him, and the two moved towards the entrance of the facility. No lights illuminated the entrance, but with his night-vision goggles Riker could see three guards standing near a door that led into the mountain. The two men moved in silence as they approached the guards. When they reached the predetermined position behind a boulder four hundred yards from the entrance, the two soldiers stopped. They waited exactly fifteen minutes, and then Morrison's voice spoke a single word into their earpieces.

"Engage."

Riker watched as the three guards fell to the ground. He could see puffs of dirt behind them and heard the ricochet of a bullet off the rocks. All three snipers had hit their marks perfectly. The guards died without even knowing they were under attack.

Riker and Timber moved forward. The night was cool

and silent except for the crunch of sand under their feet. Timber towered over Riker. He must have been six foot six. He appeared slim, but Riker could tell the height misrepresented his mass. The large man pulled a set of charges out of his pack and rigged them to the door. Once they were secure the men pulled back and waited for the next command.

Another word spoke into their comm, "Open."

There was no hesitation. Timber flipped the switch on the detonator, and a flash of light was quickly followed by a loud explosion. When Riker looked back at the mountain, there was a large hole where the door had been.

Riker was ready with smoke grenades. He launched one after the other into the mountain lair, tossing them as far as he could. Moments later, smoke poured out of the entrance. Riker and Timber stood at the ready with their rifles against their shoulders.

They didn't have to wait long until four armed men ran out of the tunnel, coughing holding assault rifles at their sides. Timber and Riker fired in unison. The terrorists didn't have time to raise their weapons. Seven were down.

"We've located the generator," another team member said into the comm.

"Take it out," replied Morrison.

Smoke continued to pour out of the entrance. Faint shouts could be heard coming from inside the complex. Riker and his teammate kept their weapons at the ready, watching the hole in the mountain. Then the smoke shifted directions. A puff of it was sucked back into the tunnel. This was exactly what Morrison had predicted. He knew that there would be an escape tunnel and the pressure in the mountain would change once it was opened. The difference would create a wind tunnel.

"Enter," came through the earpiece, and Riker moved

into the entrance with Timber. The thermal goggles that Riker wore allowed him to see clearly through the smoke, and his mask allowed him to easily breathe. They moved through the area slowly. One man would creep forward while the other covered his position. The first thirty yards were clear, and then the two men turned a corner and saw twenty men.

It was a large open cave with racks of weapons lining the room. Men with headlights were grabbing various weapons and ammo. Timber signaled to Riker, and the two moved silently away from each other, still hidden by the smoke. Once each man found cover twenty feet apart Timber gave a nod.

Riker fired three quick rounds, dropping a man with each shot. Then he took cover behind a set of crates and stayed low. The terrorists shot wildly in his general direction. Once they were focused on his location and their guns were echoing through the room, Timber began to fire. He had taken out nine men before they realized someone was attacking from a second position.

"He's over there!" a man screamed in Farsi.

Timber ducked behind his cover when they began to fire. Riker stayed low and moved quickly. Once he was flanking the remaining men he opened fire, tearing through them. When the last body fell against the stone floor of the cave, Riker ejected his magazine and slammed a fresh one into place. He looked around the room and called out, "Clear."

"Roger that," Timber replied.

The sound of gunfire was coming from somewhere farther down the compound. It seemed that the smoke coming out the escape tunnel had given away its location to Riker's teammates. Morrison had positioned snipers with lines of sight toward possible escape points. It sounded like the plan had worked. The men who tried to escape were being picked off by the team.

Riker led the way as they continued down the tunnel. After thirty yards, a side tunnel split off from the main one. The separate tunnel was blocked by a locked door. Timber shot the lock and kicked the door inward. As soon as it opened, gunfire came from down the hall. Bullets tore into the frame of the door and three rounds struck Timber in the chest, knocking him backward.

Riker put his back to the wall and readied himself for a break in the gunfire. Bullets came in a constant stream through the open door, and he couldn't get a look at the attackers. Before they were finished emptying their clips, Timber fired from his position on the ground. He squeezed off five rounds and then lay back down on the ground. No more shots came from the other side of the door.

"Shit, that really hurts," Timber said.

Riker moved into the doorway and checked the status of the attackers. Two men were dead in the hallway beyond the door. He turned back towards Timber.

"What's your status?"

He felt his chest with one hand and then staggered to his feet. "Nothing made it through the vest, but I feel like someone took a Louisville Slugger to my chest."

"Can you move?"

Timber coughed and then sucked in a deep breath. "I'm good. Let's find out what's behind door number one."

The two continued their journey into the cave moving one at a time while covering the other man. Each man moved silently in the darkness. There was a tray of cables that ran above them leading down the tunnel. The tunnel turned and then opened into a communications room.

Two men were setting fire to a server cabinet and another man directed their actions holding a flashlight in one hand and a pistol in the other. Riker recognized the face of the man with the flashlight. It was Mohamad Izad.

Riker didn't hesitate. The barrel of his rifle flashed lighting up the room. A bullet entered the right eye of the man responsible for a thousand deaths and exited the back of his head. The men destroying the computers didn't have time to do anything other than make a stupid face before Timber shot them.

"Friendlies coming in," Morison said into the headset. "We got most of them, but one man got past us. Keep your heads on a swivel."

Riker could hear an occasional shot coming from the distant tunnels. "We're in their command center. We have a confirmed kill on Izad."

"Hold your possession. I'll be there in a tick."

Timber rubbed his chest and walked over to the corpse of the terrorist leader. "Nice shot, Riker. Welcome to QS-4."

20

Riker drove down the 101 Freeway, but his mind was elsewhere. He tried to focus on the mission ahead, but the truth was that there wasn't much more he could plan until he got there and saw the layout for himself. He'd have to come up with a plan on the fly once he arrived at the house. Instead of the mission, his mind drifted to thoughts of Jessica, and her story about the gilded cage of growing up in a family with obscene wealth. Riker couldn't help but contrast that with his own experience.

On the surface, their childhoods couldn't have been more different. Rather than the coast, Riker had grown up in the heart of the Midwest. His father had drifted in and out of different odd jobs, the periods of steady income interspersed with long stretches of unemployment. Food and clothing had never been guaranteed during these times. School lunches were sometimes his only real meal of the day.

When he'd met Coach Kane and joined the wrestling team, it had not only been an outlet for his frustration and his tendency to scrap with other boys, but it had quickly become an essential part of his life. Wrestling was like a key that promised to unlock the chains that had been around his wrists for his whole life. Suddenly, college seemed like a real possibility. Coach Kane had helped him make a highlight video of his best matches to send to college recruiters. Wrestling coaches from three of the ten colleges they'd reached out to came to visit Riker and his family, and in the end, he got two full-ride scholarship offers. His future had seemed set.

But things had gone another way. Instead of college, he'd found himself in basic training the fall of his eighteenth year, on a path that had led him here. He wasn't one to bemoan missed opportunities or the road not taken, but he couldn't help but occasionally wonder what his life would be like if he'd made a few different decisions the summer after his senior year.

He glanced over at the canvas backpack on the seat next to him, loaded with equipment from Franklin's shed of wonders. A part of him had wanted to proceed with nothing more than his SIG and his knife. That was how he felt most comfortable. But he didn't know what he was walking into, so he'd decided to play it smart. He'd loaded the backpack with all the equipment he thought he might need, threw a couple larger weapons in the trunk, and headed out.

Riker pulled off the freeway and turned into a residential neighborhood on the east side of the city. He circled the block once, scoping out his target house. He didn't love what he saw. It was a large home, nowhere near the size of Tom Segman's beach house or even Franklin's bunker-like safe house, but still impressive. It was surrounded by similarly large houses. In many ways, this was the worst possible neighborhood, nice enough that people took pride in their homes and would be quick to call the cops if necessary, but not so rich that the homes had huge lots or privacy walls between them. He was going to have to do this carefully.

He circled the block a second time, considering his options. He knew that he needed to decide fast. On the off chance his targets were watching the street he couldn't risk driving past a third time. He found a spot just up the hill from the house and parked. Then he watched and waited.

There were two sedans parked in the home's driveway and a two-car garage. Up to four cars. For all Riker knew, there could be sixteen armed terrorists inside that house. The frustration mounting, Riker forced himself to draw a deep breath and find an advantage as Morrison had taught him. The most obvious one was the fact that they didn't know he was coming. The element of surprise was a powerful weapon. At the same time, he had to assume they'd be on high alert.

The house on the north side of his target had a truck in the driveway, but the house on the south-side's driveway was empty and the windows were dark. No guarantees that the house was empty, but if he needed to approach the house, he'd do it from that angle.

He also needed to consider the possibility that Franklin's intel was incorrect. After all, Riker didn't know much about his young handler, other than his apparent earnestness and his driving skills. It was not outside the realm of possibility that Franklin had gotten this wrong. That meant Riker couldn't go in guns blazing until he was absolutely certain the people inside this house were Laghaz agents.

A pair of binoculars sat in the passenger seat. Riker slid low in his seat and observed. His best bet would be to grab the next person who came out of that house, either here or by following them to their destination. Then he could interrogate that person to confirm his intelligence and to find out more information about how many people were inside and exactly how armed he should expect them to be.

He waited for nearly an hour, his body still and his mind calm. It was something that happened to him on surveillance duty. He went into an almost meditative state, with his mind focused but conscious thought pushed away. Considering it had been over six years since he'd been on a true surveillance mission, he was surprised how easily it came back to him. The quiet patience required for this work had been deeply ingrained in him during his time at QS-4, and apparently, a half-dozen years couldn't wipe it away.

A passing car slowed as it approached the house, and Riker sat up a bit straighter, automatically noting the make, model and license plate number. Then the car turned into the driveway. Two men, both of Middle Eastern descent, got out of the front seat and walked around to the rear passenger-side door.

The men looked around for a moment, making sure none of the neighbors were in the yard or clearly watching through their windows. Then they opened the door and one of the men reached inside. He pulled out a middle-aged, dark-haired woman. She held her hands in front of her, a coat draped over them. Riker noticed that she didn't use the hands to steady herself as she climbed out, instead relying on the man's hand on her shoulder to support her.

Some might not have thought anything of it, but Riker knew her wrists were bound in front of her.

The two men walked with her, one on either side, toward the house. The man on the right pressed the doorbell, and they waited for twenty seconds. Then the door opened, and they disappeared inside.

Riker silently continued watching the house, but his mind had come out of its meditative state and was in full-on strategy mode now. Any doubt in the validity of Franklin's intel was gone. Laghaz agents were inside that house, and they'd just taken a captive woman in there with them. The time for waiting was over. He'd have to be bold to make this work, but so be it.

He got out of his car, grabbed the backpack, and headed around to the trunk. He opened it and looked inside. Two weapons lay there. He was intimately familiar with both, having used one on nearly every mission with the SEALs, and the other frequently in his work with QS-4. After a moment's consideration, he pushed the M4A1 5.56 carbine aside. As much as he liked that rifle, it looked like a military weapon, and he didn't want anyone seeing him carrying it through the residential neighborhood and calling the police. Instead, he picked up the other weapon—a sawed-off Benelli M4 Super 90 shotgun. With its shortened barrel, it was small enough to slip into the side pouch of his backpack where it shouldn't attract much attention from the casual observer.

Before he closed the trunk, he unzipped the backpack and pulled out one more item, which he clutched in his hand. Then he put the backpack on, shut the trunk, and casually scrolled down the street toward the Laghaz safe house.

As he walked, he went over the plan in his mind one more time. *Plan* was perhaps giving it too much credit. It was the beginnings of a plan, and one he'd have to execute flawlessly. He had no idea what he'd find when he stepped inside that house, so he had to make sure he controlled as many factors as possible while he was still outside.

Riker had done a little research before leaving Franklin's safe house. He'd discovered that despite its sometimes negative reputation for crime, Los Angeles actually boasted a police response time well above the national average. In New York, for example, the average call was answered in 9.1 minutes. In Los Angeles, it was 5.7. Though his research hadn't shown this, Riker knew that probably varied greatly depending on the neighborhood. In some areas where the police were more hesitant to go after dark, that number was probably much larger. In a nice neighborhood like this one, it would likely be less.

To be on the safe side, Riker decided he would give himself half the reported time. He'd assume the police would arrive two minutes and forty-five seconds after they were called. He would have to work fast.

Riker reached the driveway and turned in, walking up the far side and hoping the cars would partially block a view of him from the house. He crouched next to the car closest to the garage and stuck the item in his hand on the vehicle's undercarriage—an explosive charge rigged for remote detonation.

Once the explosive was secure, Riker stood up and moved into position, ducking around the south side of the garage. He checked his equipment one last time. The SIG. Two extra magazines. The sawed-off Benelli shotgun with extra shells. His knife. Once everything was in place, he pulled the detonator out of his pocket. The moment he pressed the detonator, everyone in this neighborhood would be calling the police. Everyone except the people inside this house, Riker thought. They'd take matters into their own hands, which was exactly what Riker needed them to do.

Two minutes and forty-five seconds. That was how long he had to make this happen.

Riker drew a deep breath and started his mental clock.

21

Riker crouched along the side of the house. Above him muffled voices came from a window. He heard a man with an accent asking the woman who else knew about the exchange. He heard crying and the unmistakable snap of a fist against flesh.

After the fight at Segman's house, Riker knew that there was only one way things would end for the woman. One man would be no match for a house full of enemies. If they were experienced, they would flank a single enemy and it would only be a matter of time before they successfully eliminated the target. Riker knew that he needed to be more than one man.

If the location was under attack from a larger force, the men inside would react the same way they had at the safe house. They would take what was valuable and escape. His plan was simple, but not easy. He needed to attack the home from three positions at once.

Riker allowed himself one glance into the window above him. He saw two men in the living room. One was working on a computer with papers on the desk around him. The other was sitting on a couch watching TV with an assault rifle across his lap. The glimpse was all he needed.

He made note of the time. It was 6:59 PM. In two minutes and forty-five seconds he would leave this place with the woman or he would be dead. He felt his senses heighten and his heart rate quicken. The seconds slowly ticked forward on his watch. When the numbers turned to 7:00 he sprang into action.

Riker aimed the shotgun and fired. The glass of the window shattered inward and a spread of shot tore into the man on the couch. He was twelve feet from Riker and his body crumpled from the tight formation of the blast.

Not pausing to fully assess the damage, Riker turned and ran towards the back of the home. He pulled the detonator from his pocket and blew the charge under the car while he sprinted along the side of the house. His finger pressed the button, and he heard an explosion from the front of the home. Glass shattered, metal crunched, and car alarms went off throughout the neighborhood.

The sound of the explosion still echoed as Riker reached the back door. He kicked it in and saw a man with an assault rifle moving away from him toward the front of the house. The man started to turn toward Riker, but he only made half the turn. Riker squeezed the trigger of the shotgun, and the man flew backward down the hall.

Now Riker could hear men yelling from inside the home. The language was Farsi, and Riker caught some of the words that overlapped each other.

"Babak is down!"

"Form up."

"Grab the intel."

Riker didn't hesitate. Ducking back outside, he ran to the side of the home that he hadn't attacked from yet. He hugged the wall of the house and crouched at the corner. Then he heard two gunshots from inside the home. His heart sank and he fought to keep anger from overtaking him. The quick double-tap could only mean that the woman was dead.

Then one of the windows slid open and the barrel of a rifle poked out. Riker ducked behind the corner of the house and counted to five. When he peeked back around the corner, a man stood just outside of the window and another had one leg out. Riker put a blast of shot into the middle of the man standing guard. He pulled the trigger a second time and the semi-automatic weapon barked again. The leg that was coming through the window jerked hard to the side and the pants shredded just like the flesh beneath them. A high-pitched scream came from inside the house.

Riker ran to the back door as the screaming continued. He crouched low and went by the door frame, checking to see if anyone was attempting to come out the back. There was no one in sight. He yelled into the empty hall, "Formation two on my command. Remember to check your blind spots. Mark!"

When the last word escaped his mouth, he gave the door a kick and continued to the opposite side of the house. He waited at the corner and listened for a moment. From inside the home he heard, "Go, go, go!"

Riker sprinted along the outside of the house until he reached the front corner. He waited, making note that there were six shells left in his weapon. He heard the front door burst open and footsteps race across the concrete driveway. Riker held his position. Everything inside him wanted to move around the corner and open fire, but he held. He heard the grunts of the man with the injured leg but he continued to wait.

The second he heard a car door shut, he slipped around the corner to the front of the house. He was to the back left of the car and he saw one man in the driver's seat. The rear door was open and a man was shoving the injured guy into the back of the car. A fourth man was scanning the area, holding an assault rifle. Riker was glad that he was focused on the door they'd just come through, ready for the attackers to catch up to his group. Riker fired his shotgun, hitting the man with the rifle in the face. The force jerked his head back hard enough to lift his feet off the ground. Before remaining portions of the man's head hit the pavement, Riker shot off two quick rounds into the backseat, killing both men.

He moved at full speed while he fired, coming around the side of the car. The driver slammed on the gas and the car lurched forward, dropping a body out the back seat. The driver kept his head down, but Riker had a target. He fired through the back passenger window into the steering wheel. One of the hands on that wheel turned to shredded meat, and the car angled sharply, crashing into a tree on the side of the driveway.

Riker moved around to the front passenger window and a bullet shattered the glass from inside of the car. The driver had his pistol in his left hand, ready to fire another round. Riker didn't give him the chance. The shotgun yelled out its song one last time, and a large hole appeared in the chest of the driver.

Riker turned towards the house, making sure that no one else was coming. Once the firefight with the fleeing terrorist was over, he felt a stinging sensation in his neck. He touched the side of his neck and his fingers came away wet with blood. Sharp shards of glass protruded from his skin. A quick check in the side-view mirror of the car revealed some of the glass from the car window stuck in his neck and upper chest. The bleeding was light and it didn't appear to have caused any major damage. He left the glass in place and went back through the front door of the home. He moved through the house much more quickly than he would have preferred, clearing each room.

He found the woman lying next to a chair with a gunshot wound to the head and chest. Pushing down the revulsion, he pulled out his cellphone and snapped a picture of the dead woman. There was no one else in the house, just bodies of the men Riker had shot. The computer and papers were also missing from the table. Riker checked his watch. It was 7:02. He didn't hear sirens yet, but he knew they would arrive soon.

He ran back to the cars in the driveway. The one that he used the charge on still smoldered. The other car had what he was looking for. Next to the body of the driver was a carrying case. Riker looked inside and saw papers and a laptop. He grabbed the case and then touched the pockets of the driver. His phone was in his pant pocket. Riker was glad that the man hadn't carried the phone in his breast pocket. If he had, it would be nothing more than shrapnel torn apart by the shotgun blast. Riker pressed the button on the phone and it asked for a password. He pressed the dead man's index finger to the button at the base of the screen. The phone unlocked.

Riker jogged back to his car while turning off the passcode setting on the phone. When he opened the car door, he heard the faint sound of sirens. He drove away three minutes after his first shot.

Riker walked into the safe house with the computer bag. He set it on the table and went into the kitchen without saying a word. Everyone else came to meet him there.

"Was the information good?" Franklin asked as he walked in. "Are you okay?" He stared at the dried blood covering Riker's neck and staining the collar of his shirt.

"The info was good, but things didn't go as smoothly as I'd hoped. I think I'm okay, but there are some shards of glass in my neck."

Riker filled a glass of water and sat at the table, telling the other three about the events at the house. He gave them the information in a clear manner, with no emotion or embellishment. It was like any other debrief he'd ever given. Franklin sat quietly, making mental notes about everything Riker said. Simon's mouth gaped open. Jessica gasped when Riker told them he found the body of the woman he'd tried to save.

Finally, Riker pulled out his phone and showed them the picture of the dead woman. "Ring any bells?"

Simon's face went pale. "That's Stella. She's the guard I paid to look the other way while I took the weapons."

Riker said nothing, but his face hardened. He touched the side of his neck and pulled his hand back as soon as it brushed against the glass embedded in his skin.

"Should we take you to a hospital?" Jessica asked.

"I'll be fine. I could use a hand getting the glass out. Any volunteers?"

"I'm trained in first aid," Franklin said. "Let me get some supplies."

"I've got the medical," Jessica interjected. "You work on getting into that computer."

Franklin looked at Riker for approval. He gave a silent nod and Franklin grabbed the computer bag.

Riker pulled the phone he had taken off the dead man out of his pocket. "Here's the phone I took. Check the notes.

I'm willing to bet you find the password to the computer there."

Franklin opened the phone and looked at the Notes apps. There were two notes in the phone. One was the number 2479; the other contained a random set of fifteen numbers, letters and symbols. The long chain unlocked the computer.

"How did you know the passcode would be on the phone?" Franklin asked.

"The weak link in every security system is always the people involved. I was sure that they would have a nearly uncrackable password to their important files. The problem with great passwords is remembering them. There also needs to be a way to get the information to the next in line if the person with the code dies. Storing it on the phone was the logical choice. Now let's hope there's something on that computer that was worth the trouble."

"What do you think the other numbers are?"

"I'm guessing a combination to a lock. Probably something that is still in the house."

Franklin went to work on the computer while Jessica took Riker into the master bath. She grabbed some clean towels and a first aid kit. Riker took off his shirt and sat in a chair next to the sink.

When Jessica saw Riker's bare back and shoulders, she stared. On top of the toned physique were a plethora of scars. Some of them crisscrossed, others were small circles, some were wavy lines of old burns. Most of them were old and fading, but some were new.

"Earth to Jessica. You going to stand there and stare, or are you going to help me get the glass out of my neck."

She snapped out of the momentary trance. "Sorry, I just didn't realize how bad you were at your job."

"Ouch. I just thought you were checking out my awesome body." Riker flexed and gave her a wink.

"It's a little hard to see the muscles under all those scars."

"Each one of those scars is a lesson. Which means I have a master's degree in what I do."

She gave him a smile. "Or it means that you are a really slow learner."

"Either way, I've got some new lessons today."

Jessica spent the next half hour pulling small slippery shards of glass out of Riker. Once she was finished, she put some ointment and bandages on his neck and they rejoined Franklin and Simon in the kitchen.

"Did you find anything useful on the computer?" Riker asked.

Simon stood up and turned to Riker. His face was pale. "There are two targets. A power station and a dam. In three days, thousands of people are going to die."

22

The information on the computer was useful, but incomplete. The type of targets and instructions for placing the explosives were there. The specific locations were not.

"Is there anything in the files that can tell us where either of these targets are? A schematic that we can use to compare against existing structures?" Riker asked Franklin.

"I'm still sifting through everything on the drive, but I doubt we'll find anything. This group definitely compartmentalizes information. I'm guessing that only one or two people at that house knew what was on the computer. None of them knew their exact target."

"Why wouldn't they tell their own guys what they were doing? They need to know that stuff," Simon said.

"Because none of them could compromise the mission," Jessica explained. "They would get the exact location of the target and the weapon they needed at the last moment. If, say, the events of tonight happened, the plan could continue."

"Exactly. Someone has that information and the weapons. We have three days to find them." Riker paced back and forth as he spoke. Motion had always helped him think through problems.

"They've got to be nearby. The targets, I mean. Let's look for dams and power plants close to the house where the guys were staying," Simon said.

Franklin frowned. "There are hundreds of plants in California alone. The locations could be anywhere within a three-day trip. That means anywhere in the county is an option. We don't have time to play a game of probabilities."

"You're right," Riker said. "We need to utilize all of our resources for this. Get QS-4 on the phone. We need them to throw everything they have at this."

Franklin looked like Riker had slapped him. "Morrison's instructions were clear. He said to stay focused on Simon and let them handle the weapons. They will not help us. They're going to be more than displeased if we even request acknowledgment."

"Are you serious? I know the protocol, but this isn't an arms deal we're trying to stop. It's not just some bad guy that might do more bad stuff in the future. This is a major attack on American soil that is three days away. If there has ever been a time to break protocol, this is it."

Franklin paused for a moment. "Why don't we make an attempt to...."

Riker cut him off. "Don't try to reason your way out of this. We are talking about events that will cost thousands of lives and have ripples that will change the world. Contact them now and let them know what is going on. We need to use everything in our arsenal to stop this."

Franklin paused once more and then looked Riker in the eye. "I agree. I'll reach out to them now."

Franklin and Riker went into the office to contact QS-4. Franklin made a call that went straight to the voicemail of an ice cream shop. He left an encrypted message. Five minutes later, his phone rang. He picked up and Riker could hear someone chewing Franklin out.

Franklin tried to speak a few times, but he was cut off by the person on the other end of the line each time. Eventually he was given a chance to respond.

"I know I broke protocol, but there is going to be a major attack on American soil. It will happen three days from now."

The voice continued to tear into Franklin. This time he stood with the phone to his ear saying nothing. After two minutes of silence Franklin said, "I understand," and he hung up the phone.

Riker knew what Franklin would tell him before he spoke. "Leviathan Protocol stands. We are on our own. They were very clear on that point."

"You need to get back on the phone. We need to find a way to contact Morrison. Whoever you spoke with was probably just a buffer person with no power other than to tell you exactly what they did."

"That *was* Morrison. He is the highest point of contact that I can reach."

Riker's face turned red. His fists tightened and his knuckles went white. Franklin took two steps back from him.

"That son of a bitch. Why wouldn't he help us? He has always been an honorable man." Riker's mind flashed back to dozens of times Morrison had accepted breaks from protocol when they made sense. He was the one who had taught Riker to see the bigger picture. Apparently, things had changed a lot over the last six years.

"So we're it," Riker said. "Two rich kids and a handler who is still green behind the ears. This all falls on us."

"It seems that way," Franklin said.

Riker turned and left the room. His anger was consuming him and he needed to get it under control. Without saying a word he went to the backyard and stood under the night sky. The light pollution of the city washed away most of the stars, but there were a few he could focus on. He forced himself to stand still and watch the sky while his mind worked on the external and internal problems he faced.

First, he thought of Morrison. His mentor had earned his respect a thousand times over. He ran through every reason that he could think of that Morrison would not help. There was only one explaination that made sense, though he didn't like the implication. He took a few deep breaths, and his anger dissipated, allowing him to focus on the task at hand.

He needed to find the weapons. Asking the witnesses was out since he just killed everyone at the house. Time was too short for him to search the property before the authorities arrived. Going back now would be pointless. If there was anything left to find the police would have it in evidence by now.

Riker entered the house much more composed than when he'd left it. He found everyone in the living room watching the TV.

"Hey, I'm going to need my phone back for a bit," Simon said.

TMZ was running on the TV and there was a story about the disappearance of Simon Buckner. The reporter told of a home break-in and his sudden exit from an exclusive club.

"Can you get him a secure connection on the computer to post a cover story?" Riker said to Franklin.

"Not a problem. I think the story should involve Jessica

as well. If her family isn't looking for her already, they will be soon."

"Perfect," Simon said with a smile. "I can just post a shot of us in bed under the covers. That will take care of both our stories."

"If you do, I'll just follow it up with this post." She made a disappointed look and held her thumb and forefinger an inch apart. "Hashtag little vacation."

"Very funny. We can come up with something else. I was just trying to keep it simple."

"Whatever you say I need you to do it now," Riker said. "We don't need anyone else trying to track you down, complicating the situation even more. Franklin, I want you to approve the message and the photos. Make sure there is nothing that gives away our location.

"After that we need to find out where they are keeping the weapons. I think we should start by getting a look at the crime scene report from the police. They may have found a lead when they searched the house."

Franklin thought about it for a moment. "What are you suggesting? We walk into the police station and ask the detectives what they found?"

"I was hoping that you could hack into their system. Use some of that knowledge you picked up at Brown."

"Getting info from the police is not an issue," Jessica said.

"Yeah, even I could get that." Simon agreed.

Riker let out a laugh. "I'm guessing that both your families donate a lot of money to the LAPD."

"You never know when or how many times you may need a little help getting out of trouble," Simon said.

Jessica looked at Riker. "I can get you full access to the

department. I'll let them know you are a PI working with my family. Everything will be off the books."

"Okay, let's get to work. The faster we can get a lead, the faster we can find those weapons."

"I've got it," Franklin said. "You get some rest."

"I'm fine. This needs to get done."

"Like I said, I've got it. I will work with these two on finding our next lead. You get some rest. We need you on top of your game when it's time for action. Now stop arguing so I can get to work."

Riker smiled at the sudden authority in Franklin's voice. "Fair enough. Just make sure we have a target by morning."

Once the thought of rest entered his mind, Riker realized that he was exhausted. His bedroom had its own bathroom, and he used it to rinse off the dirt and sweat from the day's battle. He was wearing the only clothes that he had, so he left them in the bathroom to air out and slid under the covers in the buff.

Moments after he lay down the door cracked open.

"You still awake?" Jessica whispered.

Riker sat up and turned on the light by the bed. "Yeah, did you find something?"

She walked into the room, closing the door behind her. She took a seat on the bed next to Riker. "The police were attacked at the crime scene at Tom Segman's house. Someone came back to get the security footage from the house. Franklin is working with my contacts. He said that he has a few ideas to figure out who took it and where they went."

"Do they need my help?"

"Not yet. I just wanted to give you an update and check on my patient." She softly ran a hand down Riker's neck.

The small wounds from the glass shards had scabbed over. Freckles of red scattered his neck.

"I never properly thanked you for saving my life." Her hand continued to move down his chest. She leaned in close, bringing her lips to his.

Just before they kissed he said, "You don't owe me anything Jessica. I didn't help you with any intentions of a ... reward."

She smiled and shook her head. "Obviously. I just said that so I didn't seem slutty."

The kiss started slow and soft but the attraction between them quickly moved to passion. She climbed on top of him and their mouths and tongues pressed hard against each other. Jessica pulled off her shirt, revealing a body that kings of old would have started wars over.

Riker went somewhere that he hadn't gone in a very long time. In the throes of passion, nothing else matters. Just this moment with this woman. All of his guilt, regrets, and self-loathing were gone. The thoughts of the mission and the weight that lay on his shoulders disappeared. Their bodies entangled, and nothing but the moment mattered.

When the two were finished, they rested under the sheets, both covered in a thin layer of sweat and well satisfied. Jessica lay with her head on his chest and a leg wrapped around his. Riker drifted into the most restful sleep he'd had in years.

23

Riker woke early, but he lay in bed for a long while staring at the ceiling, not daring to move. He felt Jessica next to him, her body just barely touching his. He felt the rhythmic rise and fall of her breathing and knew she was still asleep.

Part of him wished they could lie like that forever. As long as he didn't move, everything would be perfect.

He'd been through this before. He knew that a passionate first night together could sometimes be followed by an awkward morning. When you woke up with someone and neither of you knew what to say, it could kill the afterglow pretty quickly. Riker fiercely didn't want that to happen. He liked this woman a lot. More than he'd liked anyone in a very long time.

And yet, he couldn't lie here much longer. There were lives at stake, and that trumped this new... fling? Relationship? Whatever it was. This woman had awoken a part of Riker he'd feared might be dead forever. And yet, there was still work to be done.

He'd almost mustered the willpower to get out of bed when he felt Jessica stir. She was on her back, and she rolled toward him and put a hand on his bare chest. She wore an easy smile, as if she'd just woken up from a pleasant dream.

He reached over and brushed her hair off her shoulder. "Morning."

"Morning. Let me ask you something, super spy. Anybody ever told you that you snore like a lumberjack?"

Riker let out an indignant laugh. "I do not!"

"How do you know? You have to count on your bedmates to tell you, right? And I'm telling you."

"No way." Riker shook his head, a smile on his face. "If I'd ever so much as let out a whimper in my sleep, my old boss would have trained it out of me. Trust me, he was a bear for the details."

Jessica sat up and the sheet fell away. She didn't bother covering her body. Riker drank it in. She was even more beautiful in the morning light.

"Ah, but that was a long time ago. You said it yourself. You've been out of the game a while. You're old. Maybe you snore now."

Riker gave her a long look. "Seriously. Did I snore?"

"I'll never tell," she said with a wicked smile.

Riker just shook his head. The fact that things were still as easy between the two of them as they had been the previous night gave him the strength to get out of bed. He started toward the bathroom, then paused and looked back at her. "I'm going to take a shower. Care to join me?"

She didn't bother answering. Instead, she stood up and walked to the bathroom, taking her time about it, giving him a long look at her naked form in motion.

They stayed in the shower until the water went cold.

When they finally dressed and headed into the living room, they found Franklin and Simon sitting on the couches. Franklin was on his laptop, and Simon was flipping channels on the TV. Franklin greeted them with a nod. Simon said nothing, but he wore a goofy grin.

"Did you two, um, sleep well?" Franklin asked, not quite meeting their eyes.

"Yeah, they did," Simon said.

Jessica rolled her eyes. "Seriously? You guys ever heard of being gentlemen and just pretending you didn't see... whatever it was you saw?"

"It was more hearing than seeing. And what I heard went on for a while." Simon grinned at Riker and held up his hand for a fist bump. "My man."

Riker ignored the fist. "Can we please change the subject?"

"What? I think you two make a cute couple." Simon sat up straight, as if realizing something. "Wait, I introduced you. That means if you get married, you're practically obligated to make me best man."

"Really any other topic would be fine," Riker muttered.

Jessica leaned up against him. "Well, no use trying to hide it now."

Simon pointed at Riker's face. "Look at that, Jessica. You made him blush!"

Riker sank down onto the couch next to Franklin.

The handler glanced up, the tiniest of smiles on his face. "He's right though. You do make a cute couple." His smile disappeared when he saw Riker's expression. He quickly started typing on his laptop. "Okay, what do you say we get back to work?"

A new page popped up on the screen, and Riker leaned over. It looked like sports scores.

"What is that?" he asked.

"Arkansas youth hockey."

"Is hockey big in Arkansas?" Simon asked.

"Not at all. None of these teams are even real. It's a way for my employers to communicate with me. The box scores are a kind of code." He stared at it for a long moment, his lips moving a little while he decoded the message. He put a hand to his mouth.

"What is it?" Jessica asked.

"They're pulling me back." His voice sounded hollow. "I'm to leave you this safe house and provide remote support only."

"What the hell?" Simon asked.

Riker frowned. "Apparently Morrison really didn't like you calling him."

"He may have alluded to not loving me being so personally involved when we talked." Franklin slowly closed the laptop and stared blankly at the wall.

"It's not good news for sure," Riker said. "But we have to keep moving forward. Let's find out what we can about these bad guys."

As Franklin slowly gathered his belongings, the others started working. Jessica took the desktop computer and Riker worked on the laptop. Franklin even tossed Simon a burner phone so he could research.

After a few minutes, Simon pointed the phone at Jessica. "Smile, girl."

She gave him a withering look, but he snapped the photo.

"Guess that'll have to do."

Riker ignored him. He'd only begun his own research when Jessica spoke.

"I think I have something."

Riker walked over and stood behind her, his hand resting lightly on her shoulder. "What am I looking at?"

"Financial records. That address where you got the laptop? It's owned by a corporation. Gadsberry, Inc."

"Who the hell are they?"

"Nobody. That's the point. It's a shell company. It was used to buy that home, and as far as I can tell, nothing else."

"So does that help us?" Riker asked.

"Not sure. Maybe. Working on it."

Riker trudged back to his spot on the couch and continued tapping at his laptop. In truth, the longer he kept at it, the more he realized that he probably wasn't going to be the one to crack this thing. That didn't mean he was going to give up though.

Five minutes later, Simon spoke up. "Got it!"

Everyone else stopped and turned to him.

He angled his phone toward the others. Its screen displayed a photo of a Middle Eastern man petting a dog. "Tell me that's not the guy from the club, Riker? The one you shot on the motorcycle."

Riker studied it for a moment. "Maybe, but I can't be sure. Where'd you get this?"

"Tinder. I built a fake profile using Jessica's pic and I'm cruising for guys. For research. Terrorists get horny, too, right?"

Jessica raised a skeptical eyebrow. "And how does finding a dead terrorist's Tinder profile help us?"

Simon thought a moment, then sighed. "I'll try something else."

For the next twenty minutes, the only sound was the clicking of keys, most of it coming from Jessica's computer. Finally, she looked over to Riker.

"This is it. Has to be."

Riker walked back over, this time bringing his laptop. "Tell me."

Jessica tapped her carefully manicured fingernail on the screen, indicating the name of a company--Figaro Enterprises. "This is where the twisted paper trail ends. These guys are careful. Each company only buys one property. But I was able to trace it back to this parent company. Their subsidiaries own a few homes throughout the L.A. area. And one warehouse in Santa Monica. I'm thinking that's our best bet."

Franklin stepped into the room, a travel bag in his hand. "If you're launching two major attacks, I'm guessing you'd want something bigger than a home. They'd want to train. Drill. Practice for the big events."

"What's the address?" Simon asked.

Jessica scrolled down a little. "7849 Rovello Drive."

Simon let out a little whistle. "That area's crawling with soundstages. I think Keanu Reeves trained for John Wick for like six months in a facility on that street."

"So a little gunfire might not be out of the ordinary?" Riker observed.

"Definitely not. Explosions. Gunfire. Whatever. That's the day-to-day in that neighborhood."

Franklin looked at Riker. "Ideal for keeping your terrorist organization sharp."

Riker touched Jessica's arm. "You found all this in the public record?"

"Some of it," she said sheepishly. "I may have sent an email or two. Nothing that will raise suspicion. I promise."

Riker felt a twinge of pride. This wouldn't have been the team he'd have selected for a job like this, but they were surprising him. Likely the group of hardened soldiers he would have called in would still be trying to boot up the computer. In that time, Jessica had practically performed an audit on the terrorists.

"Okay, let's see what we can find out about this warehouse," Riker said. "I want blueprints, what security system they use if any, previous owners. Whatever we can find to make this job easier."

He picked up the laptop, but Franklin set down his travel bag and snatched the computer out of Riker's hands.

"You might be deadly when it comes to combat," Franklin said, "but we both know I'm better with this particular weapon."

Riker didn't argue the point. "What about the orders on the hockey website? Morrison isn't one to take kindly to disobedient employees. Especially handlers fresh out of college."

"I'll tell him I forgot to check it." Franklin sat down on the couch and opened the laptop. "That excuse won't last forever, but it'll buy me a day or so."

Riker felt an unexpected rush of gratitude. Franklin was underselling the risk of what he was doing. Ignoring orders would end his career with QS-4, plain and simple. Morrison wasn't going to accept the excuse of forgetting to check the orders. Franklin was giving up a career with limitless potential, both financially and politically, and he was doing it without complaint. Because it was the right thing to do. Riker had to admit that he'd underestimated the handler.

"I've got the name of the exterminator they use," Jessica said a few minutes later.

"Good," Riker said. "Possibly useful. But keep looking."

Five minutes after that, Franklin let out a triumphant laugh. "Got blueprints."

"Let me see."

Franklin passed the laptop to Riker. He studied the layout, and he didn't like what he saw. Entrances at either end. Wide-open spaces in between. There was no telling what modifications Laghaz had made to the property. If none, they'd be walking into an open area with little to no cover. If Laghaz had built out the space, they'd be walking into the complete unknown.

"We need more guys," Riker said, more to himself than anyone else.

"Take me," Simon said.

The others looked at him, surprised.

"What? I've been to the shooting range plenty of times. I can do this."

Riker tried to answer as gently as possible. This was a big change from the Simon he'd met two days before. "I appreciate that, but the shooting range is target practice, not combat."

"Come on, man." Simon's face was flushed at the implication that he couldn't handle himself in combat. "You keep underestimating me. Give me a chance."

"It's not about underestimating you. It's about risk assessment. My mission is to keep you alive. There's no way I'm putting you into a battle, no matter how capable you might be. Sorry."

Simon sighed, then nodded. "Yeah, okay. I get it."

"I don't," Jessica said. "If not for Simon, how are you going to pull this off. You said yourself what you need are more guys."

Riker considered that, mentally flipping through the list of people he might be able to call. The list was surprisingly short. Pretty much all of his former colleagues were either dead or still in QS-4.

Thankfully, someone else did have an answer.

"I think I might have an idea," Franklin said.

24

Riker crouched down next to the blueprints on the floor, going over the plan one more time. He glanced at the men around him. There were four of them, each dressed in a black T-shirt, dark pants, and boots. Outfits that wouldn't stand out on the street, but also worked for what they were planning—a tactical strike on the warehouse in Santa Monica that Riker believed was Laghaz's local headquarters.

He had to admit, Franklin had come through on this one. It was early afternoon, only a few hours after they'd found out about the existence of the warehouse, and Franklin had managed to round out four qualified mercenaries-for-hire. They were now gathered in a storage facility in Burbank, the blueprints laid out in front of them.

"What's communications look like?" one of the men, a guy who'd introduced himself as Saber, asked. He was on the shorter side—maybe five foot seven—and wiry, but he had a hardness around the eyes that spoke of experience. He looked like many of the guys Riker had worked with in Special Forces. Unlike what the movies would have people believe, most Special Forces operatives were below average height; Riker's big frame was the exception rather than the norm.

Riker took some handheld radios and burner phones out of his pack and began to hand them out. "We synchronize our watches and attack the pre-ordained time. We'll use the radios to communicate pre and post mission. If we need to communicate silently, we text with the burner phones."

"These are pretty old school," the man code-named Jameson said as he looked at the radios. "You sure we can't get whisper mics?"

Riker shot him a look. "Our time and resources are limited. We go with what we have."

Jameson grimaced, but said nothing.

Riker looked around at the others before continuing. Besides Jameson and Saber, the other men were Greco and Wendig. Greco was about Saber's height, but bulkier. He was quiet, but his eyes showed he was taking it all in. Wendig was the oldest of the group. He had to be closer to fifty than to forty. He kept making jokes—nobody laughed, but only Jameson seemed bothered. Riker sensed a clash coming between the two of them.

Despite his gratefulness for Franklin's fast work, he couldn't help but be a little nervous. He'd be going into battle with guys he didn't know. It had happened before, both in his Navy days and in QS-4, but back then there had been an organization to train and vet the fighters. All he had now was Franklin's vague assurances that these men could handle themselves.

Riker was half tempted to ask them about their backgrounds, but he knew guys like this could get squirrelly about those kinds of questions. There's a chance they'd start thinking this was a setup and walk. The only question he'd asked was if any of them were trained to use a sniper rifle. Only Saber had answered in the affirmative.

As much as Riker didn't like it, he'd have to trust that Franklin had gotten him the right guys for the job.

Riker had seriously considered bringing Franklin along for the mission too. The guy had military experience and had proven he could handle himself in intense circumstances. Even the handlers in Morrison's organization had rigorous and specialized combat training. *Everyone's a fighter under my watch*, the man had often told Riker. *Anyone who's not ready to do his part when the shit hits the fan isn't worthy of collecting the same paycheck as you and me.*

For his part, Franklin was more than game to join in the mission. Now that he'd disobeyed Morrison, he didn't see why he had any reason to continue following QS-4's rules about no handlers in the field. He was all-in, and he wanted to help in any way he could.

Eventually, Riker had decided against involving him directly. He'd done it for two reasons. First, he needed to make sure Simon was safe. If Riker took a bullet on their mission that night, he had to know that someone would protect him. Second, there were the weapons to consider. He needed someone to continue that part of the mission if he died.

And Jessica. Riker was doing his best not to think about her and the night they'd spent together. He needed to focus, not drift off into fantasies like a teenage boy in algebra class. She was another reason Franklin couldn't be part of the mission. The thought of leaving her alone with only Simon to help her escape the angry members of Laghaz put a lump in Riker's throat. He wouldn't allow it to happen.

Riker pointed a finger at the main entrance to the warehouse on the blueprint. It was surrounded by a small parking lot. That would be the battleground. "Wendig and I will strike here. We'll go in hard and fast. Thirty seconds later, Jameson and Greco join in from here." He pointed to the back entrance. "Your goal is to flush the guys toward us. We want everyone in that building to come out the front door."

Jameson scowled.

"Something to say?" Riker asked.

"Yeah. It's a bad plan. Sorry, but you asked." He squinted at the blueprint. "Fuck this whole sniper situation. We should charge inside with everything we have. We'll catch them holding their dicks. They won't even have time to grab their weapons."

Riker stood up from where he'd been crouching next to the blueprints and turned to Jameson. "Thanks for your time, but your services will no longer be required."

Jameson stared at him in surprise for a long moment. "You're kidding."

"I'm not." Riker's expression was hard. "You can go."

As much as he hated to lose a man when they were already likely to be so outnumbered, he knew it was the right call. Besides the tension between Wendig and Jameson, he couldn't go into battle with a man who was going to question his orders. He hadn't seen a lot of Jameson, but he'd seen enough to know he didn't want to entrust the man with his life. That made the decision easy.

"What the hell?" Jameson gestured toward Saber. "He asked about communications, and you're not shitcanning him."

There was a big difference between asking a question

and telling your employer that his plan sucked, but Riker wasn't going to waste his time explaining that to Jameson.

"You can go," he repeated. "I'm not going to tell you again."

Jameson shook his head. "No way. I was promised a thousand dollars. You want me to leave? Pay up."

Riker had the money Franklin had given him in his pocket. Five grand in cash—enough to pay each of them plus a little extra. He felt the bulk of folded paper pressing against his leg. But no way was he going to give it to this guy now. These other men were about to put their lives on the line for that money. Giving a share to a guy who wasn't going into battle with them would be a surefire way to kill their motivation.

Instead, Riker lowered his right hand as if he were reaching into his pocket, then brought it up fast, catching Jameson under the chin in a vicious uppercut. The man's head snapped back, and he staggered.

Riker didn't let the moment pass. While Jameson was still off-balance, he surged forward, catching Jameson in a double leg takedown. As they hit the ground, Riker jammed his right arm under Jameson's shoulder, grabbed the man's arm and twisted, putting it into a painful armlock.

Jameson cried out, unable to move. From the panicked look in his eyes, he'd never been on the receiving end of an armlock and he wasn't enjoying the experience.

"Tell me what I want to hear," Riker said.

Jameson looked back at him with wide eyes, as if he had no idea what Riker was talking about. For all his bravado, Jameson wasn't the brightest light on the Christmas tree.

Riker waited.

Finally, Jameson got it. "I'll go. You don't have to pay me. I'll go."

Riker released the arm, and Jameson collapsed to the floor.

The room was silent as the two of them stood up. Riker turned away from Jameson, subtly letting his body language indicate that he was done with him, but he kept the man in his periphery. When Jameson was back on his feet, he hesitated for just a moment. Riker knew he was considering making a move. He turned his head and glared at Jameson.

The man's posture slumped, defeated, and he left without another word.

When he was gone, Riker turned to the others. "I'm sorry it had to go down like that, but we don't have the time for games. Or for insubordination."

"You don't have to apologize to us," Saber said with a grin. "That guy was an asshole."

"Amen," Wendig added.

"Good," Riker said. "Then let's get back to it."

Riker adjusted the plan for their newly reduced numbers. He'd be entering the front of the warehouse alone now, with Wendig and Greco teaming up to go in the back. The group talked through the logistics.

After about ten minutes of discussion, Saber pointed at the road along the south side of the building. "I have a question. This street. What kind of traffic are we looking at?"

Riker considered that. He hadn't revealed the address of the warehouse to the team yet, wanting to keep security as tight as possible. Now that Jameson was out, he was doubly glad he hadn't. There was a chance Jameson's wounded pride would lead him to place an ill-advised call to the authorities before that night's festivities.

"You're worried about police?" Riker asked.

Saber considered that, then nodded. "You said strange

noises aren't unheard of in this area. But still. If we're driving the fight into the parking lot, things could get loud."

Riker thought about that. There was a concrete wall around the parking lot, but the man had a point. "One second."

Riker pulled out his burner phone and touched the only number in the contact list.

A moment later, Franklin picked up. "Hey, how's it going with our new recruits?"

"They'll do. Most of them, anyway."

"Good. What do you need from us?"

"Actually, I need to talk to Simon."

There was a long pause. Franklin sounded surprised when he spoke again. "Okay, one moment."

Simon's voice came on the line. "Hey, buddy, what's up?"

"I need a distraction a few blocks from the warehouse tonight. Think you can make that happen?"

"How loud do you want it?"

"Loud enough to cover up the sounds of the fight, but not so loud that the police shut it down."

Simon considered that. "Can you get me a picture of the corner near the warehouse?"

"Sure. What are you going to do with it?"

"I'll put it on the 'gram. Caption it with the street rave hashtag. Tag a few people."

Riker's eyes narrowed, no idea what half those words meant in the context Simon was using them. "Will it cause enough commotion to drown out a minor battle?"

"Oh yeah," Simon said with a chuckle. "You get me that picture, and they'll show up in droves. That block is going to be hopping. You'll have all the cover you need."

"Okay. I'll get it to you soon."

Riker ended the call and turned back to the others.

"I take it we've got some cover?" Saber asked.

"That we do." Riker turned back to the blueprints. "Let's go over the plan one more time."

The team went back to work. With any luck, by the end of the night, they would have both the stolen weapons and the American leader of Laghaz in custody.

25

An hour after the sun dipped below the horizon, cars started to stream into the area. Riker could hear pounding and construction three blocks away, and two streams of light reached out to the heavens. Whatever distraction Simon had planned, subtlety was not part of it.

Several explosions went off overhead and showers of colored sparks rained down. Then the music started. Riker hoped that it was more pleasant closer to the source. Where he and his team were positioned, the only sound was the teeth-rattling bass. A crowd cheered on occasion and more fireworks shot into the sky.

Riker's team waited on a rooftop with a full view of the front and one side of the warehouse. They watched the building through binoculars. When the first fireworks went off, two men came out of the building. They held assault rifles and wore headsets.

"Looks like the distraction has a downside," Saber said. "They will be armed and on full alert."

Riker shook his head. "No disadvantage there. In fact, it will work in our favor. When I attack from the front, they will move out to meet me quickly. I'll drop back and move to the far side of the building. If they pursue me, their backs will be to your position. If you are good at your job, they should drop before they know they are under attack."

Saber tapped on the side of his B+T APR 308. He had attached a silencer, and two additional magazines were sitting next to the weapon. "This bad boy is dialed in. I can promise that there will be no wasted shots at this range. How long do you want me to wait before I start the attack?"

"As long as possible. I want as many of them exposed as we can get." Riker turned to Wendig and Greco. "Once Saber fires his first shot, I want you two to advance from the rear. Anyone left inside should be focused on the frontal attack. Use your silenced pistols until they are aware of you. Then you can break out the rifles. We will be outnumbered so don't take chances. Just go for kill shots. Any questions?"

"What if they don't take the bait?" Wendig asked.

"If they run from me, you two will be waiting for them at the back of the building. I'll make my way in after them. We good?" The group was silent, and Riker took that as a yes. "Get into position and wait for my signal."

Riker moved slowly around the block, staying in the shadows. When he reached the corner, he climbed the concrete wall that surrounded the parking lot. Once inside, he found cover behind a work truck at the end of the parking lot. A guard with an assault rifle stood by the front door, illuminated by the harsh light mounted on the front of the building.

Riker used the truck to steady his rifle. He took aim and fired. Before the guard had time to register the flash and crack of the shot, a bullet tore through his right knee cap. He fell to the ground screaming. Riker was a hundred yards from the man and he watched him tap his headset.

"Tell Chatti!" the man screamed. "We're under attack."

As the man yelled into the mic, he dragged himself towards his rifle which now lay a few feet from him. Blood streamed from the wound, and Riker respected the man for keeping a level head while enduring the pain. Still, Riker squeezed the trigger again. This time the guard's head jerked back, and he lay silent.

As the beat from the nearby dance party bounced through the parking lot, the door to the building slammed open. The barrel of a rifle poked out, followed by a man's face. He scanned the area, looking for the attackers. Riker had the angle and could have delivered a kill shot, but he waited.

The man called out and a second person crouched low and moved from inside the building. He checked on the fallen guard and took cover behind a nearby car. Once he was behind the vehicle, Riker fired two quick shots into the engine block, making sure they felt the pressure of the assault. Half a second later, the rattle of an assault rifle came from the man in the doorway.

Riker moved to the other end of the truck and lay prone near the back tire. Another man came out of the warehouse and started crossing the parking lot. Riker squeezed the trigger, putting a bullet through his shin. The man fell to the ground screaming, and Riker moved back behind the truck. The injured man's friends answered in kind, sending a volley of gunfire tearing into the truck. Glass shattered and all four side windows were blown out by the rounds.

Riker watched the sides of the truck. He needed to make sure no one flanked him. The fact that he was putting so much trust into one of the mercs Franklin had hired felt way riskier now that he was pinned down.

Voices called out, some in English, some in Farsi. Even if

Riker hadn't known the language, he would have understood the message. The men were calling out move orders. One would yell that he was moving, and two others would rattle off rounds into the truck, pinning Riker down. When their fire stopped, Riker stayed low and inched his barrel over the hood of the truck, firing off a few rounds in the general direction of the building. The attacking team moved tactically and effectively. These were the most professionally-trained terrorists that he had ever faced.

Riker tried to count the voices over the bursts of fire and the pounding of the bass. He thought there were five, but it could have been six. He held his rifle at the ready and watched the back of the truck, waiting for an attacker to find a line of sight to him.

The shouts and gunfire were getting close. Riker guessed that they were twenty feet away. Another burst of fire started, but this time it stopped much sooner than the previous volleys.

Riker held his position. After a few moments without gunfire, he moved to the back of the truck and cautiously glanced toward the attackers. He could see three of them lying face down, pools of blood around their heads.

Riker's phone buzzed in his pocket. He took cover and checked the screen. There was a simple message from Saber.

You're clear

Riker ejected the magazine from his rifle and put in a fresh one. He was prepared to fire into the car next to the building, hoping to lure out another enemy. Then he heard the rattle of assault rifles coming from inside the building. The sound intensified into a constant stream of bullets--a firefight was taking place inside the building.

Riker crouched and moved from car to car as he

approached the door to the warehouse. On his way, he saw two more dead men lying face down on the pavement just like the other three.

Once he reached the building, Riker hugged the wall and moved towards the entrance. He heard the screams of an injured man over shouts and gunfire. Just past the threshold, he could see that the layout was drastically different than the blueprints. Rooms lined one side of the warehouse. Shelves and stacks of hard plastic crates lined the other wall. A pathway led between them to an open area with two vehicles parked inside of a roll-up door.

One man had his back to Riker near the entrance. He was hiding behind a set of crates and firing at the other end of the warehouse with an assault rifle.

Riker pulled out his knife and slid in behind the man. He caught Riker's movement at the last second, but it was too late. The blade sliced through his neck, and Riker pulled the man to the ground. Blood sprayed from the severed artery, and the man went limp in seconds.

Looking over the crate, Riker could see Wendig lying in a pool of blood near the exit at the far side of the building. Wendig held his abdomen with both hands and moaned. Greco was pinned behind one of the SUVs parked near the exit. Four men fired at his position. Bullets ricocheted off the windows and sides of the vehicle, which must have had some major upgrades.

The men fired two at a time while two more moved to flank Greco. They called out commands in Farsi.

Riker aimed his rifle at the man approaching Greco's position. Before he pulled the trigger, Greco peeked around the front of the SUV and fired at one terrorist. His shot missed, but the man closest took advantage. His rifle was at the ready, and Greco took a bullet to the head.

With Greco down, Riker was alone with four men in the building. While their attention was still on Greco, Riker fired a shot, hitting a man center mass. He quickly moved the sights of his rifle to the man who had killed Greco and fired again. The man fell forward, collapsing onto his face.

Before Riker could move to a third target, he caught movement to his left. Someone had come out of the rooms on that side of the building. He ducked down just as the man fired, narrowly avoiding a bullet to the head.

The man that had fired yelled out in Farsi. "Take the device and go. I'll be right behind you."

Riker recognized orders when he heard them. This man was in charge. What was the name the man outside had shouted into his radio? Chatti, Riker remembered.

A barrage of gunfire tore into the crate in front of Riker and the wall behind him. He heard the sound of the garage door going up and an engine starting. Riker crouched in a runner's position behind the crates, tensing his muscles and waiting for a break in the fire.

The instant the automatic fire stopped, Riker sprang, running forward toward Chatti. Riker raised his rifle and fired, but Chatti's reaction time matched his. Chatti ducked into the room as bullets splintered the doorframe. Riker saw that he had ejected the magazine from his rifle and hadn't loaded a fresh one. Riker continued to fire and advance on the shooter's position.

He sprinted across the short distance, hoping to finish Chatti before he could ready his weapon. Riker continued firing as he charged through the door at an angle. The muzzle of his rifle had barely crossed the doorway and a hand shot out and grabbed the hot metal.

A hard pull on the weapon dragged him into the room. He released his grip on the weapon but kept moving forward. He grabbed the pistol in his belt and brought it up to finish the attacker. Chatti released the barrel of Riker's weapon and grabbed Riker's wrist, stopping the hand from coming up.

Riker threw a hard jab with his empty hand, but Chatti ducked the punch and countered with one of his own. The hook caught Riker in the ribs. The pain was intense, and for a brief moment, Riker wondered how Chatti had gotten the leverage for such a powerful blow in these tight quarters.

Chatti drew back his hand for another punch, but Riker brought his knee up into the man's chest, repaying the blow to the ribs. The hit lifted Chatti off the ground an inch, and his grip loosened on Riker's wrist. Riker took full advantage and twisted out of the grip, freeing his right hand and the pistol it held. He moved his aim to the center of Chatti's chest. As he squeezed the trigger, Chatti brought a hand down on Riker's arm. The shot hit the man in his thigh instead of his chest. Riker had never fought an opponent who was so much faster than he was.

To Riker's surprise, Chatti brought the leg that had just been shot up for a kick. He braced his back against the wall and kicked Riker, sending him stumbling back across the room. Riker hit a desk and fell backward on top of it. He kept his grip on his weapon and his sights on his target. Raising himself up, he fired. Chatti dove through the doorway, narrowly missing a bullet.

Riker hopped back off the desk and pointed his weapon at the door frame for a moment. He could hear the pounding of footsteps on the warehouse's concrete floor. Riker charged after him, running out the door just in time to see Chatti climbing into the other SUV. Riker raised his pistol and fired a desperate shot from fifty feet away. The door closed, and Riker's bullet scratched the glass an inch from Chatti's temple.

The tires chirped as the car lurched forward. The driver swerved just enough to catch Wendig under the wheels as it drove out of the warehouse. Riker fired two shots at the back window of the vehicle, but they ricocheted off the bullet-proof glass.

Riker's mind was making connections he wasn't sure he was ready to face, but he needed to confirm his suspicion. He ran over to one of the downed terrorists and picked up the radio from his belt. He pressed the button on the radio and spoke a code phrase he hadn't used in over six years. "ATR."

Two quick responses came.

"A1 clear."

"A3 Clear"

Riker gritted his teeth. The responses told him everything he needed to know. Then another voice came over the radio.

"I finally meet the great Matthew Riker, and who does he bring with him?" Chatti said. "A bunch of low-rent mercs?"

Riker blinked hard. This guy knew his name. "Apparently that's all I needed to take down your command center and put a bullet in your leg. I'm guessing you're Chatti?"

The response crackled as the radio moved out of range. "I'm going to savor your demise. What you did today changed nothing."

Riker put the radio down and looked around at the carnage of the warehouse. He thought back to the command Chatti had given his men. He'd said, "Take the device and go." Device, not devices.

Riker grabbed the radio and spoke into it. "Saber, thanks for the help out there. Over."

"That's what I'm here for. How we looking? Over."

"We're clear. Come down and give me a hand searching for a weapon."

26

Riker waited near the warehouse entryway until Saber joined him. Only a few minutes ago, this place had been a cacophony of sounds—gunfire, heavy feet on the concrete floor, the screams of dying men. Now it was almost eerily quiet. All Riker could hear was the thumping of the bass from the street party outside.

Saber trotted up, his rifle slung over his back.

Riker held up his hand and the two men bumped fists. "That was some quality work."

"You too," Saber said. He looked a little shell-shocked. "Greco and Wendig?"

Riker just shook his head.

"Damn." He glanced back at the parking lot where the signs of their handiwork were clear. "They knew what they were getting into, but still. Damn."

"Franklin will make sure their families get the money. Small consolation, but it's something." Riker paused. "If it helps, they died for a good cause."

"No offense, but it doesn't. I've never had a job the client didn't claim was for a good cause." Saber shook his head. "Come on, let's do this."

Riker nodded and led the way into the converted warehouse. The signs of the battle were all around them. Bodies, blood, and chunks of wood from the torn-up crates lay strewn around the room. Riker walked through the storage area and down the long hallway that led to the other end of the building.

"Looks like they made some updates to this place since those blueprints you had," Saber observed.

"Looks like. Their leader took off, but let's make sure nobody's hiding out, waiting to put a bullet in our backs." Riker stopped at the first door, waited for Saber to give him a nod, and threw the door open. The two men rushed in and quickly cleared the room. There was no one inside, but there was a plethora of workout equipment. The room was as well-equipped as most professional gyms.

Saber let out a soft whistle. "When you want to terrorize a nation while still getting your reps in."

Riker said nothing. He didn't like the looks of this. These guys had been embedded here for a while.

As they continued searching the building, they didn't find any people, but they did find plenty to confirm Riker's suspicions. There was a kitchen. A two-lane shooting range that ran half the length of the building. Even a rec room complete with couch, a big-screen TV, and a PlayStation 4.

"Call of Duty." Saber nodded to the TV screen, which showed a paused first-person shooter video game. "Guess they were tired of shooting guys in real life and wanted to do it virtually."

Riker led them to the door to the final room. The door was half-open, but unlike most of the other rooms, this one had a lock. Commercial grade, too. If it had been locked, it would have been a pain in the ass to get past. As it was, Riker just pushed the door open with his foot and stepped inside.

The room was a large office. A desk chair sat in front of a bank of three monitors, all of them glowing. Someone must have been working at the computer when they'd attacked. The person had rushed out to join in the fight.

Riker chuckled. "Mighty nice of them to leave the computer unlocked for us."

"Hey, QuickBooks!" Saber meandered over and sat down in front of the computer.

"Quick what?"

"It's accounting software." He studied the screen. "I don't particularly like the way they've got it setup though. I prefer a cleaner layout."

"Big QuickBooks user?" Riker scanned the rest of the room, but he didn't see anything that would be useful.

"Well Riker, the merc thing isn't exactly the steadiest gig in the world. I've been studying for my CPA. I figure if I can be as deadly with my bookkeeping as I am with my rifle, maybe I can stop shooting people for a living."

That was a sentiment Riker could fully relate to. He just hoped Saber was able to get out of this lifestyle more permanently than he had. He reached into his pocket and pulled out a piece of equipment Franklin had insisted he bring—a one terabyte thumb drive. He tossed it to Saber. "Copy everything from the hard drive onto this."

"You got it." Saber inserted the thumb drive into a USB port and got to work. "It's going to take a few minutes for the files to transfer."

"That's fine. I'll start digging through the rest of the facility while you do that."

He was almost to the door when Saber spoke again.

"What the hell?"

Riker stopped. "What is it?"

"I'm going over their books and looking at the payments received. This list…"

Riker walked back over and looked at the monitor over the other man's shoulder. The screen showed a list of names and dollar figures.

"Check it out." He pointed at one of the names—Juniper Withholdings.

"You know these guys?" Riker asked.

"Know them? I've worked for them. They hire mercs like me to go down and protect their interests in South America. They pay well, too."

"So I see." The dollar figure next to their name was eight hundred thousand.

"What's a legit company like Juniper doing working with terrorists?"

Riker scanned the list and recognized a few companies he'd worked with back in his QS-4 days. "I don't think these guys were terrorists. Not the kind we thought, anyway."

"You're thinking Laghaz is a front for something else?" Saber asked, the surprise clear in his voice.

Riker wasn't ready to comment on that just yet. The pieces were still coming together in his mind.

"Riker, what the hell's going on here?"

The computer dinged before Riker could answer.

"Files are done transferring."

"Good," Riker said. "Let's keep investigating."

After Saber tossed the thumb drive to Riker, they headed back to the storage area near the entrance. Riker took a long look at the crates near the wall, considering them. Then he pulled out his knife and pried one open.

Inside, he found a row of six M17 pistols, all sitting

snugly in perfectly carved foam inserts. He took out the first row and set it on the ground.

Saber nodded toward them. "Nice pistols. Mind if I help myself to a little bonus?"

"I wouldn't. We don't know where they got these weapons or how they're registered. My policy is to never fire a weapon of unknown origin. But it's your call."

"You know your problem, Riker? You're too damn sensible." Saber frowned, but he didn't pick up any of the weapons.

Riker kept working, unloading row after row of weapons until the crate was empty. Then he moved onto the next one.

"What exactly are you doing?" Saber asked.

"Following a hunch."

In the second crate, Riker found MK 16 SCAR-L rifles, situated as nicely as the handguns had been. He got to work unloading.

"You know, my work for Juniper was one of the toughest jobs I ever had." Saber walked over and leaned against the wall, watching Riker work with a skeptical eye.

"Yeah?" He could tell that Saber had a story to share. He just needed a little prompting. "What kind of thing did you do for them?"

"I had been out of the Army for a couple years at that point. Bouncing from job to job. Bored out of my skull and half going crazy, wondering if this was my life now. You know how it is."

"Yeah."

"But then an old buddy calls me. Says he's got a new gig I might be interested in. This company—Juniper—they extract minerals in the South American rainforest. Thing is, getting the minerals out is tricky. You've got your environmental groups that want to stop you. You've got bandits who want to rob you. So they hire experienced soldiers to come down and protect their interests. Two months of work, and it pays more than I'd make in a year at the lame jobs I'd been working. So I talk to one of their people, and a week later, I'm on a plane down to Brazil."

Riker finished unloading the second crate. Setting the last rifle on the floor. He looked at the remaining four crates. After a moment, he selected the second one on the right and popped it open. More M17s. He started unloading.

"It was exciting to get back to a bit of soldiering, but I was not prepared for the rainforest. The humidity. The bugs. It was hellish. Then one night, we're in our bunks when a bunch of dudes with automatic weapons charge in and hold us at gunpoint. They'd killed the two guys we had on guard duty, and they forced the rest of us to stay in our beds while they pillaged the minerals we were supposed to be guarding. It was terrifying. And a little humiliating."

Riker finished unloading the handguns. He stood looking at the empty case for a long moment.

"I thought the bosses were going to tear us a new one," Saber continued, "but they couldn't have been nicer. They sent us home with full pay. My buddy told me what happened after that. I guess there's a black-ops group they work with. Some real bad-ass heavy-hitter types. They brought them in once we were gone. According to my buddy, they managed to recover every ounce those guys stole from us, and they left a strong enough impression on the locals that no one's bothered messing with Juniper in that area since. It makes you think, doesn't it?"

Riker turned to the other man. "How so?"

"Why would Juniper hire terrorists?"

Riker turned back to the crate. He stuck his knife in one

of the seams at the bottom of the crate. And then a second. With a twist of the wrist, the false bottom popped open.

Saber's mouth dropped open in surprise. "How'd you know that was there?"

"Lucky guess." He removed a piece of foam, revealing what was underneath. He recognized it immediately from an image Franklin had shown him—it was one of the stolen detonators and the explosive devices.

A wave of relief swept through Riker. The recovered weapon represented potentially thousands of lives saved.

"Let's check the other crates."

Saber nodded, and the two men got to work.

As they reached the bottom of the final crate without uncovering anything further, Riker's feeling of relief began to fade. There was still one weapon out there. And he was certain that the leader of Laghaz—or whoever they really were—wasn't among the dead men in the warehouse.

He hoped the thumb drive in his pocket contained some indication of where the terrorist/mercenary group was planning to strike.

He pulled out his phone and tapped Franklin's number. The man answered on the first ring.

"What happened? Are you all right?"

"Yeah," Riker said. "We lost two guys, but I made it."

"Damn." There was a long pause. "The weapons?"

"We recovered one."

"That's wonderful!"

"I'm on my way back to the house. And when I get there, we need to have a serious conversation. I figured out who these guys are working for."

"What do you mean?"

"Not over the phone. I'll see you soon."

27

Eleven years earlier.

FROM BRICKLAYERS TO ACCOUNTANTS, the worst jobs always went to the new guy. Riker's first solo mission with QS-4 was no exception.

"You ready to get out and stretch your legs?" Morrison asked Riker one day as he was coming in from the practice range.

After the mission to kill Mohamad Izad, Riker and his new teammates had been promptly flown back to the States, and Riker had gotten his first look at QS-4's headquarters in southwest Virginia.

"Close enough to D.C., but not too close, if you catch my drift," Morrison had explained.

To call the campus impressive would have been an understatement. It contrasted with Riker's military experience in a thousand little ways, from the quality of the food in the cafeteria to the excellent water pressure. It was clear that the bigwigs at QS-4 had the comfort of their employees in mind when they'd designed this place.

Riker had been wide-eyed and speechless during the initial tour of the facilities.

Timber grinned and slapped him on the back. "Just don't go soft on us, Scarecrow."

"I'll do my best."

And so he had, pushing himself even harder than usual in his daily training regime. It had now been a week since they'd returned from the mission, and Riker's thoughts had turned to what was next. Based on Morrison's sudden appearance outside the shooting range, he was about to find out.

"Yes, sir. Where are we headed?" Riker asked enthusiastically.

"*We* aren't going anywhere. You are taking on a solo mission. Nothing major, but it needs to be done."

"A solo mission, sir?"

"Do you have an issue with that?" Morrison asked.

"No, sir. I'm just surprised to have one this early on in my time with the organization." Riker paused and watched Morrison's slight change in facial expression. "This is a test, isn't it? You want to see how I do in the field alone?"

Morrison gave a slight nod. "I consider it more of an assessment. This job is an exercise in patience. Your handler will fill you in on the details."

A few hours later, Riker was briefed on an intercept mission. The mission was simple. He had to wait until a package exchanged hands. Then he was to retrieve said package. If it could be done without any deaths that would be preferred, but the other way worked too.

The exchange was part of an underground supply

network. The items were typically weapons. Normally, it was a small explosive. QS-4 would examine the retrieved item to try and find the point of origin. This allowed them to fill some of the cracks in legitimate weapon distributors and militaries.

Normally these kinds of missions weren't bad. The problem with this one was the drop window. This network used vague timelines, making them hard to stop. They had a five-day window when the drop was to take place. Riker was supposed to watch the location every minute of the day until the exchange happened. That meant a potential one hundred and twenty hours of sitting and waiting. Sleeping was out until the drop occurred, and any bathroom breaks needed to be quick.

The exchange would likely only take a few minutes, and if the operative was not watching closely, they would miss it. That meant they would wait out the remainder of the five days and have nothing to show at the end. The mission objectively sucked. Apparently, this was the first mission assigned to most QS-4 operatives.

After packing some supplies, Riker was ready to head to Cairo. Morrison came to see him off.

"Your handler will be available if you get into trouble, but I doubt that will happen. I would prefer if you took care of this on your own. I expect my men to get efficient results operating under their own discretion."

"Understood."

After Morrison left, Timber found him. He wore a smirk on his face. "You going on the intercept mission?"

"Yep, I'm headed out now," Riker said.

"Have fun with that bullshit."

"What makes you say it's bullshit? It sounds slow, but simple."

"I spent five straight days watching a tree in a park when

Morrison sent me on that wild goose chase. I never took my eyes off the drop site. It was a long five days."

"You never took your eyes off the location?"

"Maybe I took a dump, but that's it. I didn't sleep, I had rations next to me and I pissed in a bottle. I'm pretty sure there is no drop. Morrison just does it to test out the new guys. He wants to see if you can stick to an order even if it sucks."

"Has anyone ever intercepted the package?"

Timber hesitated for a moment. "Well, two guys have. That's out of forty who tried. Doesn't mean I missed it. All I'm saying is that you should prepare for a long five days."

"Thanks for the heads up."

Riker took five days' worth of gear and headed out.

Five days later, he sent a message to his handler that he was still working the mission. Ten days after that, he still hadn't returned.

Riker finally showed up at QS-4 headquarters three weeks after he'd left for the mission. Morrison waited when he entered the building. Riker came in with a beard and a loaded rucksack.

"That was a long five days," Morrison said.

"An extremely long five days," Riker agreed.

"Clean up and head in for the debrief," Morrison said and then walked away.

After a shower and shave Riker felt like a new man. He sat in a conference room across from Morrison and his handler. There was a small case, a stack of files and a laptop computer on the table between them.

"I see that you brought something back. Explain these items and the missing time." Morrison's face didn't give away any emotion. Riker couldn't tell if he was pissed, happy, or indifferent.

"The case is the item that I intercepted at the drop. The files contain contacts and future exchange locations. The laptop contains the encryption key to determine the exact time for the drops."

The handler's mouth dropped open. "That's impossible. The drops have huge time windows. It's how the supply chain has functioned for as long as it has."

Morrison's expression didn't change, and he ignored the handler. "Now I know what you were up to. Why did it take longer than the expected five days?"

"I spent three and a half days waiting for the drop. I had nothing to do but keep my eyes on an alley and think. You said that your operatives had a lot of discretion for their missions. I started to think about my objectives. The point of the mission was to stop this underground supplier from getting weapons into the wrong hands. Sending operatives out to sit and wait for five days at a time didn't seem like the most effective way to do that.

"After eighty-one hours of staring at an alley, the exchange finally took place. Instead of waiting across the street, I was waiting in the alley. I stood next to a dumpster and camouflaged myself with trash. I was close enough to hear the exchange and see the money transfer hands."

"You just stood in place for three and a half days? Like a scarecrow?" the handler asked.

"I don't recommend it."

Morrison gave a slight nod. "Continue."

"I subdued both men and took the device. I questioned the men for the next two days. They were both very stubborn, but I was patient. Eventually, they gave me the locations to which they were to deliver their respective items.

"I spent four days learning the security and routines of the buyer who was purchasing the bomb. I learned he was most vulnerable while traveling between businesses. I captured him, and he was kind enough to inform me how they know when to meet up for the exchange. There is a second encryption buried in the message for the location. It requires an additional key. That key was on his computer." Riker nodded towards the laptop.

Morrison made a strange harrumphing sound. "That leaves an unexplained week and a stack of papers."

Riker nodded curtly. "After I was finished with the buyer and the key, I went to pay the supplier a visit. I hoped it would only take a day, he'd turned rabbit after his man never returned from the exchange. Luckily I'd left my two informants alive. This time when I asked for more information, they were eager to comply.

"Eventually I was able to track down the leader of the supply chain in Cairo. He was much more difficult to subdue. After the botched exchange, he surrounded himself with security and bunkered down. I had to fight my way through his forces. Eventually I got to him, but he died in the firefight so I could not question him. Fortunately, his protected location contained a lot of documentation about the organization and his clients." Riker nodded to the stack of files.

"Holy shit, we have to get this info to the data guys," the handler said.

Morrison stared at Riker for a long moment. "Would you say that you successfully completed your mission?"

Riker tilted his head in surprise. He'd expected Morrison to be blown away. "I'd say success is a bit of an understatement."

"So that's a yes?"

"You bet your ass that's a yes, sir." Riker responded, a bit more forcefully than was necessary.

Morrison made the harrumphing sound again, and the slightest smile formed at the corner of Morrison's mouth. Apparently, the sound meant he was pleased. "I agree. You still have a lot to learn, but you have shown that you are worthy of the lessons."

Riker stifled a bemused chuckle. He still didn't know if Morrison was a smug jerk or the most skilled mentor he had ever had. Somehow it felt as if both were true.

Morrison turned to the handler. "Get this data down to the guys in the lab. I'll take the weapon to lock up."

The handler left with the papers and computer.

Morrison stared at Riker for a long moment. "I know that most commanders would either put on a show about how pissed they were that you went outside the parameters of the mission, or they'd tell you what a great job you did and then take credit for the results."

"I can already tell that you aren't most commanders," Riker said.

"No, and QS-4 isn't a normal outfit. I'm not going to take credit for anything you did, because we aren't here to get medals or pretend we are better than we actually are. You did a good job, and the world will be a better place for it. That's all the reward anyone here gets. And I didn't react the first way, either. Guess that means *I* passed *your* test, too."

Riker smiled. "Yes. You told me that I had control of my missions. You said that the way the operation was completed should be in the agent's hands. I didn't believe you when you said it, but I believe you now."

Morrison stood up. "My assessment is that you have a lot of potential. I will make sure that you realize every bit of it."

28

Franklin, Jessica, and Simon were all waiting for him in the living room when he arrived back at the safe house. Simon looked blurry-eyed, as if he might fall back to sleep at any moment, but the others looked far too nervous to sleep.

Jessica greeted him with a big hug. "Thank God you're all right."

Riker couldn't help but smile. That was the most pleasant greeting he'd ever received after a mission. He wanted nothing more than to return to the bedroom with Jessica, slide between the sheets, and not leave for a couple days. Unfortunately, there was a lot of work to do before that could happen.

Riker pulled away after a moment and set the thumb drive on the coffee table. "The contents of their hard drive, as requested."

Franklin's eyes lit up. "Wonderful!"

"How'd the street rave thing work out as a distraction?" Simon asked.

"Very well," Riker admitted. "You did good, man."

Simon beamed proudly.

"What did you mean on the phone?" Franklin asked. "The guys aren't working for Laghaz?"

Riker took a seat on the couch. "Not exactly. Laghaz doesn't really exist."

Franklin stopped what he was doing. "What?"

"They are a front. A boogie man to be used as an ugly scapegoat. When there is a job that needs to be blamed on a terrorist organization, Laghaz takes the fall."

Franklin and Simon sat with their mouths open, trying to take in what Riker had just said. Jessica focused on the new information.

"If they are a front, who's backing them?" Jessica asked, taking a seat beside him.

"QS-4."

The room was silent for a long moment. Then Franklin shook his head. "That's impossible."

"I didn't want to believe it at first, either. But the pieces fit. Think about it." Riker leaned forward, looking the handler in the eyes. "Morrison comes to me, someone who's been off the books with QS-4 for six years, and asks me to protect Simon. Makes a big deal about this mission being Lone Wolf status. Why the secrecy?"

"To avoid potential embarrassment to Simon's father."

Riker chuckled. "I've known Morrison for a long time. If there's anything he cares about less than a politician being embarrassed, I don't know what it is."

"Maybe," Franklin allowed. "But it's hardly proof."

"When we found out about the weapons and told Morrison, he told us to back off, right? The only way that makes any kind of sense is if he *had* to say that. I believe the whole reason he gave me this mission was because he knew there was no way in hell I'd stop hunting the weapons just because of orders."

Simon nodded sagely. "I've only known you for like three days, and I already know you don't follow orders."

Riker continued. "The thing that finally pulled it together in my mind was Chatti, the leader of Laghaz. He knew my name. He said he'd been wanting to meet me. After the fight, I called out a code on the radio that only QS-4 operatives would understand. They answered immediately."

Simon thought for a moment. "So QS-4, like, created this fake terrorist group?"

"If you have people hiring you to do shady stuff, it would be very handy to blame it on terrorists," Jessica pointed out.

Franklin's face was pale as he stared at the floor. "I'm still not sure I buy it. Morrison would never approve of those methods."

"Exactly," Riker said. "That's why he got me involved. QS-4 doesn't exactly handle dissent among the ranks very well, so he can't openly object to what they're doing. He can't even risk openly telling you what he wants me to do. So he brings in a retired operative as a ghost agent to handle things."

"Handle things how?" Franklin asked.

"Recover the weapons. Stop Laghaz." Jessica's voice was distant as she thought it through.

"So Morrison isn't really trying to save my life?" Simon asked. "I'm hurt."

"I'm sure he cares about that too," Riker said with a smile. "It's probably just eight or nine on his list of worries."

Franklin ran a hand through his hair. "This... this is a lot to take in. You might be retired, but I am not. You're saying the company I work for employs terrorist-like methods."

"I'm also saying Morrison trusted you enough to assign you to be my handler. I have no doubt that he is risking everything to have us stop this attack. Things have gone wrong inside of QS-4. I'm guessing Morrison is trying to set them right." Riker pointed toward the thumb drive on the coffee table. "I know it's tough to hear, but we don't have a lot of time to process our emotions. We need to find out what's on that drive."

Franklin nodded slowly. He looked almost relieved to have something else to focus on.

The four team members spent the next few hours looking through the files Riker had brought back. At first, things seemed promising, as they quickly discovered possible attack targets. The problem was the sheer number. There were two hundred and sixteen specified targets in one folder. Each target had a record of the property, satellite photos, and schematics.

"I don't get it," Simon said. "Maybe they want to use the prototypes to manufacture more? Or maybe they didn't choose the final targets yet."

"That's not it. This is another form of encryption. We just need to crack it." Riker stared at a screen that held two hundred and sixteen dots on it across the US.

"How the hell do we even start to figure it out?" Simon's frustration came through in his voice.

"Let's start by trying to work it backward. Jessica, bring up any locations that are a twelve-hour drive from the command center that we hit. They had a lot of vehicles at the warehouse and lots of gear. They wouldn't try to fly all of that out, which means they were close to one of the targets. Since the attack is supposed to take place in two days and they haven't left yet, the target must be fairly close."

After laying a radius over the map of possible targets, Jessica said, "There are forty-one possible targets in that range. Still a lot of options."

"Look for the biggest targets," Franklin said while looking over Jessica's shoulder. "Either dams that would cause the most damage if they were destroyed or power plants that support the largest number of end-users. Terrorists always go for the biggest impact."

"Wait." Riker rubbed his chin. "Your logic is sound, but it isn't right in this case. This isn't a normal terrorist cell. If they were, they would target the most people or the biggest financial target. Those bombs could easily get into a football stadium and kill a hundred thousand people. Why aren't those the targets? These aren't religious zealots. QS-4 is behind this, which means someone hired them. There's a logical motive here, one that involves money or power"

"Then what do you suggest?"

Riker looked at the remaining targets on Jessica's screen. He didn't have an answer yet.

"Why the bombs?" Simon said.

"For their destructive power," Franklin answered with annoyance.

"No, I mean why these bombs? The destructive power is only half the tech. The other half is their new detonators. They work differently."

"Check for any updated security systems," Riker said. "See if you can find any articles about better protections against communications."

Franklin pounded on his keyboard and flipped through a series of windows. "The newest protective measures create dead zones. They kill all cell signals and flatten most wireless communication waves. They're designed to prevent wireless cyberattacks, but it would also prevent the signal from reaching an explosive device."

"I'm guessing that this new tech will get around that

system just fine. Can you tell what facilities are using the new defensive measures?"

Jessica and Franklin searched the records and checked any press release they could find.

"One of the remaining targets is using that tech," Jessica said. "It's a power plant out by Bakersfield."

Franklin brought up the target. "That makes no sense. You were right. Destroying that plant wouldn't have a lot of impact. It might bring down half the city, but nowhere near the impact something around L.A. or San Francisco would have."

Riker knew there was a clue he was missing. He relaxed his mind and then it came to him.

"Jessica, what file number was that target?"

"What do you mean?"

"The folder that had all the targets listed in numerical order. Is that plant number 24?"

She checked the folders. "Yeah, how did you know that?"

"Check number 79. Tell me if that one has the same defensive measures."

Franklin brought up the file. "It does. It's a dam in Georgia. Do you think that's the other target?"

"I know it is. The series of numbers on the phone that I took off the guy in the first stash house. It was 2479. I thought it was for a lock. It was actually a key to this code. 24 and 79 are the real targets from the list."

"Damn, nice work Sherlock Holmes," Simon said with a whistle.

"It seems correct, but I still want to know why they chose these two targets. It can't be random," Franklin said.

"I agree that there is a connection." Riker rubbed his chin. "Something is very off about this entire attack. I gotta assume they were prepping the attack in Bakersfield. That's why they're hear in L.A. Now that we've weakened their operation here, they'll switch their focus to the other target."

"How do you know that?" Simon asked.

"Because it's what I would do in their situation. We need to get to that dam in Georgia before it's too late."

"Leave that to me," Jessica said. "I can get us a plane. Before you ask, no, there will be no record tying it to me."

Franklin smiled. "You are handy to have around. I should be able to get weapons for us in Georgia."

"How long will it take for you to get us a plane?" Riker asked.

"It will be ready when we get to the airport. We keep one on standby."

"Perfect. Everyone grab your stuff. I've got one call to make before we go."

Riker went into the other room and dialed a number on his burner phone. After several rings a tired Saber picked up the phone.

"Sorry to bug you so late, or early, depending on how you look at it. I could use a little help on another mission."

"You just get right to it, huh Riker? I normally don't get a second mission the same day I finish the first."

"I know it's a little unusual, but you know this one is time-sensitive. I need to get one more weapon back. Having an ace sniper will really help our odds."

"Where is it at?"

"Georgia. We leave right now."

"Shit. I have to pick up my daughter in a few hours. I don't want to bore you with the details, but I'm on the verge of losing my custody. I'm really sorry, but I can't make it work right this second."

"You're sure there's no way you can pull it off? Like I said

I could really use another guy on this, especially one I trust."

"I'm sorry man. If I had a little more time to change things around, I may have been able to make it work, but I'm not going to risk losing my kid."

"I understand. Thanks for your help yesterday."

"Glad I could help. See you around, Riker."

"See you around, Saber."

By the time Riker hung up, Franklin, Simon, and Jessica had gathered their things and were ready to head to the airport.

Riker looked at the three unlikely companions. He felt something for the first time in years. He had felt it in his wrestling career and his service in and out of the Navy. He felt as if he belonged. This was his team, and each member was a vital part. He wanted to savor the moment, but the clock continued to tick and they had work to do.

29

When the group arrived at the airport and made their way to the private jet Jessica had reserved for them, Riker's jaw dropped open. "You've gotta be kidding me."

"What?" Jessica asked, her voice innocent. "It was the first thing they had available."

Simon clapped Riker on the shoulder as they stepped out onto the tarmac and walked toward the aircraft. "You're going to love this man. It's a Bombardier Global 7500. These things are nice, even by my standards."

"Dibs on the master bedroom," Jessica said.

Riker raised an eyebrow. "There's a *master* bedroom?"

"This thing sleeps eight, so there's plenty of room for us."

"No kidding." Riker had been on his share of aircraft during his tenure with both the SEALs and QS-4, but most of those had been simple transports that favored functionality and practicality over comfort. This thing was like entering a whole new world. The jet was over a hundred feet long and looked like it was made for about twenty passengers rather than the four of them.

Franklin just shook his head and said nothing as they boarded the aircraft.

"Shouldn't the pilot be here to take our bags or whatever?" Simon asked.

"I told them we wanted privacy. I'll go to the cabin to introduce myself and let him know we're ready, but other than that, they'll leave us alone for the duration of the flight."

Riker climbed to the top of the airstair and stepped onto the plane, taking a look at the luxurious space. He set down his bag on one of the ten seats in the main cabin area.

Simon ran through the plane, excitedly checking out the four rooms. He came back and gave the others the rundown. Besides the main cabin area, there was the master suite, a second sleeping area with seats that converted to beds, and an entertainment room complete with a large television and surround sound.

"We won't be using that one," Riker said. "We've got work to do."

By the time the plane took off five minutes later, all four of them were in full research mode, with Jessica and Riker huddled over one laptop, and Simon and Franklin sharing the other. They'd be flying into Augusta, Georgia, the nearest airport to their suspected target. From there, they would drive the thirty miles north to Senhold, where the dam was located. The question on Riker's mind now was why a random dam in rural Georgia would be the target for a major operation. It didn't take him long to find the answer.

"Number one employer in Senhold is Strymond," Franklin said.

"The pharmaceutical company?" Riker asked. That certainly brought things into focus. He turned to Jessica. "Can you bring up a map of the area?"

Her fingers flew over the keyboard of her MacBook Pro, and a few seconds later, Riker was looking at the layout of the town.

She pointed at a spot on the north end of the map. "This is the dam. And this..." She moved her finger a few clicks south. "...is the corporate headquarters of Strymond. Looks like they have a production facility in town as well."

Franklin leaned back in his chair and crossed his arms. "I'm guessing the destruction of that dam would cause some major infrastructure issues for Strymond."

"Sure." Something still didn't add up for Riker. "It would cause major issues, but to what end? Why fake a terrorist attack just to mess up a portion of a global pharmaceutical company?"

"It's a misdirection," Jessica said. "No one will pay attention to the damage done to a corporation when they are talking about a terrorist attack on American soil."

"It's possible. But who is behind it and why?" Franklin asked.

"Apparently QS-4, but I have no idea why." There was hesitation in Jessica's voice. It sounded as if she was feeling the same way that Riker was. While it was clear that they'd located the correct target, there was still a piece missing. They knew the where and the who, but it felt as if they hadn't fully finished putting together the why.

"Keep in mind someone probably hired QS-4 for this operation," Riker said. "There is another player that we aren't seeing."

"Does it really matter?" Simon asked. "The bad guys want the place to go boom. We wanted it not to go boom. We stop them. That's what matters."

Riker chuckled. "I'm starting to think you would have made a decent soldier, Simon."

Jessica scratched at her chin as she stared at the map on the screen. "Okay, so if the *why* isn't our focus, what is? What do we need to figure out?"

"Operational details," Riker replied. "We're going into territory we know very little about. The terrorists have probably spent weeks mapping out the town, the dam, and the power plant. We need pictures, blueprints, anything we can find."

"On it," Simon muttered. He pulled out his phone and started tapping at the screen. The others were still browsing the power company's website when he spoke again. "Seven hundred fifty-three pictures."

Riker looked up in surprise. "Pictures of what?"

"The area around the dam. Check it out." He leaned over, showing Riker his phone. The screen displayed a grid of dozens of pictures of a nature area. "Looks like these Strymond guys have a corporate fitness program. They use the hashtag StrymondStrong on Instagram. So, I just searched with the hashtag and filtered the results to show pictures posted in and around Senhold. Turns out there's a running trail that goes past the dam."

Riker scrolled through the pictures, looking at the dam from dozens of different angles and perspectives. Taken individually, they were just lame snapshots people took to show the world they were exercising. But altogether, it provided a comprehensive layout of the area from the ground level. It was as good as most of the recon packages Riker had received for his QS-4 missions—better actually, since those had usually consisted of satellite photos and pictures taken at odd angles from concealed surveillance equipment. "This is impressive. Nice work."

Simon grinned. "I knew all those hours I spent on Instagram weren't a waste of time."

"What about the dam itself? Can you get me any pictures from inside the power plant?"

"I'll see what I can do."

They spent the next hour hard at work, digging up everything they could find on Senhold, its power network, and the dam. By the time they reached the flight's halfway point, they'd put together a pretty good packet of information. Franklin pulled the blueprint of the power plant from the file they recovered, and Jessica used the company's financial records to figure out the name of the security company that protected the dam. Simon kept digging through social media and was able to find some photos taken by local high schoolers on a tour of the dam. It wasn't as good as the #StymondStrong photos, but it was a lot better than nothing.

Riker stretched and let out a yawn.

Jessica stared at him for a long moment, then stood up and took him by the hand. "Come with me."

"Where are we going?"

"If everything you've said is true, we're going to have a hell of a lot of work waiting for us when we hit the ground. Might be a good idea to rest up, don't you think?"

"Finally, someone is talking sense!" Simon leaned back his seat and put his hands behind his head.

Riker glanced at the laptop one more time, trying to push aside the guilty feeling that he should be working. Still, they had put together all the information they were likely to find, and they could use a break. Besides, when a woman like Jessica King wanted to take you to bed, you didn't fight it.

She led him to the bedroom, and he was surprised to see a full king-size bed dominating the walled-off section of the cabin. She lay down and patted the spot next to her. "Come on, don't be shy."

"Something tells me we're not going to get a lot of rest on this flight." He lay down on the bed next to her.

"You're not wrong." She leaned in, and their lips touched in a soft, lingering kiss.

Riker pulled away and smiled at her. "I know it's cheesy, but I've always sort of wanted to join the Mile High Club. How about you?"

She let out a laugh. "I've been a member for quite some time now."

He gasped in mock surprise. "You mean I'm not the first man you've seduced on a ridiculous private jet?"

"What's the matter? Scared of a little competition?"

"Actually, I thrive on it."

Her body pressed against his as they kissed once again. Just before the passion took him completely, he broke their kiss. Something about what she'd said caused a thought. "Competition. You said competition."

"Don't tell me your ego is that fragile," she said with an eye roll.

"No, not me. Strymond. Who's their number one competitor?"

Jessica's face grew serious. "Vin-Brooks. They are the two biggest pharmaceutical companies, right? Strymond and Vin-Brooks?"

"Right." Riker's mind was moving quickly now. "They stand to profit nicely if Strymond's production drops."

Jessica nodded slowly. "If Strymond can't fulfill their contracts, or if there is a panicked sell off, Vin-Brooks could swoop in and pick them up."

"Exactly."

"So you're saying this might be a hostile takeover of the literal kind?"

"It seems to fit. Apparently the lives of thousands of people are worth less than billions of dollars in profits."

30

THE BUMP of the wheels of the plane touching the runway woke Riker. His body wanted to stay asleep, but he forced his eyes open. Jessica stretched and yawned, coming out of her own slumber. Riker never imagined there was a combination of events that would end with him waking up in a bed aboard a private jet with a beautiful woman, yet here he was. He wanted to push the rest of the world out of his mind and stay in this moment forever, but that wasn't an option.

"If I live through this mission can I get another ride on this plane?" Riker asked.

"If we all get through this, I'll give you a ride anywhere you want to go," Jessica said with a wink.

The team left the plane and found two black Cadillac Escalades that Jessica had arranged. Franklin took one and Riker took the other with Jessica and Simon. Franklin was able to find a connection in the area that would supply weapons. He left with the intent of coming back with a small arsenal.

Riker, Jessica and Simon drove by the dam. Riker wanted to be sure that layout matched up with the information they had compiled. One drive by of the dam and he was confident in their information. The pictures showed the current state of the area down to the vegetation.

"Okay, so that's the dam. What now?" Simon asked.

"Now I need to get the two of you to a safe place. Franklin lined up a house for us, that's where we're headed now." Riker drove away from the dam.

"Shouldn't we be watching this place? I mean they could be here any time," Jessica asked.

"In theory we have until tomorrow. That was their original plan."

"You know as well as I do that the plan may have changed. We have thrown a pretty big wrench into their scheme," Jessica pressed.

"That's true, the plan may be totally different now. They could show up any minute, or they could choose a completely different target. One way or another we need more information. That's why Franklin set up a house for us. We need a base of operations that you can work from. If you are here with me, then I will need to protect you while I try to defend the dam. That would most likely get all of us killed."

"I do know how to shoot a gun," Simon chimed in.

"So you have said. I don't think now is the best time for you to experience a firefight."

"You're not listening to me," Simon protested. "I can shoot. My buddy takes me all the time. I have shot hundreds of rounds in a training lot that he has access to. It is where they train actors for roles. I get that it isn't the same as a firefight, but you need help with this."

"Simon, I appreciate that you want to help, but this isn't a game. You saw Ted take a bullet to the head. With one quick discharge of a gun you can die. There is no learning curve, one mistake and that's it."

"I get it. I also get that there is a weapon out there that is about to kill a bunch of people and it's my fault. If I die trying to clean up my mess, then that's probably what I deserve."

Riker watched Simon's eyes in the rearview mirror. He could tell that the kid meant what he was saying. He definitely didn't fully understand it, but he meant it.

"Let's get the house set up and the weapons in hand. Then we can talk about what our next move is. You've already helped this mission out in some big ways. None of them involved taking a bullet or putting one into another person. I think we should keep it that way."

"That's right. Besides, someone has to stay behind and protect me." Jessica turned to Simon and batted her eyes. "I'm just a helpless girl."

"Fine. We'll talk about the plan later." Simon crossed his arms and slid down in the backseat.

The house was only five minutes away from the dam. It was an old white farmhouse with a barn next to it. There was a for sale sign in the yard. The house sat back from the road and had a forest behind it. Riker wondered if the place had internet access or cell service. The house looked as if it could have been his neighbor's in rural North Carolina.

The forest behind the house was between them and the location of the dam. Riker thought he might be able to see the dam from the roof.

Riker went to the house and found a lockbox by the door. He considered calling Franklin to get the combination, but he used his bump key instead.

"You think you're so cool with that little trick don't you?" Jessica said with a smirk.

Riker's cheeks turned a little red, and he opened the door to the house. With a half-bow he turned to Jessica. "After you, my lady."

She laughed and went into the house.

"Aren't you the cutest couple?" Simon said as he walked by Riker. "How did you find this place?"

"Franklin looked up vacant homes for sale. He called the realtor and negotiated a horrible deal on a week's rent."

"I hope he put a big deposit down. The houses we stay in tend to get shot up."

Riker laughed. "Maybe we should have had Jessica buy the place. Then we could do all the damage we wanted."

"I'm fine with that," Jessica said as she went into the kitchen.

Riker shook his head. He thought of all the teams he had been on. Almost every one of the guys came from nothing, or at least not much. Each one of them worked their asses off and wanted to prove their worth to the world. They had all made fun of the rich and privileged, especially anyone who was born into that life.

He remembered joining in making fun of people like that. Riker had an idea that these two were not the average rich kids, but they had made him realize there wasn't a one-size-fits-all mold for people. He didn't fit into one and neither did they. Both had performed well under bad circumstances. He would have expected them to put their own lives ahead of everyone else, but here they were helping take down a terrorist plot. They might not know how to fight, but they were a good team. Even Franklin had proven himself more than a cog in the machine.

The similarities between the people he was with now and those he had been with then were that they were a team. Riker had missed that, and he had forgotten how good it felt to be part of one.

The sound of a vehicle came from down the road and Riker went to the porch to see who was coming. A black Escalade came down the street and pulled into the drive. Franklin parked next to Riker's SUV.

"How'd shopping go?" Riker said.

"Come see for yourself," Franklin replied.

The two went to the back of the car and opened the hatch. Franklin removed a blanket. There was an impressive collection of firearms. In addition to three assault rifles and several pistols was an assortment of army surplus gear. There was also a case, which Riker assumed held a sniper rifle. A few cases of ammo and a single bullet-proof vest finished off the haul.

"Way to come through with the weapons," Riker said.

"I have to admit I was surprised at how easy finding military-grade weapons is in rural Georgia."

Once everything was in the house Franklin joined the others at the makeshift headquarters.

Jessica had her laptop set up on the kitchen table. "What are we looking for?" Jessica asked.

"Anything that can give us advanced warning for the attack," Franklin said.

"Such as?" Simon asked.

"Ideally I would like to tap into the air traffic control tower of the airport. Unfortunately we are going to have to come up with something else."

"I can do that," Simon said.

Franklin looked at Simon like he was a two-year-old. "You can hack into highly secured systems?"

Simon gave him an insulted look. "Yeah, of course, I can."

"Bullshit. I've known you for years, and you are not a hacker," Jessica interjected.

"Well maybe I can't do it personally, but I know a guy. You aren't the only person here with connections."

"I'll believe it when I see it," Franklin said.

Simon grabbed his phone and walked to the back of the house. "When I deliver on this, I get to sight in those rifles. I'm telling you, I'm a good shot."

Riker turned to Jessica. "Do you think he can deliver, or is he just blowing smoke?"

She shrugged. "He can be full of shit, but he normally isn't that cocky unless he knows he can come through."

Franklin pulled up his plans of the dam along with a satellite image. "We need to make a game plan for defending this place. Or at least a plan to ambush the attackers."

"How are your marksmanship skills?" Riker asked.

"Good enough to hit center mass at three hundred yards. I don't know how accurate I will be past that point. I haven't spent much time at the range in a while."

"Then we will keep you within three hundred yards. I think that I'll need to be in the dam. I can draw their attention and keep them from placing the bomb. We just need to figure out the most likely place for them to plant it. Then we can position you in a place to attack from behind while they come after me."

"That's a dumb plan," Jessica said.

Riker turned to her. "It's a good strategy. It worked at their safe house and it's the reason we have the information that we do."

"It also involves an unknown number of trained killers attacking you. A single well-placed shot and you're dead."

Riker didn't expect anyone to question his planning

when it came to battle. He especially didn't expect it from a civilian who had never seen a moment of action. Then he looked at Jessica and saw something in her eyes for the first time. It was fear. She was afraid for him.

"I know that the odds aren't great, but I've gotten this far. I'm actually pretty good at this sort of thing. I can't promise that I will make it, but I can promise that I will do everything humanly possible to get through this."

Jessica bit her lip. "Isn't there someone else that we can call in? Some way to even the odds?"

"I'll try to get some more people here in time, but my resources are limited. Especially since I'm currently violating an order," Franklin said.

"Like I said we will do everything we can to stack the odds in our favor. Besides, I have a perfect track record of not dying on a mission," Riker said with a smile.

"Actually your file said that you were clinically dead during one of the Siberian ops," Franklin said.

Riker gave him a look that clearly said shut the hell up. "I've never totally died on a mission. I expect you to be here to revive me when it's all over, okay?"

"Just make sure you make it back this time," Jessica said. "Preferably without needing to come back from the dead."

"You've got it," Riker replied.

Simon walked into the room and went over to the weapons on the couch. He picked up one of the assault rifles. He pointed it towards the window and looked through the scope. Then he slid back the bolt and checked the chamber.

"Looks like I'm going to get to sight this baby in," he said with a smile.

"What exactly do you mean?" Riker asked. "You said

you'd take care of the problem. I don't see anything fixed quite yet."

Simon looked down the barrel of the AR-15, pointing it toward the wall. "We should have access to the tower's comms and systems in the next forty minutes. I got one of the best hackers in the country on it. Relax."

"Hang on." Franklin took a step toward the other man, a furious expression on his face. "You gave details of our mission to an individual we haven't vetted?"

Simon shrugged. "Lloyd's good people. Don't stress."

Riker and Franklin exchanged a look. Riker didn't like it either. On a normal assignment with normal mission parameters, an unknown civilian learning classified details could be reason enough to abort. But they didn't have that option in this particular scenario. Laghaz was going to blow up that dam in the very near future unless they found a way to stop it.

"All right," Riker said. "We're going to have to roll with this. Simon, try not to tell anyone else about a secret terrorist plot? Everyone else, let's see if maybe we can get some work done while this Lloyd guy does his thing."

Franklin sighed. "Okay, hopefully, this guy comes through. I doubt the terrorists are flying their experimental weapon commercial."

As Franklin sat down at the table with his laptop, Jessica grabbed Riker's arm.

"Help me with something?" From the serious look in her eye, he knew better than to argue.

She led him into a bedroom on the other side of the house, closed the door, and began unbuttoning her shirt.

"Uh, what's happening now?" Riker asked.

She shot him a look. "You complaining?"

"Not at all. It's just unexpected. There's a lot going on."

She paused, her hand still on the third button. "Look, in times of stress, I get... let's say tense. It's always been this way. Just ask the incredibly lucky waiter at the charity event I spoke at last month. Trust me, to perform at the top of my game mentally, I need to be relaxed. That's where you come in."

"Okay," he said with a laugh. "Happy to help, especially since there aren't any waiters around at the moment."

"Don't make fun. Everybody reacts to stress differently. I'll bet you have an odd quirk or two when things get stressful."

Riker's mind immediately flashed back to a series of moments: a firefight in Pakistan, a helicopter crash near the Iran border, worked a knot at the bottom of the pool during a drown-proofing exercise in BUD/S, stepping between his crying mother and his drunk, angry father. In every one of those situations, time had seemed to slow as his mind receded into the background and his animal instincts took over. "I suppose you're right. And let me just say, on behalf of both myself and lucky waiters everywhere, there are worse ways to deal with stress."

She grinned and quickly undid her remaining shirt buttons. "Enough talking. We've got twenty minutes. Work fast, mister."

They emerged from the bedroom fifteen minutes later, both a little sweaty and decidedly more relaxed. Franklin kept his eyes on his keyboard, carefully not noticing that they'd been gone for the last quarter of an hour, but Simon shot Riker a wink and a quick thumbs-up.

Seven minutes later, Simon's phone buzzed. After he typed a few messages, he looked up with a smile on his face. "Perfect. It's done."

A chime came from Franklin's laptop. Franklin looked at

his screen. Windows were opening on it and the layout moved without his assistance.

"What the hell?" Franklin said as he watched an unknown person control his laptop remotely.

"Just relax, you're going to have all the access you need. Lloyd has been at this since he was a kid. He's been putting backdoors for himself into security systems for decades," Simon said.

"How is it that you know an expert hacker?" Riker asked.

"I met him freshman year of college. He was a bit of a loner, but I thought he had a cool vibe. I brought him to some parties, and we became friends."

Riker laughed. "That's it. You just happened to meet him."

"Hey, it's a very underrated skill."

"What? Meeting people?" Riker said.

"Yes. I don't just meet people—I get to know them. Lloyd and I became friends and stayed that way. You may be hanging out by yourself on a farm, but I have built relationships with hundreds of people."

"So you have learned to take advantage of others. That's not a skill," Franklin chimed in.

"That's your problem. You only network so you can use people. I just get to know them. There isn't any taking advantage, or using them. I didn't get to know Lloyd so I could have a hacker friend. He was just a cool guy that had a totally different world perspective. I'm glad that we have been friends. There was no scenario that I thought I might need a hacker. Somehow saving the world from fake terrorists wasn't on my list of things I saw coming. I help out everyone that I'm friends with if they need it, and they help me if I need it. In the meantime, we all just enjoy each other's company. That's what being friends is."

Riker put a hand on Simon's shoulder. "You're right, that is a skill, and you are much better at it than I am."

"Thanks, man." Simon looked at Franklin's screen. "It looks like you got the information you wanted."

The computer displayed the FAA control information in one of the windows. Another window showed the state police database. A third had the active 911 logs."

Jessica looked at the screen. "Way to go. Your buddy is amazing."

Franklin stared at the information with wide eyes. "I agree."

"Okay," Jessica said, "let's run it down. We have weapons. We know they're going to strike soon. We've got the layout and the security footage, not to mention the 911 dispatch system monitoring. It seems like we have everything we need, right? Is it just a waiting game now?"

Riker frowned. "I wish it were that simple. We have the intel, but that's only the first step. Now we have to figure out what to do with it."

"What do you mean?"

"Think of it like a chess match. We understand how the pieces move, but that doesn't mean we have a viable strategy to win. Laghaz and the people they're working for have likely had weeks to plan their attack. Maybe months. Whatever their plan is, it will be well-crafted. Now we have to somehow anticipate that plan and figure out a way to stop it."

"How the hell do we do that?" Simon asked.

"The first step is to put ourselves in their shoes. If I had the weapon and wanted to blow up the dam, how would I go about it? What weaknesses in security would I be looking to exploit? What time of day would I want it to go down? How many guys would I send? That's where we start. Then we hone the plan, the same way they would have. Only then can we start thinking about countermeasures."

Simon let out a sigh. "And here I thought maybe we could knock off early and go for dinner. There's a local barbeque place the #StrymondStrong people all rave about on Instagram."

"Afraid not. We've got a lot more research to do."

"Um, Riker, we might need to revise our agenda." Franklin stared at his computer screen, his face pale.

"What do you have?" Riker asked.

"Two helicopters. Neither of which filed a flight plan. I just tracked their course."

There was a sinking feeling in Riker's stomach. "Tell me."

"They're headed on a direct path for the dam. They'll arrive in thirty minutes."

Riker swallowed hard. So much for planning. It was time to go to work.

31

RIKER PULLED the Escalade over a few hundred feet from the guard station at the top of the dam. He hopped out and popped the hatchback. Franklin quickly joined him.

Franklin shot him a nervous grin. "I'd imagine an untested handler isn't exactly the guy you want by your side when going up against an unknown number of terrorists."

Grabbing a rucksack, Riker shoved a few items inside, including a set of binoculars, some zip ties, and plenty of extra rounds. He took a radio and clipped it to his belt along with a pistol. "If you're half as good at fighting as you are at finding military-grade weaponry in the middle of nowhere, I think we'll be fine."

"We're in rural Georgia. Finding weapons isn't a problem."

Riker tossed the single Kevlar vest to Franklin. "Put that on."

"Shouldn't you be wearing it?" Franklin protested.

"This isn't up for debate. The less I worry about you the more I can focus and keep both of us alive."

In truth, Riker was a little nervous about going into combat with an ally with little-to-no field experience. But he knew QS-4 required rigorous training for even their handlers. As long as the kid kept his cool and let his training guide him, he'd be fine.

Riker grabbed the soft case containing the sniper rifle and handed it to Franklin. "You're our dirt-belly." When he saw the blank expression on the handler's face, he clarified. "Our sniper. I need you to take out the choppers before they land."

"Ah. Got it."

Riker picked up an AR-15 and slung it over his shoulder. "Okay, let's do this."

They marched to the guard station, making no real attempt at a concealed approach. Best to get it over with quickly.

The single guard in the booth was reading a book, and he didn't seem to notice them until they were about fifteen feet away. Even then, he stared at them blankly, not immediately understanding the significance of the object slung on Riker's back or the case Franklin was carrying. When they were five feet away, an expression of surprised shock appeared on his face.

"It's okay," Franklin said, holding up a hand. "We are not here to start trouble. We want to help with—"

Riker reached through the open window and grabbed the man by the collar, hauling him halfway through the opening. Twisting the man, he got his arm around his neck, choking him out. Then he looked at Franklin. "Sorry. I figured that would be faster."

Climbing inside the open window, he unlocked the door, letting Franklin in. Then he dragged the guard's limp body to the storage closet, put him inside, bound his hands and legs with zip ties, and wedged a chair under the doorknob. There was no telling when the guard would wake up, and the last thing he wanted was a rogue guard shooting him in the back while he was trying to fight off QS-4 operatives.

He nodded toward the sniper rifle case. "You any good with that thing?"

"On the range." Franklin bent down, unzipped the case, and started assembling the weapon. "I've never shot down a helicopter before if that's what you're asking."

"I sort of figured. Look, there are two effective ways to do it. One is to take out the pilot. There are a lot of variables there, so it's risky. The other way is to shoot the tail rotor. It's a tougher shot, but an almost sure thing if you hit it. Without the tail rotor, they won't be able to generate enough power to stay aloft without spinning out of control. The chopper will come down fast. If you think you can make the shot, go that route."

"Got it." Franklin's voice sounded anything but confident.

"Be ready. I'm going to go check out the target."

Removing the AR-15 fifteen from his back, he headed out along the top of the dam. On his right, the water rose nearly to the top of the concrete. To his left, there was a fifty-foot drop off, and then a concrete platform that held the electrical equipment. Though he couldn't see it, he knew the dam's locks would be below that platform.

He moved to the center of the dam and crouched down. If he were planting an explosive to destroy the dam, this was where he'd place it. To ensure total destruction, he would ideally want to drill down into the concrete and plant the explosive there. Bringing down a concrete structure wasn't easy, and the placement would be paramount to success or failure. He figured that was one thing working in his favor. This wouldn't be a fast and easy job. The open terrain on the other hand... that was going to be a problem.

A sound came from his left, and he looked, spotting a small object in the southern sky. The radio on his belt chirped, and Franklin's voice came through.

"Riker."

"I see it," he said into the radio. He reached into the rucksack and pulled out the binoculars. The lens brought the helicopter into stark focus, and he immediately recognized the aircraft. The UH-1 Iroquois, otherwise known as the Huey. Though no longer in use by the US military, the chopper was still very common in the black ops world. Riker had flown in plenty of them during his time with QS-4. "Remember what I said."

"Tail rotor. Got it."

Riker stayed where he was, crouched down, binoculars to his eyes. A moment later, he heard the crack of a rifle and the helicopter began to spin, smoke rising from its tail. "Nice shot!"

But the victory was short-lived. The nose of the helicopter quickly came up, slowing the descent and bringing the chopper out of its spin. Riker cursed silently. That pilot was good. The aircraft was still going down, but it was a controlled descent, and the likelihood of a crash landing seemed low. He kept his binoculars trained on the chopper until it was twenty feet from the ground and the trees hid it from his view.

He brought the radio back to his mouth. "They're touching down. I'd guess a quarter-mile from here. That doesn't give us a lot of time."

"Any idea how many?"

"That was a Huey. Up to fourteen passengers, not including the pilot."

"Wonderful odds. Fourteen to two."

Riker's eyes went to the sky. "Perhaps a bit worse than that."

The second helicopter appeared in the southern sky, and it was headed straight for them.

"Well, shit," Franklin said.

"It's all good. Stay focused. These guys will know we shot their buddy, so they may be playing a little more aggressively. If you get a shot at the tail rotor, take it. Otherwise, go for the pilot."

Just as Riker had assumed, the second chopper took a very different line of approach. It dipped down, approaching low and fast, staying close to the trees.

Franklin's rifle cracked, but the shot hit the rear part of the hull, missing the tail completely. "Damn it!"

"It's okay," Riker said. "Don't lose your cool. Go for the pilot."

A moment later, Franklin fired again. Through his binoculars, Riker could see a hole in the glass at the front of the helicopter, but still, the aircraft kept coming. Franklin had clearly missed the pilot. The chopper turned slightly, exposing just a bit of its side. Then automatic fire spit out of the aircraft and ripped into the guard station.

"Franklin, take cover!" Riker shouted into the radio.

"I am! But their rounds are tearing through this booth like it's nothing."

"Hang on, I'll draw them off you." He took a deep breath and raised his AR-15. Attracting their attention when he had zero cover was a bad idea, but he had no other choice. If he didn't, Franklin would be a dead man.

He pulled the trigger, spraying the aircraft with a burst of gunfire. His rounds peppered the hull, but unless he'd gotten very lucky, they probably hadn't done fatal damage.

Just as he'd hoped, the helicopter swung around, focusing their attention on him. Their gun sprang to life, but Riker was already in motion. He dove off the top of the dam, splashing down into the water on the high side. His AR-15 still clutched in one hand, he kicked hard, diving deep into the chilly waters.

All around him, bullets cut through the water. It would only take one of them to end his life, and there was nothing he could do except keep swimming and pray one of the rounds didn't find him. He pushed the thought away. He concentrated on staying under, on putting as much distance as possible between himself and the spot where he'd entered the water. It wasn't much, but it was something.

Fifteen feet under water, he made his way along the concrete, heading toward the end of the dam where the guard station was located. If he managed to survive his swim, he wanted to come up somewhere where he'd have a chance at helping Franklin.

After a few moments, the bullets slowed. Riker considered heading for the surface but thought better of it. His lungs were starting to burn from the lack of oxygen, but he had plenty of experience ignoring that particular impulse. A moment later, he was glad he did. Bullets once again plunged through the water all around him. The helicopter must have circled around and come back for a second pass. Riker kept swimming hard, heading toward the guard station. When the bullets stopped for a second time, he decided it was his best chance to surface. He quickly swam up and pulled himself onto the top of the dam.

Staying low, his eyes scanned the sky. He spotted the

helicopter circling around, coming back for another pass at him. He angled the barrel of his rifle downward and retracted the bolt. Water ran out of the muzzle. He kept the barrel pointed downward for as long as possible. Firing a rifle with a wet barrel wasn't good for the weapon, and it could potentially go very wrong, but he didn't have a choice. As the helicopter circled around, he raised the weapon and squeezed off a burst of rounds at the front of the aircraft.

The helicopter spun wildly, careening toward the ground and disappearing into the trees. Riker knew he must have hit the pilot. There was no telling how many of the supposed Laghaz operatives he'd taken out, but he'd certainly improved their odds.

Now to help Franklin. He stayed low, moving in, crouching toward the guard station. Glancing past it, his breath caught in his throat. Seven men in paramilitary gear were moving toward the guard station. The men from the first chopper. Not as many as he'd feared, but still enough. They were going to get to Franklin before Riker.

He drew a deep breath and raised his rifle. He'd once again have to draw them off Franklin. With his exposed location, he knew it was a suicidal move, but he didn't see any other option.

Just as he was about to fire, another shot rang out. A man in the back of the group of seven fell down, clutching at a wound on his neck. Riker's eyes narrowed. The shot hadn't come from the guard station; it had come from the parking area.

Another shot, and a second operative went down, clutching his chest. He quickly got to his knees, hurt but not killed thanks to his Kevlar gear. The operatives were all turning toward the parking lot now, and Riker did the same. What he saw caused him to let out a soft curse.

A man was standing behind a pickup truck, using the rails of the bed to steady his rifle. He raised his head, trying to get a better look at the operatives, and Riker got a clear view of his face. It was Simon.

32

Riker sprinted towards the end of the dam. His mind raced and adrenaline fueled his muscles. He knew he needed a better position if he was going to win this battle. He also knew it would be a miracle if he and his friends made it out alive.

Three men raised their assault rifles and moved towards Simon. Some of them fired, pinning him down behind the truck 300 yards away, while others spread out, preparing to flank him. The distance and the motion of the attackers made the shots inaccurate, but they were riddling the truck with bullets and getting closer by the second.

The other three men pressed forward toward the guard station with Franklin inside. They sprayed the building with bullets to keep him pinned down. Riker watched as one of the men stopped firing his weapon and pulled a grenade from his vest. They were so concentrated on the target that they hadn't noticed Riker coming in from the top of the dam.

Riker dropped to one knee and focused on the men attacking the guard shack. His view of the man with the grenade was blocked by one of the other shooters. Riker put one bullet just under the man's chin. His body went completely limp as the bullet tore through the spinal column at the base of his neck. Before the body hit the ground, Riker saw the man with the grenade in motion. Riker aimed for his exposed neck just as he had before. The shot found its mark, but it arrived a moment too late. The grenade was already flying toward the guard station.

"Frag out!" Riker yelled. "Get out of there!"

The object flew into the open window of the guard station, and Franklin ran out. The last gunman had a bead on Franklin, and Riker could not get a clear shot without risking shooting his friend. Everything seemed to stop and Riker waited to see the tissue spray out from an exit wound in Franklin's head. Before that could happen, the grenade went off. The noise distracted the gunman just long enough for Franklin to dive into the water on the high side of the dam.

The gunman brought his rifle around, aiming it toward the water where Franklin had disappeared. Riker knew he was a moment behind the attacker. He sprang up, getting an angle on the man. The gunman spotted Riker and shot without adjusting his aim. Riker felt the bullet pass by his left ear. He fired at the stationary gunman, aiming for center mass, and two quick rounds hit the man's chest. His vest stopped the bullets, but the force of the impact dropped him to his knees.

Riker didn't hesitate. He fired twice into the gunman's face, and the man slumped to his side. Riker started to run towards the gunfire in the parking lot, and he noticed a case sitting next to the man who'd thrown the grenade—a case that looked exactly like the one in which he'd found the first stolen weapon.

The urge to stop and grab the weapon was almost overwhelming, but a scream from the parking lot redirected his attention. Riker didn't know exactly what had happened, but he knew Simon had been shot. The men were still advancing toward his position behind the truck, approaching cautiously from both sides. That meant Simon was still alive, or at least that the attackers thought it was a possibility.

The only advantage that Riker had was the distraction Simon was providing. He knew that as soon as he fired a shot at one of the men going after Simon he would be fighting the remaining two. They were two hundred yards away, and Riker needed to be close to make this work. He sprinted with everything that he had. His target was the center attacker—the one who was laying down cover fire. That man had his back to Riker, while the other two were flanking the truck ready for Simon to move or try to take a shot. He could see that both men on the side were closing in on Simon. It would be moments before they were able to finish him.

Each time his foot hit the pavement, Riker expected the gunman to hear it and turn, but the steady fire of the assault rifle muted the rest of the world. Riker pushed his body, sprinting as fast as he had ever gone. One arm pumped, matching the motion of his feet and the other clutched his assault rifle. He was close, only twenty yards away from his target, but he could see one of the men angling around the edge of the truck. He knew that he would be too late. Simon would die.

Riker was five steps from the man laying down cover fire. He focused on one thing—the back of the gunman's head. He raised his weapon while he was still in motion and fired, putting a bullet through his target.

The other two gunmen didn't seem to realize that the shot hadn't come from their ally. One of them aimed his rifle, ready to pull the trigger, but Riker fired first, hitting the man in his right temple. The last gunman didn't even notice the other man falling to the ground. He kept his focus on Simon, and that cost him his life. Riker quickly took him out.

Riker stood in the middle of the parking lot checking his surroundings. He realized that he might be the only person left alive.

"Simon, are you okay?" Riker yelled.

"Did you get them?" a weak voice asked.

"Yes, we're clear."

"Then come and help me. I'm pretty fucked up."

"I'm coming. Hold your fire."

Riker's heart was still pounding like a jackhammer as he stepped around the truck. He saw Simon leaning against the tire, his shirt soaked in blood and his rifle on the ground next to him. Riker bent down and looked at the wound. There was an entry in the front of the right shoulder. He pushed Simon forward so he could see if there was an exit wound.

"Fuck!" Simon screamed.

"Sorry, I need to know what we are dealing with." He saw that there was no exit wound. "It looks like the bullet hit your shoulder bone. I hate to tell you, but you're never going to make it in the majors."

The arm hung limp against Simon's side. "Now you have a sense of humor? I'm dying here."

Riker smiled. "No. You are badly in need of medical attention." Riker took off his shirt and pressed it hard against the wound, causing Simon to let out another string of profanity. "You will live through this."

"Are you sure? It really feels like I'm dying."

"I'm pretty sure," Riker said with a smile. "I've been shot worse."

"Bullshit. Don't try to one-up me, Riker. Let me have this one." Simon gave a half-smile through the pain.

"I'm going to get you up and to the SUV. You really do need medical attention and probably surgery to fix that shoulder." Riker helped him to his feet, and the two headed towards Riker's Escalade.

"Where's Franklin?" Simon asked.

"I don't know. I'm going to try to find him after I get you in the truck. I also need to grab the weapon."

"What the hell, man? I thought that you were good at this stuff. You lost Franklin and you left a weapon of mass destruction lying around? I'm going to have to put this in my report."

Riker laughed out loud as they reached the SUV. Simon leaned against the vehicle while Riker opened the door to the back seat.

Simon said, "Make sure to tell Jessica that I saved the day when we get back. I think it will make up for—"

Simon stopped mid-sentence as the window behind him shattered and a bullet entered his chest. The report of a rifle cracked in the distance. He collapsed to the ground, blood gushing from the wound.

Riker grabbed him, scooping him up, and ran to the other side of the SUV. While he moved, a bullet struck the car next to him and then another report followed. Once they were on the opposite side, Riker laid Simon on the ground.

Riker ripped Simon's shirt and used parts of it to pack the wound. He slid one hand to Simon's back and felt chunks of tissue surrounding a hole.

Simon gasped in half breaths and blood trickled out the

corner of his mouth. Tears welled in both eyes and he blinked them onto his face. He spoke in a quiet gasp. "Save me."

They were on the driver's side of the SUV and Riker knew it was unlikely that the sniper could hit them from his position. He had the keys and could easily get Simon in the back seat. If he left now, he might be able to get him to the hospital in time to save him.

Then he thought of the case lying near the guard station. The case holding the weapon that could end thousands of lives.

Half of his mission was in front of him, bleeding out on the pavement, and half was sitting at the edge of a dam two hundred yards away. In his heart, he knew that he couldn't accomplish both of his objectives. Painful as it was, he needed to choose.

He looked down at Simon. "Put pressure on this. I need to get the case."

Simon looked into Riker's eyes, tears still sliding down his face. He spoke in a soft whisper. "I'll die if you don't help me."

Riker forced himself to keep eye contact with the young man. "I know. You did great here. I'll make sure Jessica knows." He moved Simon's left hand onto the blood-soaked rags and pressed it down. "I've got to take care of this. You wait right here."

33

Riker slid behind a car, doing his best to push his dying friend out of his mind. He needed laser focus. All that mattered right now was the recovery of the weapon.

The way he figured it, the man who'd shot Simon must have been a survivor from the second helicopter, the one Riker had shot down. Considering there was no one in sight, he had to assume the guy was a sniper. He scanned the terrain, thinking about where he'd set up if it were he. His eyes quickly settled on the spot—a hill to the east. He thought about the trajectory of the round that had hit Simon, and the location made sense.

Now he had two options—go after the sniper first, or go after the case. The problem with the first option was that it left the case vulnerable if there were other survivors from the helicopter crash. The second option would earn him a bullet. There was a third possibility of course; he could wait. The case was fifty yards away, sitting in plain sight. Of course, that meant throwing away whatever slim chance Simon had of survival.

He moved toward the case, staying in a crouch and

putting whatever obstacles he could between himself and the assumed position of the sniper. When he was thirty yards from the case, he slipped between two cars, providing himself excellent cover. Unfortunately it was also the last bit of cover between him and the weapon. There was nothing but blue sky and the very real possibility of a sniper bullet standing between him and the case. He drew a breath, focusing his mind, preparing for the dangerous work ahead of him.

Just before he took another step, he saw movement out of his periphery and froze. Three men dressed in military gear, assault rifles at the ready, hurried out of the trees, headed for the case. Riker smiled and raised his weapon.

He forced himself to wait until they'd reached the halfway point between the trees and the case, until they were precisely in the middle of the open area Riker had just been considering crossing. Then he opened fire.

The first man went down hard and fast as Riker's bullets tore through his face. Riker knew he had to aim for the head to get past their Kevlar vests, and he was close enough that he felt comfortable doing so. As the first man fell, he shifted his aim to the second man. That one went down just as easily. In less than three seconds, he'd killed two men.

The third operative dropped to the ground, training his weapon toward the source of the gunfire. He was still searching for his attacker when Riker fired again, putting a round through his head.

All three men were down now, but the sniper still remained. Riker shifted his position, considering his next move. He could use the bodies for a little bit of cover, but it wasn't enough to give him real protection.

Something to his right caught his eye, and he flung himself backward just in time to avoid a bullet from a handgun. A man charged toward him, sprinting between the cars while Riker was still off-balance. This man was dressed like the others, but he carried himself differently. Riker recognized the way he moved immediately. The other operatives had been soldiers, but this man was a true warrior. Riker drew a sharp breath as he recognized the man—it was Chatti.

Riker rocked on his heels, getting his balance back just in time. As Chatti took aim with his handgun, Riker surged forward, letting the rifle fall from his hands. It would be no use in this close-quarter combat. He drove his shoulder into Chatti's chest, knocking him back a step. Riker raised both arms and slammed them down onto the man's forearm. Chatti's right arm hit the body of the car next to him hard, and the pistol dropped from his hand. Riker lashed out with one foot, kicking the weapon away from both of them.

Chatti reacted quickly, immediately changing positions. He shifted his weight and brought up one knee, repeatedly slamming it into Riker's stomach. Riker doubled over, and the man brought an elbow down on the back of his neck.

Chatti was strong, and his fighting style made Riker think he had Krav Maga training. He wasn't going to go down easily, but neither was Riker. Driving with his feet, Riker pushed him backward, slamming his back into the other car. Air rushed out of Chatti's lungs, but he didn't panic as most men would. Instead, he twisted, freeing himself from Riker's grip and putting a step between them.

"You killed a lot of my operatives today," Chatti said in a breathless voice. "Not to mention two very expensive helicopters." The accent was North African. Egyptian maybe.

Riker said nothing. He knew Chatti was trying to get him talking, probably to buy some time for the sniper and any other allies he had left.

"Not feeling chatty? Understandable. You don't even know what's happening here, do you? Who we are?"

This time Riker couldn't resist taking the bait. "I know you've got a hole in your left leg. How's that feeling?"

The man shook his head sadly. "Just a minor flesh wound. I learned from our last meeting, and I doubt that you will live through this encounter. No matter what they say about you, you're just a man."

Riker flashed an animalistic smile. "Do they really talk about me?"

"Unlike you, I do my research. You're Matthew Riker. Navy SEAL. QS-4 operative. Beekeeper. Had a full-ride wrestling scholarship to the University of Iowa, but a couple bad choices later, you found yourself in the military instead. How am I doing?"

"Not bad. I caught your name, Chatti. Everything else about you will be irrelevant in a few moments."

Then he remembered Simon lying on the pavement. If he was still alive, he wouldn't be for long. Riker had left his friend to die so that he could recover a weapon of mass destruction, and here he was getting caught up in his enemy's mind games instead of doing his job. The time for talking was over. All that mattered was recovering the weapon.

He reached into his pocket and pulled out a four-inch folding knife. Not a true combat weapon, but any port in a storm. He flipped it open and charged.

Chatti reacted immediately, stepping forward, cutting the distance between him and Riker. He raised both arms, positioning them between Riker's knife arm and his body, preventing Riker from being able to stab his head or torso.

That was fine with Riker. The knife had been meant as little more than a distraction. His favorite part about attacking someone with a knife was that they generally ignored your empty hand.

Riker brought his left fist up in a vicious uppercut, punching Chatti in the ribs. He pulled back the fist and hit again. And again. Chatti cried out in pain, doubling over to protect his side. Just as Riker thought he had him, Chatti's right foot snaked out; hooking behind Riker's left foot. Chatti launched his body into Riker. The next thing Riker knew, he was on his back on the asphalt, and Chatti was on top of him.

The man's hands were around Riker's neck in an instant, squeezing hard, a look of fury on his face. "You damn idiot. Sit around on some farm in North Carolina for six years, and you think you can just come off the bench and beat me? Please. I've been working every day while you were out of the game. Honing my craft. Perfecting my—"

He let out a grunt as Riker's knife sank into his side. Riker stabbed him just below the ribs, hoping to puncture a lung. He knew right away that he'd gotten the angle wrong. Still, four inches of steel is bound to do some damage just about anywhere in the torso.

Chatti was silent now, but the hands around Riker's neck didn't loosen. If anything, he squeezed harder. His face was red, and he stared down at Riker with hatred in his eyes.

Riker knew he didn't have long. In seconds, he'd be unconscious. Shortly after that, he'd be dead. He needed to make something happen now. Gripping the knife blade hard, he twisted it ninety degrees counter-clockwise.

Chatti groaned in pain, and his body shifted, weakening his position for only a moment. It was all Riker needed. Bucking his hips, he twisted his body, freeing an arm and punching Chatti in the face. He slipped out of the man's grip and executed a reversal, flipping Chatti onto his back.

He pulled the knife out of Chatti's side and raised it to his throat. Chatti grabbed Riker's wrist, holding the blade an inch away from his jugular. Riker saw his eyes flicker toward the parking lot. Riker followed his gaze and saw someone running toward the case.

The sniper. That had to be it. Chatti had been stalling Riker to give the sniper time to grab the case.

Riker slammed Chatti's head against the pavement and jumped up after the sniper. He ignored the burning pain around his neck where Chatti had nearly squeezed the life from him. The sniper spotted Riker just as he reached the case. He grabbed for his pistol, but Riker slammed into him before he could draw it. Riker wrapped his arms around the man, preventing him from getting his weapon. The momentum sent both men flying backward to the pavement. They slid and crashed into the railing along the dam.

On the ground Riker had the advantage. He spun behind the man and sank his knife into his throat.

Riker looked up to see Chatti picking up the case and holding his handgun. Blood dripped down his side, and he raised his weapon slowly. Riker pulled the sniper's body in front of him like a shield. A round cracked from Chatti's gun and slammed into the dead man's Kevlar vest.

Then another report sounded to Riker's right. He snapped his head to see Franklin peering up over the edge of the dam, firing his handgun. The shots were stopped by Chatti's Kevlar vest, but the impact knocked the air from his lungs.

Chatti returned fire and Franklin ducked back below the edge of the wall in the water. Riker had no weapon other than his knife, and bullets continued to strike the man that he held as a shield.

The bullets went wild, striking the concrete and pavement around Riker. He waited another moment and then peered around his shield. Chatti had the case and was running through the parking lot.

Franklin came back over the edge of the wall and fired at Chatti, but he missed his mark. Chatti returned fire, hitting Franklin in the center of his chest. His vest stopped the bullet, but Franklin clutched his chest and gasped as he fell backward into the water.

Riker dove in after him. His body was sinking quickly. Riker grabbed him and swam upwards against the weight of Franklin's body. They broke the surface and Franklin gasped. Riker held him against the side of the dam until he could breathe properly. When the two climbed back over the edge Chatti was gone.

34

Eleven years ago.

Riker stepped out of the workout facility, still dripping with sweat, and found Morrison standing there waiting for him, an easy smile on his face.

"Hey, Scarecrow. Getting your reps in, I see."

"Sir, yes sir." Riker was still getting used to the new codename. In many ways it felt strange, like a new pair of shoes that hadn't been completely broken in yet. But he also felt a twinge of pride at the name. He'd earned it.

"Good. Enjoying the setup?"

Riker nodded. "I gotta say, you weren't kidding about the facilities here. This place is practically a country club compared to most of the bases where I've lived."

"Our bosses spare no expense when it comes to training their operatives, I'll give them that." He paused, looking Riker up and down. "Tell you what. Go grab a shower, get cleaned up, and meet me in conference room 212 in thirty minutes."

"Yes, sir. Do we have another mission?"

"Not exactly. More like a debrief. Don't keep me waiting." With that, Morrison turned on his heels and marched off."

Riker went back to his quarters, a two-bedroom apartment on the north end of the facility, and grabbed a quick shower. The hot water felt great on his fatigued muscles, but after quickly washing himself, he turned to handle all the way toward cold. He let the freezing water wash over him for a minute, invigorating him. Then he turned off the water and climbed out.

Five minutes later, he was back in the main building of the facility, searching for conference room 212. After a few wrong turns, he eventually found it. Though he was six minutes early, Morrison and another man were already waiting for him.

Morrison gestured toward the other man. "Riker, meet Warren Bates, one of the most important people at QS-4."

"Sir," Riker said, holding out his hand.

Bates shook it, his face flush with embarrassment. "Morrison exaggerates. I'm just a pencil pusher."

Riker looked the man up and down. He certainly didn't look like the type of guy one would expect to find at the headquarters of an elite black ops organization. He looked to be in his mid-forties, and he was a good thirty pounds overweight. His pale skin told Riker the guy didn't see a lot of the great outdoors.

"Nonsense," Morrison said. "Bates is the head of our forensic accounting department. Without him, the Mohamad Izad mission wouldn't have happened."

Riker tilted his head in surprise. "How so?"

"Have a seat, Scarecrow. It's time for your first real lesson in how things work at QS-4."

Riker took a seat at one end of the long conference table. Morrison and Bates sat across from him.

Morrison looked Riker in the eyes. "You've impressed a lot of people in your short time with us. Timber won't shut up about you, and I've heard three of your other teammates mention that you were a great addition to the unit."

"Thank you, sir." Riker was truly humbled by the comment. To be considered valuable by men like the ones at QS-4 was not something to be taken lightly.

"That said, you've got room to grow if you're going to have a future here." Morrison paused, considering how best to continue. "Let me start by asking you a question. Why do you think we took down Mohamad Izad?"

The question caught Riker by surprise. "What do you mean, sir? He was a terrorist. His organization had killed American soldiers. He was a threat to the United States."

Morrison chuckled and turned to Bates. "You believe this guy? What did I tell you?"

Bates flashed a quick smile. "He's idealistic. That's not a bad thing."

"I suppose not. But tell him why we really took down Mohamad Izad."

Bates opened a file folder and pulled out a picture of a middle-aged man. He looked Middle Eastern, and he was dressed in a sharp suit. "This is Dawud Ghafoor. He's the third richest man in Afghanistan. Primarily made his money in oil, but he owns banks, investment firms, and a growing ore export business."

"Okay," Riker said. "What's he have to do with us?"

"He's our client. Izad's organization was destabilizing the region, which was a major problem for his mining operations. He paid us to take care of him."

Riker's eyes widened in surprise. "You're telling me we killed this terrorist because this rich guy told us to?"

"Two things you gotta remember about QS-4," Morrison said. "We are a for-profit organization, and someone has to pay the bills. In this case, it was Ghafoor."

Riker said nothing. He suddenly felt incredibly stupid. He'd somehow assumed he was still working for the US government, albeit through a private contractor. What the hell had he gotten himself wrapped up in here?

"Before you panic, let me make a couple things clear. We never work against the interests of the United States. In fact, we often work quite closely with them to ensure our outcomes match with theirs. And secondly, just because we're privately funded doesn't mean we can't do good. I think you'll agree that the world is a safer place without Izad in it."

Riker couldn't argue with that.

"In fact," Morrison continued, "the source of our funding isn't the biggest difference between QS-4 and the US military."

"What is?" Riker asked.

"Our methods." He turned to Bates. "Care to explain?"

Bates leaned forward. "When a client hires QS-4, they only give us an objective. The way that we accomplish that objective is up to us. That's where I come in."

Riker still wasn't following, and his face must have made that clear because Morrison jumped in.

"Think back on your military career. You're always given a task to complete, right? Take out this target. Capture this facility. Rescue this asset. We operate differently here. We look to solve the source of the problem, not just the problem itself. If you want to be successful at QS-4, that's what you need to learn to do. You can take out enemy soldiers? Fine. But if your enemy is well-funded, he'll be able to keep sending more soldiers to replace them. If you go after the enemy himself, or better yet the source of his funds, then you can end things fast. That's where Bates comes in. A good example is how we took out Izad."

"What do you mean? A bullet from my gun took him out."

"Ah, but that bullet was the end result of a long process. Tell him where it started, Bates."

The accountant grinned. "An especially cold spring in Florida."

Riker raised an eyebrow but said nothing. He had no idea how that related to Izad, and he was interested to see how these men made the connection.

"Our biggest problem with taking out Izad was political," Morrison said. "We needed the cooperation of the military. As you well know, they were working on locating his compound. We also needed to be sure we weren't mucking up any existing operations, and Uncle Sam can be a little tight-lipped when it comes to sharing info on covert operations against terrorists. That's where Florida comes in."

"Senator Jeff Kindt sits on the Military Intelligence committee. He also happens to be up for re-election next year." Bates was clearly getting excited talking about this stuff. This was his area of expertise. "There was a late freeze in Florida this spring, which means a bad orange crop this year. I knew that was going to hit Kindt's usual campaign contributors hard. That was our opportunity."

"You track stuff like that?" Riker asked.

"We track everything," Bates said with a grin. "We approached Kindt with the offer of some back-channel contributions. Our only ask was that he help us arrange a sit-down with a certain frustrated general who was sick of politics getting in the way of his operation to take out Izad."

"And the senator agreed?"

Morrison nodded. "An hour in a conference room was all it took to convince the general that we might be able to help with that particular situation. He even threw in a little something extra as part of the deal."

"What's that?" Riker asked.

"You."

Riker looked down at the table. He wasn't sure how he felt about all of this. Taking out a terrorist was one thing, but political contributions, under the table deal with generals... all of this felt a little dirty. "So you're saying that to solve the problem of Izad, you had to bribe a senator?"

"Not exactly. I'm saying there's more behind every mission than the mission itself. That's what you need to understand. See, Bates was able to determine that Izad wasn't really the source of the problem plaguing our client and the entire region. The real problem was the man funding him." Morrison leaned forward and looked Riker in the eyes. "I'm saying the mission isn't over yet."

A week later, Riker and Morrison sat at a table sipping tea halfway around the world. A jar of Afghan honey stood in the middle of the table. Morrison had raved about the honey from the Herat Province and insisted Riker try it. Riker was surprised at how much the sweet nectar improved the flavor of the tea.

A constant stream of traffic filled the road next to them and the sidewalks were bustling with people. The Balkh market in Kabul, Afghanistan, was wall-to-wall people in the middle of the day.

Riker watched as a group of four businessmen walked by. Three of the men hovered around the tallest of them. He was clearly the boss. Riker positioned his body towards Morrison and took a sip of his tea. His sunglasses hid the direction of his gaze while he observed the group of men.

Once the men had passed, he turned enough to see them enter a building two hundred yards down the road.

"So that's Tayebah? The man with deep pockets and evil intentions." Riker shook his head. "They always look less menacing than I imagine."

"Yes, it's a shame that all the evil sons of bitches in the world don't grow horns. It would certainly make tracking them down a lot easier. Instead they just look like everyone else on the street. Tell me what you know about Tayebah and his company."

Riker took a sip of tea thinking of his response. Morrison had given him the file on the man and the company. He was well aware of what Riker knew.

"Tayebah is the third generation of his family to run the business. What started as a small copper mine seventy years ago grew into one of the largest mining companies in Afghanistan. Tayebah's father expanded and diversified the business until it became what it is today. Most of it is legitimate business operations ranging from resources to telecommunications. The rest is used to funnel money to various political organizations. That includes extremists like Mohamad Izad."

Morrison sipped his tea with a blank look on his face. Riker knew that this was a test, and he realized that he was failing. He worked the puzzle in his mind and then continued.

"Those are just the details. The real question is what kind of man is Tayebah? Why would someone with a successful business and all the money in the world want to fund a group that kills his own people and other innocents?.

He uses the instabilities to put pressure on the current political figures. It helps him expand his businesses. He uses the media companies that he owns to influence the public. He makes them afraid of the very dangers that he creates. He is the kind of person who always justifies the end by the means."

Morrison set his cup down. "Go on."

"He is a narcissist who believes he is the person who is best fit to control everything. Everything he is doing is positioning himself for a political takeover. He will tear the country apart so that he can rebuild it as a ruler."

"Very good," Morrison said. "Now what do you think we should do about this?"

"Clearly we should take him out before he does any more damage." Riker stopped and thought about his answer. "It isn't just him. The massive power of his businesses should be stopped. We need to find a way to dismantle the entire operation."

The corner of Morrison's lips turned down in the slightest frown. "You're almost there. You just need to unlearn a few things. From early on we learn that things are good or bad. As a society, we need that to be true. Some corporations are good, some are bad. Some countries are good, some are bad. Governments are good or evil. That is all bullshit that we need the masses to believe. People have enough to worry about, so we have to be able to say those are the bad guys, and they need to believe us.

"That's how you were trained as a soldier. We need every man in the chain of command to attack and possibly kill any target that we say is bad. In truth, every group is a mixture of good and evil. Most of the people who work for Tayebah are just trying to put food on their plates. The copper that he mines helps fuel the economy of the country and keep it stable."

"So we should just take out Tayebah and let the machine keep running?" Riker asked.

"That's what you need to let go of. There isn't a right or wrong answer. There are an infinite number of possibilities. We retain the good and get rid of the bad, or at least as much of it as we can find."

Riker took in the statement. His entire military career had been a series of single-minded objectives. He never had to think about anything other than the practical means to accomplish the mission.

"Each government, company, and country is a constant mixture of good and bad," Morrison continued. "Thousands of people working towards something. We do our best to make sure there is more good than bad. It is why we need the best men. Not just soldiers, but men who can determine what needs to go and what should stay."

Riker looked at the congested street. Thousands of people were moving about the city. He didn't think he was qualified to judge the evil from the innocent.

"How do you suggest we divide the groups?"

Morrison smiled. "I use a low bar for good and a high bar for evil. For example, funding a group that indiscriminately bombs women and children puts you in the bad camp. Anyone who knowingly participated in that doesn't deserve to keep breathing. Anyone who supports the actions of a man like Tayebah shouldn't be in charge of anything. Anyone who isn't knowingly working towards the death and destruction of others is good enough."

"I can get behind that kind of judgment. Now, all we have to do is figure out who is involved in that side of the operation."

"That part is much easier than you would think. We just need to find the last link in the chain and put pressure on him. Then we watch until his panic goes all the way back up the chain."

The next four weeks gave Riker a crash course in infiltrating an organization. Warren Bates had given them the name of a single CFO. He worked for one of Tayebah's companies. The man signed off on all invoice payments. One of those payments made it to Mohamad Izad. That particular payment never made it onto the books of the company.

Two operatives of QS-4 posed as auditors and asked about the missing funds. That simple action put a chain of events in motion that filtered out most of the people involved with the illegal operations. QS-4 operatives tracked the movements as they happened. The CFO panicked and met with one of the executives that worked for another branch of the company. Shortly after the meeting, the CFO was killed. He was hung so that it looked like the suicide of an embezzler.

The team watched as each man in the chain reported to the one above him. They met in alleys and parking garages. Each one was observed and noted by Morrison and the other men who were part of the mission. It took two weeks before the final player met with Tayebah. Four men had been killed by the time the message reached the top.

Riker was shocked at how much of the work was done for them. All of the effort and death to cover their tracks just exposed the people involved. After the people were identified the final leg of the mission started.

Three teams were dispatched to eliminate targets on the same night. Riker and Morrison went to Tayebah's home.

The palace that he lived in was heavily guarded.

Clearing the floors and working their way to the top level allowed Riker to see the abilities of his leader first hand. Morrison was at the top of his game. Every enemy received a single controlled bullet. He was calm and calculated even in the midst of battle.

Riker focused and fought along his side. He knew that this man could teach him skills that no one else possessed. He also knew that he was in for the ride. The two men cut through the guards and found Tayebah in an office near the center of the home.

He was crouched behind his desk with an AK-47. When Riker approached, he sprayed several rounds through the door. None of the rounds came close to hitting the target. Morrison positioned himself on one side of the doorway and Riker waited on the other.

Tayebah yelled from his position. "You fools have no idea what you are doing! I am the future of our nation. I will have your families—"

Morrison swung around the frame of the door and fired before Tayebah even registered the motion. The shot hit the corner of Tayebah's head that protruded from the edge of the desk. Morrison kept his weapon at the ready and moved to the side of the desk. The body lay flat face down. He put two more rounds into him without a word.

The next day both men were on a plane headed to the States.

"We are done with the mission now right?" Riker asked.

Morrison gave a slight nod. "The root of this problem has been removed."

"Do you think that it will stick?"

"I think Tayebah is dead and he will stay that way."

"What about his company? Do you think that the people

who are left will correct the course, or will some other monster just fill in the position?"

"I'm hopeful that they will correct the course. We will monitor the movements of the company, track the people that fill the new leadership position, but honestly, it could go either way," Morrison said as he slid back in his seat.

"Does it bother you that all of this might have been for nothing?" Riker asked.

"No. Not doing anything would bother me. Sitting on the sidelines and hoping for the best would bother me. Taking out some of the worst men on earth lets me sleep like a baby."

Morrison reclined the seat and closed his eyes. Riker replayed the entire mission in his mind until the wheels touched down.

35

The run over to Simon's position hurt more with each step. Riker could tell his ribs were bruised and his throat burned with every breath. His neck pulsed with pain, reminding him how the tissue had been crushed by Chatti's fingers. Riker didn't let any of that slow him down. Simon deserved to have a friend nearby before he died.

The pool of blood around Simon had grown, and several tendrils were trailing off into cracks in the pavement. His hand still rested on the rags Riker had put on the wound. Riker knelt next to him, ready to check for a pulse. Then he saw his friend's struggled breathing. Tears continued to stream down his cheeks, and he angled his head toward Riker. He took a breath and a wheezing sound came from his chest. Simon tried to speak, but just coughed, sending a spray of red out of his mouth.

"Don't talk. I'm going to put some more pressure on the wound. It's going to hurt, but it will help stop the bleeding." Riker put both hands on the wound and pressed down. He did his best to completely cover the entry wound. Simon's face scrunched in pain and his eyes widened, but he didn't make a sound.

A ball of anger grew in the pit of Riker's stomach. He knew that he'd failed his mission. Chatti had gotten away with the weapon, and now, with no help and no supplies, Simon was about to die.

This was about more than just the mission for Riker now. For all his faults, Simon was a good kid and a good team member. He deserved better than bleeding out in a parking lot in the arms of a bitter soldier.

Franklin moved as fast as he could. He was still recovering from his near-drowning.

"Over here! I need some help." Riker's voice was hoarse when he yelled.

Franklin ran over to the SUV. He paused when he saw Simon. "What's his status?"

"Two gunshot wounds. One to the shoulder, struck bone, no exit wound. The other to the chest, in and out. Seems to have missed the lungs." Riker snapped into mission mode.

"Keep the pressure on." Franklin moved to the back of the vehicle. He opened the hatchback and pulled out a small field-medic bag. In a rush, he threw the bag on the ground next to Simon and started digging into the contents.

"I need you to get his shirt off and clear the area around the wound right now. I've got to get him stabilized."

Riker nodded, immediately doing as his handler asked.

Franklin worked in a clinical way that was typical of his personality. His tendency to learn every rule and proper technique was giving Simon a chance at life.

After a few minutes of work and well-placed chest seals, Simon seemed to be doing a bit better. He was still a long way from making it but at least there was a chance.

In the distance sirens, wailed growing louder each moment. Riker looked from Simon to Franklin.

"You need to get out of here," Franklin said. "I'll stay with and handle the authorities. There's no reason for us both to be caught up in the shit storm that's about to hit. That weapon is still out there."

Riker wanted to protest. He wanted to stay with Simon, to do anything he could to help him, but he knew Franklin was right. There was nothing more that could be said. He just nodded and climbed in the SUV.

Riker drove off in the opposite direction of the approaching first responders. He grabbed his phone and called Jessica. She picked up on the first ring.

"Are you okay?" she asked.

"Yes, I'm coming to you now."

"Simon took off. He was headed for the dam. Did you see him?"

Riker paused for a moment. "Yeah, I saw him. He saved Franklin."

"Thank God. The weapon?"

"We lost it. Chatti got away." His voice caught in his throat. "There's more. Simon is hurt. He was shot twice and things aren't looking good."

"Oh, my God. Are you taking him to a hospital?"

"I had to leave him with Franklin. The weapon is still out there, and there will be questions I can't answer about the attack."

"You just left him there?" she said in a whisper.

The disappointment in her voice stung Riker. "I had to. Franklin is with him and there were first responders on their way."

"I understand. Come and get me." She hung up the phone.

Riker and Jessica arrived at the only hospital in the area a short time later. They found Franklin in a waiting room.

"Are you okay?" Jessica asked.

"I'm fine. A couple minor cuts. Nothing worth mentioning."

"What about Simon?"

Franklin looked at the floor. "He might make it. I did what I could, but the amount of blood loss was substantial. He was barely holding on when he went into surgery."

Riker put an arm around Jessica. "I'm sure they are doing everything they can."

She took a step back and looked at both men. "I'm sure they are doing everything in their power to save him, and so am I."

"What do you mean?" Riker asked.

"I made some calls before you picked me up. The two best surgeons in Atlanta should be here any minute. Simon's Dad is on his way, too."

Franklin's face lit up with anger. "Why did you involve Senator Buckner? We have done so much to keep him out of this."

Her eyes tightened in on Franklin, and Riker thought she might be about to punch him. "I called Albert because his son might die, you asshole. Maybe Simon will want his parents beside his deathbed, and maybe they want to be here for their son."

"I understand that this is an emotional time, but we cannot let those emotions drive our decisions," Franklin said.

"Are you a fucking monster?"

Riker stepped in between the two. "We all need to calm down. We need to agree on a story to tell the senator and the local authorities."

"How can you even look at him right now?" Jessica said. "You're as cold as he is."

"Franklin is right. We should not have involved the senator. His presence will not help Simon, and it may put him in danger." He went to put a hand on her shoulder. "I did everything I could to protect Simon."

"Does that include leaving him in a parking lot to die?"

Franklin spoke quietly, but there was anger in his voice. "Please remember, if not for Riker, half this town would be dead, Simon along with them."

Riker kept his eyes locked on Jessica's. "I know this is hard to deal with. I wish that you and Simon never had to see any of this, but wishing doesn't change anything that has happened."

Jessica nodded, her eyes on her feet. She looked more defeated than Riker had ever seen her. "You two decide what to tell everyone. I'm going to check on Simon."

When she'd gone, Franklin shook his head. "Women just don't get it. They always let their emotions run the show."

"Shut up Franklin," Riker said.

The two of them sat down and waited in silence. When Riker was a SEAL, he'd always completed an after-action report. The habit had stuck with him throughout life. He replayed every moment at the dam, thinking about the things he'd done right and what he'd done wrong.

Then he thought about what Jessica had said to him. He wondered if he was really coldhearted. He wasn't sure. He thought of himself as a man of honor, but he didn't see life and death the way other people did. He feared that part of him had just killed any chance he had with Jessica.

He watched people come into the hospital until he saw the man he was looking for. Senator Albert Buckman. Riker stood up as he rushed towards the front desk, intercepting him before he got there.

"Senator, you don't know me, but we need to talk about your son."

The conversation between the two men lasted an hour. Riker was as honest as he felt he could be, not referring to QS-4 by name and minimizing the way Simon had brought the situation on himself. It ended with a firm handshake. The two men went together to the surgery wing to see if there was any news on Simon.

Jessica was there and gave the senator a hug when they arrived. "They are still working on him. They told me that he is stable at the moment."

The senator smiled. "That's great news."

Riker nodded. "I'm going to find Franklin. He was waiting to talk to the police. Let me know as soon as you find out anything else about Simon."

Jessica gave a confused look when Riker shook the senator's hand as if they were old friends.

When Riker found Franklin, he had a dazed expression on his face. "I don't know what Jessica did, but the police stopped by to make sure I was okay. They didn't even ask for a statement from me, they just said everything was taken care of."

Riker smiled. "She does solve a lot of problems."

"So what now?" Franklin asked.

Riker chewed on the question for a moment before answering. "Simon's life is out of our hands. There's still a weapon of mass destruction out there, and as of right now we have no idea where it is. I say it's time we get back to work."

"I have some thoughts on that," a voice behind Riker said.

Both men turned to see Jessica standing behind them.

"But first, I thought you'd want to know that Simon just got out of surgery. He's going to make it.

A wave of relief washed over Riker. "Thank God."

"Now about this weapon," she continued. "If you really want to see this through to the end, you're not going to do it without me."

36

"Hold still, Miro."

Miro Chatti gritted his teeth, embracing the pain that coursed through his body. "Easy for you to say. You're not the one being sewn up like a ripped pair of pants.

Enrico smiled down at him. "I seem to recall offering you an anesthetic."

"And I seem to remember declining it. I earned these injuries with my carelessness. That means I earned the pain that comes along with them. To dull it would be to follow the coward's path."

"As you wish." The short, stocky man once again inserted his needle through Chatti's flesh and pulled the suture tight. He'd been Chatti's handler for almost five years, and it wasn't the first time he'd sewn him up.

Chatti closed his eyes, savoring the sharp tang of the pain. The metal table was cold against his bare back. The knife wound was the primary source of the pain, but there were other contributing factors, none of them unbearable, but decidedly unpleasant when taken together. His right arm was a mess of painful bruises from where Riker had slammed it into the car. His leg stung where the bullet had grazed him the previous day. He'd tweaked his knee during the helicopter crash, and it ached with a dull throb. His face was raw and painful from Riker's fist. He cherished all the injuries. The pain brought clarity—it always did.

His first mistake had been underestimating Riker's dedication. Most people thought that unraveling a mystery required flashes of brilliant insight, but in truth, it was the result of simple hard work. And Riker had apparently put in the effort. He'd somehow connected Chatti, Laghaz, and the stolen weapons with a seemingly innocuous dam in rural Georgia. He'd flown across the country and beaten Chatti to the scene, actually been waiting there when Chatti's operatives arrived. As much as he didn't like the end result of the encounter, Chatti did have to admire the work ethic.

And then there had been the fight itself between Chatti and Riker. Though technically the fight had ended in a draw, it didn't feel that way. The case could even be made that he'd won since he'd left with the weapon. But he hadn't accomplished his objective, and his enemy still lived. In Chatti's book, that was a loss through and through.

Many men—especially those in Chatti's profession—would have taken the loss of a fight personally. They would have bruised egos and made excuses for why they didn't win the day. Not Chatti. Though it was rare, he had lost fights in the past. He simply took the encounter as a chance to learn more information about his enemy. He cataloged Riker's moves, his fighting style, his approach and level of aggression. The outcome of the fight was barely relevant.

Because while Chatti had lost fights in the past, he always learned from them. And he learned his lessons well. The same would be true here. The next time he faced Riker—and there would be a next time—he would crush him.

"What do you make of the other man with Riker?" Enrico asked, his voice careful as he worked. "The sniper who shot down the first chopper."

After the fight, Chatti had slipped away with the weapon, ignoring the blood loss and pain as he moved through the trees. He'd called Enrico, the only man who they'd left behind in Augusta as a failsafe, and then waited nearly an hour, bleeding in the woods. Enrico had finally picked him up and performed enough medical treatment to ensure he didn't bleed out. Then they'd driven back to Augusta. Now they were in the back room of a veterinarian's office. It was nothing but dumb luck that his injuries hadn't been more catastrophic. He easily could have died before Enrico arrived to retrieve him.

As he'd waited for Enrico in the woods, Chatti had considered his failure from many angles. The role played by the mysterious sniper had been one of them.

"I think the man is Riker's QS-4 handler."

Enrico raised an eyebrow in surprise. "In the field?"

"It's the only thing that makes sense. Seems like long odds that Riker would have picked up help locally, so the man must have come with him from LA. We know he hired mercenaries when he attacked our facility there, but most of those men died. We've been tracking the one who didn't, and he's still in LA." He paused, wincing as Enrico's needle pierced his skin once again. "The mystery shooter took out the chopper's tail rotor. It was a nice shot. He has training. But he wasn't a major factor in the fight after that. He hid in the guard station and let Riker take the risks. That leads me to believe he has limited field experience. Hence a handler."

"You're telling me our entire team was taken out by a retired mercenary who's been sitting on his ass for the past six years and a handler with no field experience?"

Chatti frowned. It was that kind of thinking that had led to their current position. "Riker's clearly kept his skills sharp. He's as good as his reputation. I won't underestimate him again. I suggest you don't either."

"With any luck, we'll never see the man again. He'll go back to his beekeeping, and we'll be on to the next job." Enrico paused. "Speaking of which, when we're done here, we need to call QS-4. Let them know the mission didn't end as we'd hoped."

Chatti shot the other man a cold stare. "That won't be necessary."

Enrico tilted his head in surprise. "The dam will be crawling with law enforcement by now. An entire team of our operatives are dead."

"And yet we persevere."

"Miro, our bosses will understand. These types of jobs are always a risky proposition. They knew going in that there were no guarantees. Will they be happy? No. But they'll accept the outcome."

Chatti lay staring up at the fluorescent lights for a long moment before he spoke again. "When I was growing up in Cairo, I ran with a group of boys. I suppose you could call us a street gang, but nothing was formalized. We were all simply poor and hungry, and we watched each other's backs. Some provided distractions while others stole. All of the merchants knew us and what we were up to. While they didn't exactly look the other way, they accepted that some small portion of their food goods would be stolen, and they seemed at peace with the stolen items going to feed hungry kids. But there was one merchant who was different."

Enrico looked up from his work. He was used to Chatti's strange asides. At first they seemed like non-sequiturs, but they always came around in the end. "He didn't take kindly to his goods being stolen?"

"He did not. And of course, that made him the most enticing target in the market. Boys tried their usual tricks on him, but he always caught them. He beat them with a bamboo rod, and they rarely tried him twice."

"But not you," Enrico surmised with a smile.

"Not me. First I tried having one of my friends provide a distraction by knocking over some fruit while I pocketed a handful of dates. He caught me and beat me bloody. The second time, I tried sneaking in the back and stealing from his storeroom. He had an alarm set up, and he caught me again. I tried on nights, in the wee hours of the morning, on holidays, but he always seemed to be there, waiting for me. Time and again, he caught me and took his rod to my back."

"Hardly seems worth it for a pocketful of dates."

Chatti ignored the comment. "Finally, I realized that the usual techniques weren't going to work with this man. I needed to try something new. So, I found out where he lived. At the busiest part of the day, I set his house on fire, then I headed to the market. When they told him his house was on fire, he left the shop in a panic. I broke a window, went inside, and ate my fill. They were the sweetest dates I've ever eaten to this day."

He paused, looking up at Enrico.

"Failure may be acceptable to our bosses, but it is not acceptable to me..." He paused, his hand going to the pistol strapped at his belt. "I know I'm not the easiest person to work with, Enrico. You've been a good handler."

Enrico looked up in surprise. Compliments from Chatti were rare indeed. "Why thank you, Chat—"

Chatti drew his pistol and fired, putting a bullet through his handler's head in one swift motion. Enrico's body hit the floor with a thud, and Chatti stared at it almost lovingly for a long while before speaking again. "But you're loyal to QS-4, and I can't have that now. I've been planning this for years. Waiting for my moment. And that moment has arrived. It's time to go solo."

37

RIKER AND FRANKLIN stood behind the yellow caution tape, watching as the firefighters checked for hot spots in the ruins of the warehouse that had once been the supposed Laghaz headquarters in Santa Monica. The morning sun cast beams of light through the tendrils of smoke still rising from the ashes.

"It looks like we can add arson to Chatti's list of crimes. He is very thorough in getting rid of all evidence of his existence."

The day since Simon had woken up in the hospital had been a whirlwind of activity. With Simon's condition stable, his father had him transported to Los Angeles where their doctor friends could take care of him. Riker, Jessica, and Franklin had traveled back via private jet and quickly gotten to work trying to locate any information on Chatti. It had not proven easy. Making matters even worse, there had been a disconcerting radio silence from QS-4. Franklin had attempted to reach out by all his usual methods, but his messages had gone unanswered. Very worrying when there was a powerful weapon on the wind.

"Any word from your back-alley sources?" Riker asked as they watched the firemen work.

Franklin shook his head. "I've tried to hire mercenaries fitting his description anonymously, but I haven't found anyone that matches Chatti. I've reached out to see if anyone has information or a connection to Laghaz, but it's like looking for the boogie man. Everyone seems to know about them, but there are no details. They have taken credit for a few attacks, but those attacks seem completely random. There are no similar targets and no similar methods."

"That's because they are boogie men. There is no Laghaz organization. It is just a front. By now, they've probably disbanded any of the members of this current iteration that aren't already dead. As much as I hate to say it, QS-4 is holding the cards here. If they want their man hidden, he's probably going to stay that way."

Franklin looked up in surprise. "So we give up?"

"No. But we may have to get creative. This isn't going to be easy."

"I agree. The question becomes how do we recover the last weapon? If Chatti doesn't have a mission, he will most likely give it to QS-4." Riker's phone buzzed, and he checked the text.

He's awake.

"I'm going to meet up with Jessica. She's said Simon is awake."

"I'll keep working on finding us some leads. Give Simon my best."

"Sure, you don't want to come?"

"Tell him I'll stop by when he is feeling better and when we have finished this."

When Riker entered the hospital room, Jessica was sitting in a chair next to the bed. Wires and tubes came from

Simon and the bed propped him up at a slight angle. His right arm was held in a sling with a temporary cast that extended over his entire shoulder.

"Hey, you up for some company?" Riker asked.

"More the merrier." Simon had a dazed smirk on his face.

Riker smiled. "I'm guessing that the pain management people are doing a good job."

"Yeah, buddy. They've got the good stuff in this place."

"That's the reason we brought you back to LA. Nothing but the best for the son of a senator," Jessica said.

"How did surgery number two go?" Riker asked.

"I'm not sure. I slept through most of it." Simon laughed.

Jessica shook her head. "The surgeon said that it will be an extensive recovery process, but he will regain full use of his right arm."

"That's great news. I told you those shoulder gunshot wounds were nothing. Especially for a hero like you."

The smile washed off Simon's face. He swallowed hard. "Don't say that. I'm no hero."

"What are you talking about? You saved Franklin's ass. Mine too. We would probably both be dead if you hadn't shown up."

"It was stupid of you to play soldier, but you're going to be okay," Jessica said. "We all are, and that's what really matters." She put her hand over Simon's.

"I'm not talking about that. Of course I was a hero at the dam." He laughed again, this time it caused him to cough and then wince in pain. "I really get it now. I'm worse than an idiot. This entire thing, all the death, it was my fault. Thousands of people could have died because of me. I stole those weapons. It was worse than reckless."

Jessica and Riker exchanged an awkward glance.

"That's true," Riker said. "It's also true that you helped do something about it. Not just the easy stuff. You really put yourself on the line. I'm not saying you shouldn't feel bad. You really fucked up, but feeling bad helps you learn. That's what separates the good men from the bad. We see our faults, we pick ourselves up, and we try to become better men. I haven't known you long, but I know you can become a great man."

Simon stared at Riker. His eyes filled with tears. "I definitely don't feel like a good man now."

"That's because you're shot and full of drugs," Jessica said with a wink. "But even with all your faults you really are a good guy."

The three sat in silence for a moment. Jessica brushed the tear from Simon's cheek.

"So what now?" Simon asked.

"The only thing you need to do is heal up. Don't worry about the other stuff."

Simon thought for a moment, then he looked at Jessica, his eyes wide. "Your fundraiser. It's in a couple days. Am I going to be out of here in time?."

"According to the doctors, you should be out by then," Jessica said. "But in no way do I expect you to attend after what you've been through."

"Are you kidding? I'm not missing a party like that." Simon's face grew serious, and he turned to Riker. "Think I need to worry about this Chatti dude? Is he still going to try to kill me?"

"I don't see why he would," Riker said. "But we're not taking any chances."

"Your dad went all out with security," Jessica added. "There are two guys outside of the room, two more at each end of the hall, and one at the entrance to the wing. Second, we don't think anyone will be after you. The attack failed and everyone knows about the weapon that they still have. There is no reason to kill you. They would be risking exposure for nothing."

He laughed. "Good thing I don't matter anymore. This is one time where it's nice not to be wanted."

"I'd still play it safe. Take advantage of the security measures and lay low for a while. Rest up and relax."

"That works for me. What about you? Are you going to get the weapon back?"

"Working on it."

"You need to put that guy down. This thing won't be over until he's dead. And I want to help in any way I can."

Riker smiled. "I think you've done enough."

"I mean it, Riker. I have a long way to go to become a better man. If there is anything that I can do, I'm in."

"Okay, tough guy," Jessica said. "For now you can heal up."

"I agree," Riker said. "We'll stop by later to check on you. For now, we have work to do."

As they walked out of the room, Riker nodded to Saber, who was sitting at the end of the hall, a baseball cap pulled low over his face. Even though the senator had hired plenty of security, Riker felt more comfortable bringing in someone he'd personally seen in action to help protect Simon.

Riker and Jessica sat in silence for the first five minutes of the drive to the house. The moments stretched out, and Riker kept his eyes locked on the road. He hadn't been alone with Jessica since Georgia. Now that he had the chance to talk with her in private, he didn't know what to say.

"How many have you lost?" Jessica asked.

The question caught Riker off-guard. "How many what?"

"Teammates, or soldiers, or men. Whatever you call them. How many have you lost?"

He took a breath. "Too many." He saw that she was not happy with that answer. "I'm not trying to be vague, but it's not something any of us talk about. Every death stays with me. I carry around their memories and their sacrifice. They are more than casual conversation."

She turned and looked in his eyes. "I didn't mean to make their loss sound casual. I've just had some time to think. Losing Simon would have been one of the most impactful things that have ever happened to me. His death would have been another in a long line for you."

Riker's knuckles turned white as he gripped the wheel.

"I'm not trying to downplay what Simon means to you," she continued. "And I'm not suggesting that you would care less than I do about his death. You just know how to deal with it. That's a skill that I never want to possess."

The color returned to his fingers. "I've never tried to hide what I am around you. I know it isn't all good, but it is real." He swallowed hard. "I've been thinking a lot too. This thing between us is actually the most real relationship I've ever had."

She smiled and put a hand on his leg. "You know, that's kind of pathetic."

His face turned a light shade of red.

"But it's also pretty sweet. I'm not done with you yet."

Riker took a hand off the wheel and put it on her thigh. He gave her a smile. "Roger that."

They arrived at the safe house to find Franklin working in the office. He didn't look up from his screen when they entered.

"Yes, Franklin, Simon's doing fine," Jessica said. "Thanks for asking."

He continued to type for another thirty seconds before responding. "Yes, that's good to hear."

"Do you have something?" Riker asked.

"I might. It's a long shot, but I think it's worth checking out. I might have a lead on Chatti."

Riker and Jessica exchanged a glance.

"I've had an algorithm running a series of keywords through the California police database based on his description. I got a lot of false hits, but I found a domestic abuse report that stood out from the rest."

"That does sound like a long shot," Riker said.

"I agree, but the description of the abuse from the victim was..." he looked from Riker to Jessica, "unusual. The woman reported some forms of torture that a civilian probably wouldn't know, let alone have experience administering."

"What's the abuser's name?" Jessica asked.

Franklin looked at them pointedly. "John Smith. I'll assume that is an alias, but the description given by the victim matches Chatti. The police never made an arrest."

"Please tell me that you have the name and location of the woman who filed the complaint," Riker said.

Franklin looked up and smiled at Riker. "I do. She still lives in LA."

Riker thought of the mystery man who knew his past. The man who'd attempted to kill thousands of people including his friends. "I'll follow up on this one. There is a psychopath out there with a bomb and it's the only lead we've got."

"Agreed," Jessica said. "Let's head out."

"I think you should stay and work with Franklin," Riker said. "We still need to follow up on the financial records, and that's kind of your thing."

She looked at him like he was an idiot. "So you want to send a big military guy by himself to question a woman who was abused by a big military guy?"

Riker and Franklin exchanged a glance.

"Point taken. Let's go."

38

Forty minutes after leaving Franklin's safe house, Riker and Jessica found themselves in front of a small ranch house just south of the 105 in LA. The exterior was better kept than most of the surrounding homes. Bars guarded windows and the space between the home and the neighbors was just farther than Riker's arm span.

Jessica led the way up the front porch and knocked on the door. They could hear motion from inside the house and Riker noticed the peephole darken. Whoever was on the other side didn't say anything.

"Miss Thomas, my name is Jessica King. I'm sorry to bother you, but I could use your help."

"What do you need my help with?"

"It's a little complicated. Can we come in and talk?"

"I don't let strangers into my home. Please go away."

Riker spoke up. "We're looking for a man we think you know. We're trying to make sure he doesn't hurt anyone else."

There was a long pause. "Who are you?"

"He's the guy who stops bad people," Jessica said. "I promise that we won't cause any trouble for you."

The door opened a crack, the chain was still attached. They could see a sliver of the woman's face. "Are you armed?"

Jessica shook her head. "No, neither of us is armed."

"Well, I am. I want you to keep that in mind." The door opened, and they went inside.

The three sat in the living room with Riker and Jessica on the couch across from the woman in a chair. She was in her early twenties and had long blonde hair. A scar ran across her left cheek. It was faded, but still visible. She had bags under her eyes and unkempt hair. As soon as she sat down, she lit a cigarette.

Jessica spoke in a soft voice. "Thank you for letting us in, Miss Thomas."

"You can call me Mary." She turned to look at Riker. "You don't look like cops. Who are you?"

"We aren't the police. I work for a private company that helps stop terrorist organizations. Jessica is helping me with the current job." Riker watched Mary take a slow drag on her cigarette when he spoke. "We are tracking a man who you may have known."

Mary didn't say anything. She just stared at Riker while he spoke.

"I'm guessing that you know exactly who I am referring to. I saw the police report you filed three years ago. That isn't the kind of thing you forget."

"No, it's not. In fact, I think about it all the time."

"If you could tell us everything you know about him, it might help us find him."

She looked at Riker skeptically. "And if you find him, what will you do with him?"

"We'll make sure he gets locked up for good," Jessica said.

Mary kept her gaze fixed on Riker.

"Based on what I know, I'd say he's not the kind of person that goes to jail," Riker said without breaking eye contact. "I will put him down or die trying. You have my word on that."

"I doubt that you will be able to get the better of him, but I hope you do." She took another drag. "What do you want to know?"

"Just tell us your story."

"I met John at a club. I guess I knew that wasn't his real name right from the start, but I went with it. I was twenty-one, and I was hot shit. At least, I thought so, and no one was arguing. Every guy in the club wanted me. I liked getting free drinks and having the power over all the guys there. I think that's why he approached me. He just wanted to prove he could get what other people couldn't. I think about that night all the time. If I would have just told him to buzz off, I would be a different person today. That didn't happen. He was charming and rich. He knew exactly what to say to peak my interest."

"Describe him to me," Riker said.

"Olive skin. A long face with black hair. His beard was short and well-kept just like his hair. He told me he was from Cairo. He has broad shoulders, and he is slim. Very athletic and very strong. Those exotic features made him stand out. He speaks with a slight Egyptian accent."

"That's him. Please go on."

"I never thought that I'd allow anyone to control me, but he had me under his thumb before I knew it was happening. I moved in with him three days after we met. A week later, I tried heroin for the first time. He never used any drugs, but he convinced me to try them so quickly. At the time, I thought I was living the dream. He had a nice place downtown, and he gave me everything I wanted. He was nice to me, and I fell for him hard.

"By the end of our first month together, I'd started using frequently. That is also around the time his true personality started to come out. He didn't beat me, but he started to treat me like garbage. One moment he was sweet and the next abusive.

"By the third month, I was a complete mess. I was using every day, and I did anything that he told me to do. I found myself standing on the balcony of his apartment when he was gone, thinking about jumping. That was the moment I realized I needed to get out.

"I left right then and there. I was high at the time. I took my clothes and my purse, nothing else. I got a cheap hotel room and decided that I would stay there until I got clean."

She slashed the butt of her cigarette into the ashtray and lit another.

"I'm guessing that you went back to him," Riker said.

"No!" She almost shouted the word. "I stayed in that hotel room for six days. I got sober and swore that I would never touch any drugs again. I definitely swore that I would never get within a mile of John." She paused, taking a deep breath. "When I woke up on the seventh day," he was in my room. Just sitting in a chair next to the bed like he belonged there."

She shivered and then took another drag.

"Go on," Jessica said.

"He told me that I was the first girl ever to leave him. He'd thrown out every other woman that he had been with. He said that I would always be memorable to him because of it. Then he told me that he wanted to make sure that I would never forget him.

"I don't even know how to describe what he did next. I was tied up and gagged. He never once seemed angry as he was torturing me. He kept telling me to stay in the moment and to learn from the pain. I've never seen anyone act like that. He finished five hours later. He kept me conscious the whole time, but I was barely holding on by the end. Then he told me that if I ever told a soul about what he had done, there would be consequences."

"Oh, my God." Jessica looked like she might be sick.

"I don't know about God, but John wasn't done with me yet. I spent a week in the hospital recovering from what he had done to me. The police asked me to file a report. At first, I told them that I had nothing to report, but a detective convinced me that he could protect me. He said that the man who did this would do it to others unless I stopped him."

"I'm guessing they didn't have any luck finding John Smith," Riker said.

She tapped ash into the tray. "That's right. His condo was empty. All of the information that the landlord had on him was fake. They couldn't find a single piece of evidence that my attacker even existed.I withdrew my charges and hoped that I would never hear from him again. I changed my name and left town, but none of that mattered.

"I came home one night, and he was in my living room. I'd bought a gun after our last encounter, and tried to get it out, but I never had a chance. He sat me down at the table in front of a needle loaded with enough heroin next to it to kill anyone. He told me I had two choices. I could shoot the drugs, or I could live through another session of pain."

"What did you do?" Jessica asked.

"It was an easy choice. I would rather die than endure that torture again. So I shot up. I remember him walking out as I started to drift off."

"How did you survive?" Riker asked.

"Dumb luck and a shitty rental. The guy in the apartment next to mine was home. He heard our conversation through the paper-thin walls and called 911. The paramedics got there in time to bring me back."

"Why did you come back to L.A.?" Jessica said.

"When I was in the hospital recovering, I found a note under my pillow. I have no idea how he put it there, but it was from him. He told me that there must be a reason I survived and that I should learn from the experience. He instructed me to stay in L.A. and not to try to hide from him. If I did, there would be consequences. So I did what he told me to do. I haven't heard from him since."

Riker and Jessica sat in silence, letting the story wash over them. Mary's hand shook as she took another puff of her smoke.

Jessica leaned forward. "Why did you tell us the story? Aren't you afraid he's still out there?"

Mary laughed. "I'm terrified. That's why I let you in. That's why I'm telling you all of this. I've been afraid every moment for the last three years. I can't make it like this much longer. If you really can use any of this to find him and kill him, it will give me my life back. If he finds out that I spoke with you, he will kill me. Either way, it's better than what I have now."

Riker stood up. "Thank you. You've given us everything we need to find him."

Jessica's eyebrows shot up in surprise. She clearly hadn't gotten the same thing Riker had from the story.

"Once this is finished, I will let you know he is gone,"

Riker said. "You are a brave woman and there is still hope for a good life."

She let out a joyless laugh. "I doubt it, but if you can find him and kill him, that would be a good start."

They left the house and headed back to see Franklin.

"What did you learn from her story?" Jessica asked. "I didn't hear any details that would help us find Chatti."

"The story told us what kind of man we are after," Riker said. "Mary was a small prize to him. He has probably seduced and controlled dozens of women. One of the encounters didn't go the way he wanted and he couldn't let it go. He risked exposure to attack her. He upended his location and probably his business because of one woman that he had very little interest in."

"How does that help us find him?"

"What he did was based on obsession, not logic. I thought that he would disappear after the job was done. I assumed that he would no longer have any interest in Simon when every logical reason said their interaction was over."

Jessica looked at Riker. "He's not going to stop. Even if the job is over, he will finish it."

Riker nodded. "Men like the one we are after would rather die than admit failure. Simon. Me. Maybe even you. He wants us all dead. And that's our key to finding him."

39

When they got back to the safe house, Franklin was working on his laptop in the dining room. He glanced up, started to ask a question, then stopped. One look at Jessica's face made it clear that she was shaken by what had just happened.

"Everything all right?" he asked.

Riker sat down across from him at the table. "Better than all right. We may have found a way to draw him out."

"I take it the woman spoke with you, then."

"She did," Jessica said, taking the seat next to Riker. Her tone of voice said the topic was closed for the moment. "What have you been up to?"

"Researching Vin-Brooks, the pharmaceutical company whose competitor just happened to be located south of that dam."

"You think they were involved?" Jessica asked.

"I'm ninety nine percent sure. The other target, the power plant, ran the grid for one of Strymond's manufacturing plants. It looks like your theory was correct. Now we need to prove it." He spun the laptop around so they could see the screen. It displayed a picture of a balding man in his late fifties. The polished smile and solid-color background had the feel of a corporate headshot. "This is Gary Kosmider. He's the Director of Operations for Vin-Brooks. If the company hired QS-4, he would know about it. Based on my research, a job of this size wouldn't go down without his approval. It's possible that his bosses know, but I can say for certain that he does."

Riker looked at the photo for a long moment, studying the man's face. He looked so normal. So professional. Yet this would hardly be the first time a man like that had ordered thousands of deaths with the stroke of a pen. "This is good work."

"Thanks. There's something else." He looked uneasy.

"What is it?" Jessica asked.

"Morrison contacted me. They haven't heard from Chatti since the dam, and his handler was found dead in a Georgia veterinary clinic. Shot through the head."

Riker sank into the seat across from Franklin. "Chatti's gone rogue."

"That's what Morrison thinks," Franklin acknowledged. "With a weapon like the one he has, he certainly has options. He could find another target. Or he could sell it and raise enough money to open his own black-ops outfit." He paused, looking at Riker. "QS-4 is decidedly more interested in us recovering the weapon now."

"I'll bet," Riker said. "But I'm guessing they still aren't going to involve themselves further."

"With the weapon on the loose and senator's son nearly killed? They are disavowing faster than I've ever seen. We're on our own." Franklin tapped on the keyboard, bringing up a news website. "Not sure if you've seen this, but it's all over the internet."

This time, the face on Franklin's laptop was much more familiar. It was Simon, grinning at the camera as he stood in front of his Lamborghini. The headline was SENATOR'S SON RECOVERING AFTER HUNTING ACCIDENT.

"Looks like his father's PR team is hard at work," Jessica said.

"They say he was accidentally shot by a hunting buddy. Twitter is all over it. Everyone loves dropping memes about a dumb rich kid who got himself shot playing with guns."

"Poor Simon," Jessica said.

Franklin glanced up at Jessica, hesitating before asking his question. "So, the woman you spoke with. What did you learn?"

Jessica swallowed hard, steeling herself for the conversation. "She told us all about this so-called John Smith character. More than I ever wanted to know. How he stalked her. Tortured her. Made her life a living hell."

"My God," Franklin said.

Jessica looked down at her hands for a long moment. "I kept thinking during Mary's story. What if this guy decides his new obsession is torturing Simon? Or me?"

"I won't let that happen."

"I know that. And even if it is a risk, that weapon is out there. We don't have a choice, do we? God help us, but we have to stop this guy. There's no one else."

Riker put his hand over hers. "I know it's not easy, but we're in this together. I'll be right there by your side."

She glanced over at Riker. "I'm still not comfortable involving Simon."

"Fill me in?" Franklin said.

Riker leaned forward. "I know how this guy thinks. He's not going to be satisfied until he finished the task he set out to accomplish."

"Killing Simon and Jessica."

Riker nodded. "He could easily let it go. Maybe Simon saw his face. Big deal. So did Mary. A guy like this can disappear into the ether. They'll never see him again, and he's egotistical enough to believe he'll never be arrested. So why's he care?"

"Because he's wired that way," Franklin surmised.

"Exactly. He wants us dead, so we use that knowledge to draw him out. Simon will be out of the hospital in two days, which just happens to be in time for—"

"My fundraiser," Jessica finished. "We make it known that Simon is going to be making his first public appearance since the accident. The tabloids will run with it from there."

"Good," Riker said. "Simon seems pretty eager to make amends for stealing the weapon. He'll agree to it."

"Of course he will." Jessica's voice was cold.

"What do you mean by that?"

"You're his hero. Of course he's going to agree to anything you ask."

"I thought you were okay with this."

"I'm pretty far from okay with it," she answered. "I understand that it has to be done, but that doesn't mean I like it. Simon... for everything he's been given in life, he's still so naive. He's been directionless his whole life. He's going to jump at the chance to do something that saves lives, even if it's stupid. Look at what he did at the dam. I just hate to see him in harm's way again."

Riker squeezed her hand. "I get that. I really do. But he's already in harm's way. This John Smith is coming after him, one way or another. What we're doing will control the situation. Smith comes after him in public, and we'll be ready to take him out. Trust me, this is safer for Simon."

Franklin rubbed at his chin for a moment, deep in

thought. "What if he doesn't want to wait? What if he goes after Simon in the hospital? Or maybe he waits until the publicity dies down."

Riker shook his head. "I don't think it'll play out like that. He'll be impatient to get the job done. Failure hangs heavy on a man like Chatti. The only way to ease the burden will be to make it right by finishing what he set out to do."

"And the hospital?" Jessica asked.

"I'll head over there after this. If Chatti wants to get Simon, he'll need to go through me. He'll know that means a fight, and I doubt he'll want to risk that in a hospital."

"Won't you be at the fundraiser too?" Franklin asked.

"Yes. But we don't have to be public about that part."

Jessica drew a deep breath. "Okay. I'm in for this plan. However, I do have one condition."

"Name it."

"If we do this, we do it all the way. I don't want to be looking over my shoulder the rest of my life, and I don't want Simon to be, either. Chatti doesn't leave the fundraiser alive. That's my condition."

Riker gave her a smile. He was glad to see she understood the seriousness of what they were up against. "As much as I hate to admit it, Chatti and I are similar in some ways. When I set my mind to a job, I don't stop until it's done. He won't leave the fundraiser alive. You have my word."

Franklin grinned. "Then we're in agreement. Chatti has to die!" He cleared his throat, wiping the smile off of his face. "Sorry, that came out a little more enthusiastic than I intended."

"Too late," Riker said. "We know you love murder now. That's definitely going in my post-mission report."

"Report?" Franklin looked horrified for a moment, then he scowled at Riker. "Very funny."

Riker pushed himself to his feet. "I guess I'm off to the hospital. Jessica, you'll take care of the arrangements we talked about for the fundraiser?"

"That I can do. Already dialing my publicist." She pulled out her phone, tapped the screen a few times, and held it to her ear. "Renee, how are you, girl?" She listened a moment, then continued. "You still have that connection at the *L.A. Times*? Good. I have a story for them. It's about Simon Buckner."

As she spoke, Riker walked to the bedroom at the back of the house and gathered his meager belongings. He'd be spending the next couple of nights sleeping in an uncomfortable chair at the hospital, probably waking at every sound, wondering if it was Chatti coming to finish Simon off. He didn't mind. He'd spent longer periods of time in worse places, and if there was one thing he'd learned from Morrison, it was patience. His codename was Scarecrow, after all.

With his things in a small duffle bag, he made his way back to the dining room, where Jessica was finishing up her conversation with the publicist.

"That's wonderful. Just let me know when the story is going to drop. Then we'll forward the article to *TMZ*, and the rest will take care of itself." She paused, her eyes going to Franklin's laptop. "Actually, I just thought of something else you can help me with. I need a last-minute invitation to the fundraiser sent out to someone. Gary Kosmider, Director of Operations for the Vin-Brooks Corporation."

40

The most upscale events that Riker had attended all related to the military. His graduation from BUD/S training was a proud moment, but it mostly involved a ceremony attended by family members. He had been to a few political fundraisers which required a tux, but they'd been in small rooms and served a modest dinner. Tonight's event was on a completely different level.

The fundraiser was held at the International Ballroom at the Beverly Hilton. Jessica told him that she hosted it at this location since a lot of the attendees were familiar with the venue. Apparently, it was where they hosted the *Golden Globes*.

They'd booked a room in the hotel where Franklin had spent the last two days setting up a makeshift command center. He had full access to the hotel security system and all of its internal cameras. They had an adequate communications setup, consisting of a discrete earpiece and mic for each member of the team. Riker had spent the last day familiarizing himself with the hotel. He had entered every mechanical room and committed the entire layout to memory. He'd found the weaknesses and blind spots that he thought might be exploited by an assassin.

Simon entered the building on the morning of the event. His mobility was still limited and in truth he should not have been out of bed. He was brought in through the service entrance in a wheelchair complete with an attachment that helped to support the cast that immobilized his arm and shoulder. Riker did not want him to enter on the red carpet with the rest of the attendees. With all the commotion, the area was impossible to secure, and it would be the most likely area for an attack.

Riker brought Simon down to the ballroom in his chair after the guests started to arrive. They came in through a side entrance and set up in the corner of the main room. Jessica had arranged a change in the decorations that involved a large display blocking Simon from view at almost every angle. This helped reduce the risk of any snipers. If Chatti wanted Simon, he would have to get him up close.

The news story that Jessica had planted was the final lure for Chatti. It told the story of an incompetent hunter who'd shot Simon, and it contained multiple thinly-veiled digs at Chatti. Riker hoped it would be enough to draw him out.

Two of the guests seated at Simon's table were bodyguards provided by his father. Riker hoped that he hadn't misjudged his opponent. Most men would call off a hit with this many variables. They would wait for a better opportunity. Riker felt that Chatti would relish the challenge and react in the opposite manner.

Riker sat down next to Simon and scanned the room. He watched for subtle movements in the shadows and guests that didn't fit into the crowd.

"You know, if I'm going to die this is a good place to do it," Simon said.

Riker snapped out of his focus and looked at Simon. "What? Why here?"

"Are you kidding me? Look around, this is the who's who of Hollywood along with the social elite of the west coast. Plus the food is amazing. Have you tried these?"

Simon used his good arm to push over a plate of small morsels with toothpicks sticking out of them. It looked like marbled bites of steak with a light green sauce. The smell was intoxicating.

Riker frowned. "I'm glad that you are enjoying the event, but I think we should be concentrating on keeping you alive at the moment."

"You can enjoy food and keep me alive. I don't want you to run out of energy in the middle of a fight to the death." Simon pushed the tray a little closer to Riker.

With a shake of his head Riker, grabbed one of the hors d'oeuvre and ate it in one bite. The flavor exploded in his mouth, and he thought of a restaurant in New York that had recently surprised him with equally delicious food. He let out a soft yum.

"Ha, I told you they were awesome." Simon's phone buzzed, and he looked down at a text. "Jessica just arrived. She should be walking in at any moment."

Riker stood up and took a step to the side so he could see the main entrance. The entire venue seemed to take a breath when Jessica stepped inside. Her white dress gave the illusion of weightlessness as it hugged her form. It was sleeveless and cut low enough to show the perfect curves of her chest. The dress was long and waved lines of fabric touched the ground, covering her feet. When she moved from guest to guest, it truly looked as if she floated just above the floor. Riker watched her mingle through the room and understood what inspired poetry.

"I know," Simon said. "She cleans up pretty good. Now put your tongue back in your mouth and keep me alive."

"You were right," Riker said, his eyes still fixed on Jessica. "This would be a good place to die."

Simon touched the earpiece and spoke. "You hear that, Franklin? Riker said that I was right."

"Yes, I heard," Franklin responded through the earpiece.

"I just wanted it on the record. I think it's the first time he said that to me."

Jessica made her way over to the table. "You boys look nice this evening."

"I know," Simon said with a smirk. "We put on these fancy tuxedos and you just show up in an old dress."

She hit him in his good arm. "Don't be a dick. This event is always a lot of pressure. This year I need to raise a record-setting amount of money and keep you alive."

"He's just afraid to say how beautiful you are," Riker said. "I think you literally took the breath away from everyone here when you walked in."

She gave him a soft smile, and he put an arm around the small of her back, drawing her in close. She leaned in and kissed him softly on the lips for a moment that felt like a lifetime.

Jessica stepped back. "Careful, big guy. You probably don't want the press to get a picture of us together."

"Some things are worth the risk."

"Do I need to remind everyone that this is not meant to be a social engagement," Franklin said through their earpieces.

"Actually that's exactly what it is meant to be," Jessica responded.

"You know what I mean. We have a mission to do."

"Roger that," Riker said as he stepped back and composed himself. "Jessica, work the room and find Gary Kosmider. Find out what state of mind he's in. See if you can get him to slip up with any information. Franklin, watch the video feeds. Let me know the moment you see anything unusual, no matter how small. I'll stay here with Simon watching the floor."

"I'll sit here and look like a target for a psychotic killer," Simon added.

"Good luck everyone," Franklin said.

For the next two hours, Riker watched the stars mingle and drink. According to Franklin, every person in the room was accounted for. There were no party crashers. The waitstaff was the only x-factor. Jessica had barely managed to move for the last hour. As the host she was constantly surrounded by the elite seeking her attention.

Riker's biggest distractions were the people talking to Simon. They seemed to be split between those concerned for his health after the gunshot wound and friends of him giving him a hard time. The common thread was that everyone liked Simon. Riker had to admit he had a good nature and was fun to be around.

"Riker, the cameras on the roof terrace went down," Franklin said.

"All of them?"

"Yes. The feed isn't live anymore. It is just a still from four minutes ago."

"Check the feeds in the tower stairwell."

"Got it. There are four men in tuxedos moving down toward your level. Wait, one exited on floor five."

"Shit, I was hoping that we would be facing a lone wolf. Does it look like our guy is one of them?"

"I'm not sure. I haven't gotten a good look at their faces, and I never saw him up close."

"I'm going to the base of the stairs to intercept. Keep track of their locations."

Riker stood and turned to the bodyguards at the table. "Watch him." Then he raced to the stairwell.

Franklin spoke again a moment later. "Two of them are still coming down the stairs. They are moving fast."

Riker stood to the right of the door next to the handle. Adrenaline filled his body, and he forced his breath to steady.

"They just hit the second floor, and another one peeled off. The other two will be on your position in a moment."

He faced the edge of the door, waiting for it to open. He drew his left hand back, tensing the muscles in his arm and shoulder as the footsteps echoed on the other side of the door. The steps were coming fast, he hoped that they were close to one another. If they were too far apart the second man might have time to draw his weapon.

The door swung open, and the moment Riker saw his target his fist shot out. He angled his hand down so that the knuckle protruded forward. The blow struck the man in the throat. His head jerked back, and Riker followed the punch with a hard kick to the stomach. The first man flew backward into the second; he gripped his own throat and made a harsh hissing sound while he fell.

The second man was knocked backward, stumbling as he tried to reach inside of his coat, but the back of his heels hit the stairs. He fell back smashing onto the hard steps. Riker pressed the attack and pounced on the man. He brought both hands down in an arcing motion. They connected with the man's chest just below the sternum. All of the air escaped his lungs in a gasp.

Riker turned him over and pulled out a couple of the thick black zip ties that he had tucked into his pants. He secured the man's hands and feet together and then repeated the process on the first man. He took a 9mm pistol and a knife from each of them.

"Where are the other two?" he asked into his microphone.

"One is coming down the elevator," Franklin answered. "The other just reached the stairwell at the other end of the hall.

Riker left the men in the stairwell and ran out the door to the elevator bank. There were four elevators and two were approaching the lobby.

"Which one is he in?"

"To your right, closest to the lobby."

Riker ran over to the elevator. "You're sure this is the one?"

"Yes, I'm watching the live feeds. I see you."

The digital readout above the doors said two. Riker crouched down, shifting his center of gravity. His wrestling coaches had pounded this stance into his muscle memory. It allowed for explosive attacks on your opponents.

The doors slid open, and the man inside spotted Riker. He reached for his gun, but his reaction was too slow. Riker shot forward, gripping the man around his knees. He took him down hard and spun around behind him. Seconds later, the man was unconscious with Riker's arm around his neck.

Riker left him in the elevator, bound like the others. "What's the status on the last one?"

"He's headed to the ballroom."

Riker sprinted towards the entrance, narrowly avoiding knocking over a few people. One man yelled, "Hey you're that guy from the gym!"

Riker didn't pause. He turned the corner to see five men in tuxes with their back to him. "Which one?"

"The one walking by the table. Next to the woman in the green dress."

Riker took a few quick steps until he was directly behind the man. Then he reached an arm around his neck and hooked his wrist with the other hand. Riker put every ounce of force into the hold. The man grabbed at Riker's arm for a moment and then went limp.

A few partygoers turned and looked as Riker lowered the man to the floor. Riker spoke loud enough that everyone could hear. "Sorry, he had a little too much to drink."

Jessica's voice filled his ear. "Riker, it's Chatti. He's here. He just took Simon."

41

RIKER'S HEART sank at the sound of Jessica's words in his ear. *He just took Simon.*

Not killed Simon, but took him. On the one hand, that news was reassuring. There was still a chance of saving him. On the other... The story of the man's ex-girlfriend flashed in Riker's mind. Perhaps being taken by this particular individual wasn't all that much better than taking a quick bullet to the head.

It also raised a baffling question. Why hadn't he straight out killed Simon? Why go to the trouble of dragging around an injured man? Simon couldn't move very quickly, and he stuck out like a sore thumb in his odd combination of giant cast and formalwear. Was it a situation like it had been with Mary? Did he want revenge against Simon, or...

In a flash, Riker suddenly understood. This whole time, they'd assumed that Simon was the dangling thread their enemy would need to clip to feel the job was finished. They'd planned this entire elaborate trap from that perspective. But that wasn't accurate. Simon was certainly part of it, but there was another element they hadn't considered—

Riker. Riker had defeated him twice, and that wouldn't sit well with a man like this.

Chatti didn't just want to kill Simon. He also wanted to beat Riker.

Hope sprang up in Riker's chest. That meant Chatti wouldn't kill Simon yet. He'd want to use him to draw Riker out.

"Riker, what do we do?" Jessica asked through his earpiece. "He could be anywhere in the hotel. Or he could be on his way out."

It was Franklin who answered. "I'm on it. Scanning through the security footage. If this guy is still on the hotel property, I'll find his ass."

Riker started to answer, then stopped, remembering that Simon had an earpiece too. "Guys, our communications have been compromised."

There was a long pause.

"Copy that," Franklin answered.

Nothing but silence from Jessica.

Then another voice spoke through his earpiece. He recognized this one—Chatti. "Smart, Riker. This comm system is top-notch. I'm guessing your new girlfriend footed the bill?"

Riker stood stone still, his eyes scanning the people gathered near the entrance. He didn't bother answering. There was a good chance this was meant as a distraction.

"Very thoughtful of you to provide me with this high-quality audio experience."

Riker took a deep breath and tried to focus. Chatti had gotten the better of him a number of times, but every time Riker had beaten him it was because he'd been able to put himself inside the guy's head. The man had similar training to Riker's, which meant they would have been trained on the same strategies. If Riker were trying to draw an enemy out and take him down in the Beverly Hilton, where would he do it?

He ran through the luxury hotel's layout in his mind, flipping through the possibilities like the pages in a book. There was a courtyard with a fountain on the west side of the hotel. That would provide a decent venue, but it was also in clear sight of dozens of hotel windows. His enemy wouldn't want that. The pool area was certainly out on a beautiful night like this. The service entrance was crawling with caterers because of the fundraiser. The main entrance had been transformed into a red carpet receiving area, and the secondary entrance would be busy due to the repurposing of the main one.

Then it hit him. He knew where he'd go.

The phone in his pocket buzzed. He pulled it out and saw a text from Jessica. *Where?*

As he started walking, he tapped out a quick reply. *Parking garage.* Then he deleted it and typed, *Rooftop terrace.* The farther he could get Jessica from this mess the better.

He cut through the lobby, ignoring friendly greetings from the staff. His mind was focused on reaching his goal. He was almost to the parking garage when his enemy's voice once again filled his ear.

"I gotta say, I admire the confidence it takes to use a high-profile event like this as a honey pot to draw me in. I saw right through your ruse the moment I spotted the first article, of course. But I still admired it. Honestly, you've impressed me during this entire operation. Getting to Simon before I did. Taking out my guys at the warehouse in Santa Monica. The thing at the dam. All impressive work."

"The best thing about all of those encounters was your incompetence," Jessica said.

"Jessica King, I can't wait to get to know you. I hope that Riker gets to see our encounter, but that is unlikely."

Riker suppressed the urge to respond. A guy like this wouldn't just talk to hear the sound of his own voice. He was trying to get inside Riker's head. If he could mentally engage Riker in a discussion, Riker would be distracted from the fight that was surely coming.

Chatti continued, "The thing you don't seem to understand about me is that I'm basically you."

Riker thought back to Mary, and this time he couldn't help but respond. "You're nothing like me."

"Well, I am younger. Faster. Smarter. I'm the version of you who never gave up."

"Parking garage, level two," Franklin said.

"Yes, come and get me."

Riker grimaced. Chatti was exactly where Riker expected, but now Jessica would most likely be headed to the same location.

Riker stepped into the parking garage. Scanning the first level with his eyes, he saw nothing, but there were plenty of places to hide. He proceeded slowly, looking behind every vehicle. Even though Franklin had confirmed his location, Riker didn't want to be caught off guard in a trap. When his search proved fruitless, he moved on to level two.

He'd explored half of the second level before the man spoke in his ear again.

"You know, I read about your last mission. The one that made you quit. Hell of a thing."

Riker didn't answer.

"To pull off something like that and walk away afterward? Can't say that I fully understand the mindset."

Riker paused, fairly certain he heard something in the distance. He pulled out the earpiece and dropped it on the concrete floor. He heard a voice up ahead, near the turn that led to the third level. Chatti's accent was clear.

He stepped around the corner weapon raised and saw Simon standing in the middle of the drive, frozen. Behind him, Riker could just glimpse another figure. Chatti was perfectly positioned to allow Riker no possibility of a clean shot.

"That's close enough," Chatti said.

Riker stopped. He let his gun hand hang at his side, loose, but kept it ready to swing upward and fire at any moment if he saw the opportunity.

"Nice of you to join us. What do you say we finish what we started at the dam?"

"Seems unavoidable at this point." Riker took in the scene in front of him, searching for any advantage, but finding little to work with. The man had positioned his back to the open garage, so there was no cornering him against the wall. He tracked Riker's every move, subtly shifting his position as Riker did, keeping Simon perfectly between them. "Simon, you should head back to the party and let us work this out."

"I don't think so," Chatti said. "He's already dead. Just doesn't know it yet."

"For a black ops guy, you sure talk a lot."

Before the man could answer, Riker spotted something that sent a chill through him. Simon's eyes flickered up and to the right. It was a telltale sign that he was about to make a move. What that move was, Riker didn't know. Could have been a thrown elbow or a kick backward at the man's groin or one of a hundred other things Simon had seen in some action movie. It didn't matter. Any one of them would get him killed.

The man behind Simon couldn't see his eyes, but there

would be other tells. He'd tense up a moment before he made his move. He'd instinctively draw in a larger breath than normal. A professional like this guy would spot anyone of those signs and put a bullet through Simon's head before he could even start whatever hero shit he had planned.

Riker had only an instant to save Simon's life. He didn't stop to think—he just charged.

Chatti didn't react immediately, perhaps because the move was so outside of any strategy he would have expected from a highly-trained former QS-4 operative.

Instead of trying to get around Simon, Riker headed directly for him. Lowering his shoulder, he slammed it into Simon's left side, knocking him to the right. Simon went sprawling to the concrete, letting out a cry of pain as he landed. Riker felt a momentary twinge of guilt at knocking an already seriously injured man to the concrete, but he quickly pushed it aside. Better to aggravate Simon's existing injuries than to see a bullet put through his head.

All three men hit the ground hard. Chatti quickly recovered and shifted the pistol in his hand from pointing at Simon to aiming at Riker, who was still hunched over. Riker sprang up, twisting as the other man fired. The shot went wide. Riker brought his elbow down hard on the man's forearm, remembering the way he'd slammed it into the car at the dam, hoping it was still bruised and sore from that encounter.

As if in confirmation, Chatti let out a grunt of pain, and the pistol clattered to the floor. But just as quickly, the man's other hand reached out, grabbing Riker's wrist and twisting hard, causing Riker to lose his own pistol. In an instant, Chatti had Riker's handgun.

Rather than go after the gun, Riker surged forward, driving hard with his legs. He had the angle he wanted now.

Instead of knocking the man to the side as he had with Simon, he wrapped his arms around him and kept going, lifting Chatti off his feet. He slammed the man's back into the concrete wall.

Chatti let out a grunt, but he managed to keep his feet under him. He brought down a hard elbow on Riker's shoulder, sending him to the ground.

Riker tensed, expecting a bullet. Instead, he heard a little laugh.

"Well, now it's a party," the man said.

Riker looked up and saw the man staring at something across the parking garage. Following his gaze, he saw Jessica standing there, a pistol in her hand, pointed at the man.

"Don't move," she said.

Chatti laughed again. "A nine millimeter at thirty feet? I think I'll take my chances. Be patient, little girl. I'll get to you momentarily. Then we'll have some fun."

Before Chatti finished the last word, Jessica fired. The bullet struck the wall three feet to his right. Chatti returned fire with much more accuracy. Her left leg buckled backward at the knee, and she screamed out in pain.

That was when Riker's brain stopped working.

He grabbed Chatti, bringing him to the ground in an instant with a single leg takedown, grabbing him behind the knee and driving his head into the inside of his leg. Chatti let out a surprised grunt as Riker covered him up, pinning him to the ground as he tried to get an arm around Chatti's neck.

Chatti brought his knees in, stopping Riker from getting a full cover. Then he brought back his empty hand and punched Riker in the kidney. His fist kept moving, repeating the punch again and again.

Pushing the pain away, Riker got one hand around Chatti's neck. With his other hand, he grabbed the man's gun hand, twisting until he heard a snap from the wrist. Even then, Chatti's grip didn't go completely slack, and his punches paused for only a moment before resuming with even more intensity.

High-pitched screams echoed through the garage. They mixed with groans from Simon. Jessica's cries fueled Riker with wrath.

Riker ripped the pistol from Chatti's broken hand. He held Chatti's head down by the neck, pressing it against the concrete. Then Riker drove the barrel into the man's right eye. The eyeball gave a bit of resistance, but Riker kept pushing until he felt it rupture. Angling the barrel toward the center of Chatti's head, Riker pulled the trigger, sending a bullet through the eye socket and into the man's brain.

For a moment, all was silent in the parking garage. Then Jessica's sobs came.

Riker got to his feet and flicked his wrist, sending blood and viscera cascading off the barrel of his pistol and to the concrete. He raced over to Jessica.

Her face was turning white while her beautiful dress grew crimson. Riker lifted the dress and saw her knee was shattered. He took off his belt and fastened a tourniquet around her leg just above the knee.

Simon yelled from the ground behind him. "Is she okay?"

"Jessica, stay with me," Riker said, holding her hand.

Jessica just nodded.

Franklin ran into the garage. He took in the scene, Chatti lying on the ground, missing a portion of his face, Simon moaning and Riker hunched over Jessica. He took out his phone and called for the paramedics.

Hours later, Riker walked into Simon's hospital room to

find Franklin already sitting by the bed. Simon had a fresh set of stitches, bandages and pain meds.

"Any word on Jessica?" Simon asked.

"She's still in surgery. The wound was bad, but they have the top doctors working on her," Riker said.

"When she gets out of the hospital, don't tackle her. I can tell you first hand that getting laid out by a special ops guy really sucks."

"Sorry about that," Riker said.

"I'm just kidding," Simon said. "I'll take a hit from you over a bullet to the head any day. Seriously thanks for saving my life... again."

"No problem, but let's try to keep you out of life and death situations from here on out."

"It should be easy now that this is over," Simon said.

"It's not over yet. We still have work to do."

"The weapon, right?" Franklin asked. "We still need to recover it."

Riker pulled a slip of paper out of his pocket and handed it to Franklin. "I had a little chat with one of Chatti's men before the police got to him. I found him trying the slink away from the ballroom. After about five minutes of quality time with me, he was happy to give me the address where they stashed the weapon. I need you to go get it."

"I can do that," Franklin said. "But what will you be doing?"

"Finishing this once and for all. The men who ordered the attack still need to answer for their crimes."

42

"How bad is it?" Ava Bray asked.

Nathaniel Hester, CEO of Vin-Brooks Pharmaceutical, took a sip of his scotch before answering. He looked up and down the table, feeling a twinge of pride at the men and women gathered around him. Three vice presidents, two board members, his CFO, and his COO. There were others on the company's senior leadership team, but these were the ones who mattered. The people who really called the shots and made the company the success that it was. They worked hard, and they were very handsomely rewarded for their efforts.

Two days ago Hester had learned that Gary Kosmider, their Director of Operations, had disappeared after attending a fundraiser in Los Angeles. He'd immediately put his investigators on it, and it hadn't taken long for them to learn that Kosmider had fled the country. That answer had only led to more questions. What could make a powerful man like Kosmider drop off the grid and head to Asia without a word to his employers? Even more disconcerting, Kosmider had been the point man on a project they were internally referring to as Gemini. The project was an aggressive attempt to increase their market share by crippling their key competitor. It had recently hit a few snags.

But the leadership team had come together, flown out to Hester's vacation house on Lake Tahoe, and committed themselves to working the problem.

"I'm not going to sugarcoat it," Hester said. "It's bad."

"I don't understand." Frank Mendoza, CFO, leaned forward, a scowl on his face. "I've worked with Gary for eighteen years. He wouldn't just take off without saying anything. That's not his style."

Bray shook her head. "Things weren't exactly going smoothly with Gemini. Any chance he turned himself into the Feds? Maybe struck a deal?"

"No way. Not Gary."

Bray didn't look convinced. "But if he did…"

"Let's not speculate," Hester said. "There's something else we need to discuss. Another complication."

The others waited, their faces serious.

"A man contacted me last night on my personal cell phone. No idea how he got the number. He knew about Gemini. About the stolen weapons and what went down in Georgia. He claims he has proof, and he's threatening to go public."

"What's he want?" Bray asked.

"Fifty million dollars."

Silence once again fell over the table.

Finally, Bray spoke again. "Ridiculous. We're not considering paying him, are we?"

"That's what we're here to discuss." Hester took another sip of his scotch, enjoying the sweet burn of the liquid as it ran down his throat. "I've been considering the problem, and I have my answer. But I want to hear what you all think first."

Dylan Barton, the COO, was the first to speak. "If he actually has proof and goes public, we'd be looking at a public relations nightmare. The stock would take a big hit. But we could claim that Kosmider acted alone without our knowledge. I think we'd survive."

"And legally speaking?" Bray asked.

"We were careful," Barton said. "There are layers of protection. There's not a single e-mail that can tie any of us to Gemini. We didn't even discuss it over the phone. In-person meetings only. It would be impossible for them to prove we had any knowledge of the project, let alone involvement."

"What a shitshow," Mendoza grumbled. "QS-4 better give us a refund."

"I disagree," Hester said.

The others turned to him in surprise.

"We're not paying the blackmailer, of course. That goes without saying. We'll string him along to buy ourselves a little time. Then we'll contact QS-4 and tell them to get back to work."

"You want them to hit the dam again?"

"No, that would be too suspicious. I'll recommend they stage an attack on our competitor's San Francisco office. Higher population, so there will be more collateral damage, but we'll have to live with that."

"And the blackmailer?" Mendoza asked.

"If we lean on QS-4, I'll bet we can get them to take out our blackmailer as part of the deal. They owe us after botching the job so badly so far." He looked around the table and saw most of the heads nodding. "Then we're in agreement?"

Before anyone could answer, Hester's cell phone rang. He took it out of his pocket, intending to silence it, but then he saw the number.

"It's him. The blackmailer." He pressed the answer icon and held the phone to his ear. "Didn't think I'd hear from you again so soon."

ON A SMALL FISHING boat across the lake from Hester's vacation house, Riker heard the CEO's voice come through his cellphone.

"Didn't think I'd hear from you again so soon."

"Have you thought about my offer?" Riker asked.

There was a long pause. "I have. I'm working with my team now."

"Good. When can I expect my money?"

"That's exactly what we're trying to hammer out. These things take time. Gathering that kind of money without raising all kinds of eyebrows is going to be difficult. You'll have to be patient with us."

Riker bristled at the sound of the CEO's smooth voice. It was the voice of a man who was used to getting what he wanted out of life.

The past two days had been a whirlwind of research and very little sleep for Riker. While he was grateful to Jessica, Franklin, and Simon for their help in taking down Miro Chatti, he had refused to let them participate in this final stage of his operation. He hadn't even told them what he was up to—he'd simply told them he'd be in touch and left the hospital.

Gary Kosmider had proven to be a valuable source of information. He'd been all too eager to talk when Riker tracked him down and leaned on him. He'd confirmed their suspicions that Vin-Brooks was QS-4's client, and he'd gladly accepted Riker's suggestion that he leave the country and never come back. Kosmider had confirmed that Vin-Brooks had planned the operation against their competitors at the very highest level.

Riker had worked the problem just like Morrison had taught him so many years ago in Afghanistan. He'd created disruptions for his target and watched to see how they reacted. His blackmail demand had done exactly what he'd hoped it would do—it had forced the CEO to gather the people he most trusted. The same people who had been in on his plan to hurt his competitor by harming a town full of innocent people.

"I need you to do something for me," Riker said.

The condescending smile was clear in Hester's voice when he answered. "Fifty million dollars isn't enough?"

"I want you to answer a question. How do you justify what you've done?"

There was a long pause. "Excuse me?"

"How do you sleep at night? Look at yourself in the mirror? Go to your grandkid's soccer game and act like everything is normal? You ordered the deaths of hundreds of people, all to make a buck."

"You're not seeing the big picture." Hester's voice was different now. Clearly, he wasn't used to being spoken to as Riker had. "I'm not saying I was involved in what almost happened in Georgia, but as a thought experiment, sure, let's pretend that I was. And let's pretend the operation had been successful. Would innocent people have been hurt? Perhaps. But lives would have been improved, too. Our company stock would have skyrocketed in value, improving the lives of every one of our investors, big and small. We would have been able to create new jobs, lifting people out of poverty and changing their lives forever. Who's to say that the good wouldn't have outweighed the bad?"

Riker pushed down the feeling of revulsion that rose up in him at the man's words. He raised his binoculars and peered at the man's house. He could just make out some figures through the floor-to-ceiling window that looked out over the lake. He wondered if Hester was one of the men he could see.

"You know something, Hester, all my life men have been ordering me around. Sending me into dangerous situations. They all had their justifications about how it was for the greater good. But you know something funny? They didn't believe in the cause so much that they were willing to step out on the battlefield. They'd give the orders, but they never paid the price for their decisions."

"That's a very cynical way to look at the world," Hester said. "Leadership has its own challenges. Giving orders is more difficult than you think."

"Maybe. But I'm done taking orders. And I'm done watching men like you walk away from their heinous actions without consequences. Mr. Hester, it's time for you to pay for what you've done."

Riker ended the call and slipped the phone into his pocket. Then he picked up the remote detonator off the seat next to him, and he flipped the switch.

Across the lake, flames erupted from Hester's house. Glass exploded outward from the floor-to-ceiling window, and Riker knew that everyone in that room was dead. It hadn't taken some new superweapon for him to do the job, just a simple homemade bomb.

Riker felt nothing as he watched Hester's house burn. No guilt. No triumph. It was a job that had needed to be done, and he'd done it. That was all. Hester and his friends had owed the world a moral debt, and now that price had been paid.

Riker started the engine and guided the boat to the opposite shore. The mission was over. It was time to return to his friends.

43

THE DOOR to the hospital room squeaked as it slowly swung open. Simon looked up from the bed.

"You up for a visitor?" Riker asked.

"Get your ass in here," Simon said with a smile.

"You sound good. I thought you would still be in a lot of pain."

Simon laughed. "Pain management my friend."

"How did the surgery go?"

"The ortho was pretty pissed that you messed up the work he did the first time. It's going to be a while before my shoulder is fully functional."

"Sorry, man. I had to improvise. I know that hit must have hurt like hell."

"You've got that right, but you definitely don't need to apologize. I'll take a bum shoulder over a bullet to the head any day."

Riker smiled. "Fair enough."

The smile faded from Simon's face. "No man, I really mean it. I owe you a debt that I can never repay. I'm not just talking about the parking garage. I really understand what you did for me. I never should have lived through the mess that I got myself into." He paused for a moment and looked down. "You really did more than just get me through alive. I meant what I said the other day. From here on out, I'm going to do my part to make the world a better place."

"That's great. I think you will." Riker hoped that Simon's new sentiment would stick once he was out of the hospital. A big part of him believed that it would. "I really just came by to let you know that everything is taken care of. You don't need to worry about anyone coming after you."

"What about the attacks? Are they going to try to hit another target?"

Riker shook his head. "The odds of them planning another attack is zero percent."

"Oh. You *took care of them*?"

"Like I said, you don't need to worry anymore."

"So what's next?"

"Nothing, the mission is over. Time for you to go back to normal life."

"No, I mean what's next for you? Are you off to some exotic location? Maybe dance the tango with a beautiful woman while infiltrating an enemy headquarters?"

"Very funny. I'm heading back to my farm. I've got to tend to my hives."

"What about Jessica?"

Riker looked away. "I was hoping that you could give her a message for me. My flight leaves in a few hours, and I was going to head straight to the airport from here."

Simon's expression turned serious. "I'm going to stop you right there. I'm not giving her any message, because you're going to do that in person. You can't leave without saying goodbye to her."

"I don't think there is much to say. She has an amazing

life here, and I've got to head back to North Carolina. My responsibility might be small in comparison, but it means a lot to me."

Simon sat up in his bed. He winced at the pain but propped himself up to be closer to eye level with Riker.

"I've known Jessica a long time. I don't think I've ever seen her connect to anyone like she has with you. I'm going to take a wild guess and say that you haven't had a lot of good relationships in your past. I know that there is something special between the two of you. This experience has shown me that you can't ignore that. You may never have a chance to go back to it."

"That's the reason I don't think I should see her. People who spend a lot of time around me tend to end up dead. Hell, Jessica almost died in that parking garage. She's been hurt enough already, and if I see her I'm not sure that I will be able to leave."

"You need to learn to be a little tougher. I've been meaning to teach you how to do it."

Riker laughed. "Okay, I'll work at it. Maybe someday I'll be as tough as you."

"Go see her. You owe it to her, and you owe it to yourself." Simon picked up his phone from the side of the bed. He typed in a text message. "I let her know that you are on your way over. She's expecting you in fifteen minutes, so you better hurry."

"Thanks, Simon. You take care of yourself."

"See you around, Riker."

The doorman was waiting for Riker at Jessica's building. As he rode the elevator to the penthouse, a smile touched the corners of his mouth. He remembered the last time he'd been there, and the experience of meeting Jessica for the first time.

The smile left as quickly as it had come. He tried to think of what to say to her, but the doors opened before he had a plan.

She stood in her doorway just as she had the first time they met. This time she was balanced on crutches and her leg was in a massive cast. "I'm glad you came. I honestly didn't know if you would."

"I didn't know either. A friend of ours assured me it was the right thing to do."

"I can't stand forever, Riker." She motioned him inside. "How's our boy doing?"

"As good as can be expected. I'm sure he'll be running around the clubs in no time, although he says that he is going to change the focus of his life."

"My guess is he'll do both."

"And you? How are you doing?"

"My knee's never going to be the same." She hesitated, not quite able to meet his eyes. "And there are nightmares."

"There always are. Even for me."

He followed her inside, and they sat on the terrace overlooking the city. The sun lit her face, and Riker took in the image. He studied her in that moment like he studied the layout of a new city. Committing every detail to memory, holding onto it forever.

"I saw that you finished the mission." Her eyes were sad when she spoke. "There was a report of a gas explosion that killed eight members of Vin-Brooks' board. They are holding services for Nathaniel Hester, treating him like a fallen hero."

"It doesn't really matter what anyone thinks of him. I carved out the cancer from the company. Hopefully, it will take a better path now that they are gone."

"Time will tell." She turned and looked out over the city.

"I've been thinking a lot. This world, the one you live in, it's so complicated. You remember Mary?"

"Chatti's ex? Sure."

"I went to see her. I told her Chatti's dead. The look of relief on her face... It was like she was finally free."

Riker waited for her to continue.

"On the other hand, there are the Vin-Brooks board members. I've seen you kill before, but only when it was life or death. These men and women were just sitting in a house."

The tone of her voice told Riker everything that he needed to know. "It is different, but these people were the masterminds of one of the largest attempted attacks on US soil. They spent their lives acquiring power. It got to them, and they became monsters. A phone call to the police or the FBI would not have stopped them."

"You don't have to explain it. My logical brain tells me it was the right thing. Somehow it just doesn't feel that way."

"I wish I could say the same. I've seen men like that succeed firsthand, and I will never hesitate to stop them."

"So now that it's over, what are you going to do?"

"I'm headed back to North Carolina. I leave in a few hours. If you ever find yourself in Henderson County you should stop by."

She smiled. "I don't think I've ever heard of it. Is there anything to see there?"

"Nothing. That's one of my favorite things about the place. That and the honey."

"Maybe I'll swing by to taste some after I've had a little time to process all of this."

"I'll save my best jar just in case you decide to come."

"I'll keep that in mind."

He smiled. "What are you going to do now that high-speed chases and gunfights are out of the picture?"

She stared off into the distance. "It will take me a few weeks to get caught up on everything that I missed while I was in the hospital. This year's fundraiser was actually our most successful."

"Really? Should I stop by next year and stop a brutal killer?"

"I think we can get by without those kinds of theatrics two years in a row. Word got out that Simon and I were attacked by a carjacker in the parking garage. Simon played it up, saying that the best thing to help him get through the trauma was to donate to my foundation. The elites ate it up."

"That's great. I guess you can go back to saving the world on your terms, and I can go back to tending to my bees."

"Our worlds sound pretty different when you say it like that."

"Indeed they do." Riker checked his watch, he probably had more time to stay, but there was no sense in drawing it out. "I think I had better go. I don't want to miss my flight."

She nodded, but she didn't get up yet. "Riker, what happened in the parking garage... will I ever get over it? Will I ever go back to the way I was?"

"Yes. And no." He spoke evenly, careful not to let any emotion into his voice, just laying it out for her. "After a while, you'll think about it less often. It won't monopolize your mind. But will you ever be the same? No, not exactly. You've seen combat. That changes you. It doesn't have to be a bad thing or a good thing. It's just part of who you are."

She slowly walked him to the elevator, wedging her crutches under her arms, and she pressed the button. Then she grabbed him and pulled him in tight and hard. He wrapped his arms around her and brought his lips to hers.

The kiss was passionate and lasted until the doors opened with a chime.

Her eyes remained closed for a moment as she regained her balance on the crutches and stepped back. "Just something for you to remember me by."

He let out a soft breath and nodded. He stepped onto the elevator just before the doors closed.

At the airport, he sat at the gate, thinking of that kiss. His phone rang, but no number displayed.

"Riker."

"I believe you are supposed to answer Scarecrow," Franklin said.

Riker shifted the phone to his other ear, sitting up a bit straighter. "I take it you were able to recover the weapon?"

"Yes, it was the address you gave me. I took it out to the desert and set it off in the middle of the night. Figured it was better than letting it fall into the wrong hands again."

Riker smiled. Franklin had come a long way in the short time Riker had known him. "Not that I mind talking to you, but I didn't expect to hear from you again."

"This is not in my official capacity. In fact, that's what I wanted to call you about."

"Go on," Riker said.

"I was instructed by our mutual friend that this was just a training exercise for me. My report is to indicate that the exercise I participated in was a successful learning experience. I never officially met with any active operatives."

"I assumed that would be the case. Can you get him a message for me?"

"Of course."

Riker thought for a moment. "Tell him if he ever wants to grab a beer with me, I'll be at the usual spot. Same time as always."

"Got it. Will he know what that means?"

"Let's hope so. I'd very much like to speak to him."

"I'm not sure that I fully understand the situation. Is it something that you would care to explain to me?"

Riker smiled. "If I end up working another mission, I hope you're my handler."

With that, he hung up the phone and turned it off. He thought of his home and his bees and couldn't wait to get there, but there was something else he needed to do first. He walked to the ticket counter.

"Can I help you, sir?" the ticket agent asked.

"Yes. I'd like to change my ticket."

EPILOGUE

THREE DAYS LATER, Riker sat in a nondescript neighborhood bar in north St. Louis, nursing his beer. It was eight o'clock on a Monday night, and there were only three other patrons. A couple occupied the booth in the corner, sitting too close and giggling too loudly. Riker expected they'd be leaving soon. The other customer was an old man four seats away from Riker. He was downing whiskey as if it was Gatorade. His eyes were fixed on the TV in the corner, which was playing a quiz show. The old man answered every question aloud, and he had yet to guess the correct answer even once, which Riker thought was sort of impressive.

Riker focused on his beer, staring into the glass, appearing deep in thought. The last thing he wanted was a conversation, so he did his best to look unapproachable. So far, it was working. Even the bartender had left him alone after sliding him the frosty glass.

The bell over the door chimed, and a broad figure entered the bar. Riker could see the man's shape in his periphery, and he didn't bother looking up. The man walked over and took the stool next to Riker.

Riker stayed quiet until the man had ordered and the bartender had set the glass in front of him. Only after the bartender retreated to the other end of the bar did Riker speak. "Guess you got the message."

Morrison grunted noncommittally. "The usual place, huh? We only shared a beer once. Took me a hell of a long time to remember what this dive was called. I do remember that *Monday Night Football* was on. The place was going wild for the Rams. Wonder how many Rams fans are left here now that the team's moved to L.A.?"

Riker turned and looked at his old mentor for the first time. The man looked older than he had even ten days before in Riker's kitchen. "I'm glad you remembered. Wasn't sure you would."

Morrison took a pull on his beer. "You made a hell of a mess for me, Riker."

"Just like old times, then."

"The thing with the Vin-Brooks leadership. It was too far."

"It was what you taught me. Don't just complete the mission. Solve for the reason for the mission."

Morrison frowned, but he didn't argue the point. "You're lucky I came alone. A lot of the folks higher on the org chart would like to see you out of commission."

"Are you?" Riker asked. "Really alone, I mean. Nobody listening?"

"As far as I know. But these days? I'm as alone as I ever am, I'll say that much."

Riker nodded. That was good enough for him. Morrison was a cautious man. "So are you going to tell me why the hell you sent me to stop a QS-4 mission? Did QS-4 even know I was out there?"

"Oh, they knew."

"And they were okay with you sending me to stop Chatti? One of their own agents?"

There was the hint of mischief in Morrison's eyes when he spoke again. "I didn't send you to stop Chatti, remember? I sent you to protect Simon. Chatti was effective, but everyone in QS-4 knew what kind of man he was. We all knew he wouldn't leave Simon alone just because he was a senator's son. So I recommended we send you as an insurance policy against a senator digging a little too deeply into our business. I assured them we had you by the balls and that you'd protect Simon and nothing more. Since you'd never met Chatti, you wouldn't even know he was QS-4. That made you the ideal candidate."

"Uh-huh," Riker said. "So why'd you really send me?"

Morrison made a noise that sounded like a harrumph. "Because I knew you'd figure it out. If I had your handler tell you to stay away from the weapons, I knew you'd go after them even harder. Same old Scarecrow shit all over again."

Riker smiled, but then his face grew serious. "You trained Chatti. I could tell when I fought him. That's the kind of man you're bringing on these days?"

Morrison shifted uncomfortably. "I did train him. For a while. But I had concerns about his stability. I recommended that he be removed from field duty. Upper management disagreed. Say what you will about the man, but Chatti got results. At least until he ran up against you."

Riker raised an eyebrow. "Are things so bad at QS-4 that you are working to stop your own missions now?"

"I'd say they're even worse than that." Morrison took a long drink, then set the glass down hard. "Look, you know as well as anyone that we've always walked the line. I told you a long time ago that everyone needs to find that line for themselves."

"I take it QS-4 has crossed yours?"

"More and more often. This new generation of leaders... We've always been a for-profit company, but the money is all that matters to these guys. They'll take any job. Chatti's a great example of that. As long as he was generating profits, the higher-ups wouldn't take him out of the field. Instead, they came up with this idiotic Laghaz idea. Let Chatti run a faux terrorist organization. That way, QS-4 gets their profits and they can deny all knowledge if things go south." He shook his head sadly.

"And I thought things were bad when I left." Riker knocked back the rest of his beer, then looked into his mentor's eyes. "One more thing. I'm done working for QS-4. And I want them to know. Our original agreement was that I got to retire and in exchange, I'd never get involved in anything remotely resembling fieldwork again. I believe your words were, I wasn't even allowed to touch a weapon. Correct?"

Morrison nodded. "But things have changed."

"Yes, they have. QS-4 broke the agreement. They put a weapon into my hands and sent me out into the field. As far as I'm concerned, that deal is null and void. I'd like to propose a new one. I go home. I do whatever the hell I want, and QS-4 never bothers me again."

Morrison stared at him blankly for a moment. "I'm waiting for the other part. The part my bosses would have even a sliver of a chance at agreeing to."

"There is no more. That's it. That's what you take back and sell them. As far as I'm concerned, it's a pretty easy sale."

"Riker, I know I trained you better than this." Morrison's voice was hard. "I go back with that, we're both dead men."

"I don't think so. You said it yourself. Upper management is only interested in profit. Killing me is going to be a lot more expensive than letting me get on with my life."

"Not sure about that. Bullets are cheap, and we buy them in bulk."

"It's not the bullet that's the expensive part. It's what comes after. See, I had a little talk with Senator Buckner before I left L.A. I didn't reveal too much, but I made it clear that if anything happened to me in the foreseeable future, QS-4 was responsible. Turns out, he's very grateful that his son is still alive, and he is apt to be a bit vindictive if I turn up dead. QS-4 may be moonlighting with pharmaceutical companies, but I know government contracts are still their bread and butter. If I die, those go up in smoke."

"I see." The old man's eyes narrowed as they always did when he was assessing the viability of a plan. "I think I can sell that to upper management. You're a brilliant bastard, but you're still a pain in the ass, Riker."

"Always was." Riker paused. "One last question. Why involve Franklin? Did you really think I needed a handler?"

"It wasn't for your benefit. It was for his. Look, Franklin's a pompous, Ivy League asshole sometimes, but I sort of like the kid. He has potential. He just lacks field experience. I thought it might do him some good to work with a guy who's been around the block a few times. A guy who isn't afraid to do the right thing even when it's difficult." Morrison was quiet for a long moment before he spoke again. "Riker, I'm doing what I can to right the ship at QS-4. If it turns out that I can't, that ship may need to be sunk. I won't be able to do that alone. I'll need people I can trust. I'm hoping Franklin will be one of them, but I'll need more. I may need the help of someone outside the organization. Do you understand what I'm saying?"

Riker didn't answer. He didn't need to.

Instead, he eyed his empty glass. "I think I'd like to enjoy my first beer in six years as a truly free man. Care to join me?"

Morrison stood up from his stool. "As much as I'd love to, I have work to do. Reports to file. Bosses to placate."

Riker nodded. "Let's do it again in another decade or so."

"Deal." Morrison started to leave, then paused. "When you get home, you might want to take a really close look around your house. Make sure there aren't any electronic devices you didn't put there. Not saying there are, but in this day and age, a man can't be too careful." He rapped his knuckles on the bar and turned back toward the door. "See you around, Riker."

When Morrison was gone, Riker called to the bartender and ordered another beer. He felt like a weight he'd been carrying for a very long time had been lifted. He was no longer in hiding. He suddenly had a whole life in front of him.

He could do anything he wanted, and the thing he wanted most was to go home. After drinking his beer, he headed to the airport. Two hours later, he was on a plane, eyes closed, enjoying the peaceful sleep of a free man.

AUTHOR'S NOTE

Thanks so much for reading GHOST AGENT. It was a lot of fun writing Riker as part of a team and seeing his more vulnerable side as he experienced his relationship with Jessica.

The next Riker novel, LONG WAY HOME, will be out soon. In the meantime, I'd like to offer you a free short novelette about Riker's time with QS-4. It's called NO LOOSE ENDS.

Visit my website at www.jtbaier.com to join the email group and get your free copy.

Thanks again, and happy reading.

J.T. Baier

CPSIA information can be obtained
at www.ICGtesting.com
Printed in the USA
BVHW081847021222
653303BV00009B/1267